"I might as well apologize again," he rumbled.

"For what?" Shelby stared into mossy green eyes turned dark.

"For doing what I've been thinking about since you first touched me."

His mouth covered hers, and she felt warm all over. She clutched his forearms, aware his hands had crept to circle her waist. He deepened the kiss and groaned, then pulled her against his hard body.

BODYWORK

BY MARIE HARTE

A No Box Books Publication

This book is a work of fiction. The names, characters, places, and plot points stem from the writer's imagination. They are fictitious and not to be interpreted as real. Any resemblance to persons, living or dead, actual events, locations or organizations is entirely coincidental.

ISBN-13: 978-1537764474
Bodywork

Cover by Tibbs Design, No Box Books Design
Edited by TINB Inc.

No Box Books

http://marieharte.com

THE WORKS

Bodywork

Working Out

Wetwork

RELATED BOOKS

A Sure Thing

Just the Thing

The Only Thing

CHAPTER ONE

SHANE COLLINS SCRAMBLED TO FIND THE BUFFED, BLACK leather oxford to match the existing one on his left foot. Getting in at four a.m. had been hell, but waking three hours later to blaring rock music, courtesy of his uninvited younger brother who'd seen fit to sleep over, made his already sour mood worse. His head ached, his eyes burned, and he wanted nothing more than to go back to sleep.

Which he already had, before he'd remembered he had an important meeting with the Graces this morning.

Son of a bitch. He searched frantically for his missing shoe while tucking in a white pressed shirt. He searched under the bed, in the closet, even in the bathroom, for God's sake.

Glancing at his watch for the twentieth time that morning, he ripped the shoe off his left foot and threw on a similar pair. Then he donned his sport coat. Clothes, check. Shoes, check. Now to find his briefcase. He thought he'd left it on the coffee table when he'd come home.

Where the hell was it? Desperation festered into annoyance as he spied an empty pizza box on the couch. His younger brother was such a pain in the ass. He cursed George to an eternity of high school as he spied a familiar handle sticking out from under the sofa. Pulling it free, he also found his missing shoe covered in something sticky.

Not having the time or inclination to guess what might be covering it, he tossed the shoe, grabbed his case and hustled to the door. Where the car keys should have been hanging, a note had been punched over the hook. Swearing, he ripped it free and read it.

Hey bro, since I have football practice early this morning and after school, I'm borrowing the car. I'll return it after practice. Coach'll skin me if I'm late again. Hope you have a good day catching up on sleep. Thanks a million. I owe you one—Geo.

Angry, frustrated, and at fault for not clueing his brother into his last minute change of schedule, he forced himself to calm down. He ran a hand through his hair and thought hard about his options. It'd be tough to get a cab during the early morning commute hour. Shane needed a ride.

Inspiration sparked and he quickly dialed Mac's cell.

His best friend answered on the second ring. "Yo."

Shane heard the sound of music in the background. *Please be close.* "Mac? It's Shane. I need a favor."

"Don't tell me. You slept through your alarm, your brother crashed your car while you were gone, and you need a ride to work." Mac's rumble was laced with humor.

"Close enough. Man, I'm begging. I need a ride like yesterday."

"I'm next in line at Sofa's. You got lucky this morning."

"Perfect. Look Mac, I'm leaving my place now. Grab me a special and I'll be there in two minutes." Shane disconnected, pocketed his cell phone, and raced out the door. Sofa's Coffee sat a few blocks from his house, and he sprinted the entire way, grateful for this reprieve and really needing a caffeine boost. The run to grab his ride was definitely worth a hot blast of java.

He spotted Mac sitting in his car outside the shop and thanked God for his friend's caffeine addiction. With his attention focused on Mac, Shane didn't see the woman standing in his way until he ran into her.

She yelped against his chest before she stumbled away and righted herself.

"*Shit.*" He leaped back as pain hit him squarely in the stomach. Plucking the scorching fabric from his body, he noticed a dark brown stain spreading over his once pristine shirt. He cursed again and looked down into amber eyes filled with irritation. "Thanks a lot, lady." He'd be lucky if he made it on time, and now this. Before she could tear a strip off his already late hide, he raced to Mac's waiting car, fumbling at his shirt buttons.

Mac raised a brow as he slammed inside.

"Not now, Jameson," Shane snapped. "Just get me to Harmon & Sons as soon as you can."

"Aye aye, boss." The bastard had the nerve to laugh.

As Mac drove, Shane hurriedly changed out of his ruined shirt and undershirt into a clean set he saved in his briefcase for occasions like these. Wrinkles he could handle, but the coffee stain wouldn't fly. At least his coat would hide most of the rumpled mess. He only hoped Mr. Grace wouldn't be on time for this morning's appointment in—he swallowed hard—twenty minutes.

Then he inhaled and took in the heavenly scent of coffee. Mac nodded him to the second up sitting in the cup holder. After a hesitant sip, Shane guzzled the brew like a thirsting man.

"You're welcome." Mac's eyes twinkled as he put his foot

down on the accelerator. "Don't worry, buddy. You need to be somewhere in a hurry, I'm your man. Just remember, that's another one you owe me."

♥

Shelby Vanzant stared morosely at her crunched coffee cup bleeding all over the cement sidewalk. She'd been dying for a mocha latte. Yet the only one satisfied with her purchase was a yappy little Chihuahua tied to a nearby tree licking up her spilled drink. She frowned at the rat-sized creature in distaste. "I didn't know dogs liked coffee."

Her best friend joined her and shook her head at the dog still licking the ground. "This is Seattle. Everyone and everything in this city loves coffee. Tough break," Maggie sympathized. "I'll wait while you get another one."

"I don't want to wait in line *again*."

Maggie placed her hands on her hips. "We're not walking anywhere together until you've had your daily fix. No coffee, no conversation."

Shelby muttered under her breath but returned minutes later with a smile and a steaming cup. She rejoined Maggie, and they crossed the street to resume their bi-weekly walk around Green Lake. As Shelby drank, she couldn't help seeing the humor in the situation.

"Considering this is our day to discuss the idiocy of men, I'd say I'm off to a good start. My first client today is a woman, at least. Nine o'clock on the dot, and she's never late. Not like that moron running like his shirt was on fire."

"After running into you it might have been." Maggie chuckled. "Sofa's makes their coffee *hot*."

"Good. Serves him right." They moved to the side while a

trio of joggers passed. "Why is it whenever I run into a man, I get a frog instead of the prince? Even this morning, instead of Mr. Tall, Dark, and Handsome, I got Mr. Tall, Clumsy, and Rude. Why is that?"

"Who knows? But at least your rude man was sexy. I mean, did you happen to check him out when you were giving him third degree burns?"

"I didn't burn him." Not on purpose. Shelby flushed. "It wasn't my fault. He flew out of nowhere and bumped into *me.* Then he acted like it was all my fault and stormed off before I could say a thing."

She slurped her coffee.

They walked in silence, and Shelby's thoughts shifted from Mr. Rude to appreciate the clear blue sky. Seattle had a clear day. Mark that one for the books. The weather wasn't as dismal as was commonly thought. When it turned as warm as it had been lately, she took advantage of the August heat wave—*heat wave* being a relative term. This morning notched in at a comfortable sixty-eight degrees. If they were lucky and the weatherman guessed correctly, the temperature might reach a high of eighty-two.

Too bad she had no one at home to show off her new red bikini.

She sighed.

Maggie groaned. "After two years of these walks, you'd think I'd be used to this three mile loop." Another painful groan. The woman could exaggerate misery like nobody's business. "I know we need our exercise, but I distinctly recall telling you aerobics is my thing, not walking."

"Considering my line of work, you should be used to my healthy habits. I'm just glad Shantell lets you work a later shift every Tuesday."

"Me too. Shantell's a gem, and working at her gallery is a godsend. But someday I'll be my own boss, like you. Bodyworks has really flourished since you opened it." Maggie rotated her neck. "Maybe I'll book an appointment soon. I think I might have strained my neck the other day."

Bodyworks, Shelby's massage therapy clinic, was her pride and joy. Thanks to her business, she'd not only found a source of income, but her best friend. Bumping into Maggie Doran on her first day of work had been fate. They had immediately clicked and been thick as thieves ever since.

Shelby linked her arm through Maggie's. "Tell me about the latest masterpiece you've been designing."

While Maggie explained her work in detail, Shelby thought about how much she enjoyed Tuesday walks with her BFF. They had similar attitudes about men and life, though in appearance they were quite different. Whereas Maggie was a pretty blonde with a petite yet curvy body, Shelby felt like the queen of average. Neither fat nor skinny, with brown hair and brown eyes, she had even features and a nice complexion. Her olive skin tanned quite well whenever she had a chance to see the sun.

"Okay, I can tell when you're zoning out on me."

Busted.

"So, back to Mr. Rude," Maggie's continued. "Did you happen to notice that thick black hair and his frosty green eyes?"

"No, but obviously you did. All I noticed was that he stood several inches taller than me and had a nice set of abs." At Maggie's raised brow, she explained. "When the coffee scalded him, the liquid made his white shirt transparent."

"Thank God for wet, white shirts." Maggie sighed, and they laughed together.

They picked up the pace after tossing their empty cups in the trash, completing a quarter of the three-mile course around the lake. As they walked, Shelby considered Green Lake and thought again about moving out here. Only her proximity to work, in her current house in Queen Anne, stopped her.

Though the lake had several signs warning about the algae and the danger of swimming, it rippled calmly under the cool breeze, giving the ducks a safe place to gather. Fresh clumps of flowers decorated rock formations that dotted the trail, and when the wind blew, she inhaled the sweet smells of lavender and magnolia.

"Could you pick up the pace a little, Methuselah?" Maggie glanced at her watch again. "I have to be at work before Wednesday."

"Sorry." Shelby lengthened her stride. "I was just taking in the sweet smells around us in an attempt to forget that idiot from this morning." She barely avoided a pair of sweaty men running by like their hair was on fire. Joggers. Ech. Who the hell ran without a reason?

Maggie poked her in the side.

"Ow."

"You know what your problem is?"

"No, but I'm sure you're going to tell me."

"You confuse every good-looking guy with Rick. Just because Rick was a complete ass, who not only used you but cheated on you, doesn't mean every hot guy will do the same. Dumping him was totally the right thing to do."

"Thanks, Maggie. I feel so much better now." Shelby didn't want to discuss Rick the Prick on such a nice day, but Maggie was like a dog with a bone; she never let go.

"No. I think you need to be honest about this. It's been six months since you caught him sleeping with that trashy blond bimbo. Don't go there," Maggie warned, her blue eyes flashing. "I can call her a bimbo. You, of the dark-haired variety, cannot."

Maggie's self-esteem should have been higher than a kite considering the number of dates she had. But being seen as a blond plaything bothered her.

Shelby, on the other hand, would have paid to be considered a hottie, brainless or not. Apparently she wasn't the only one with issues. "Okay. I won't say how humiliating it was to walk in on Rick sitting in his chair with that slutty woman's lips around his—"

"*Exactly.* No need to rehash all that unpleasantness," Maggie interrupted. "The point you seem to ignore every time we have this discussion is that Rick really was a dick for the way he acted. Most guys aren't that bad. What about the guy you dated before the prick?" she asked, grinning. "Bobby something or other. He wasn't bad looking and seemed pretty nice."

Shelby flinched. "Bobby Wiener was his name, and there you go grinning again. Do you know how hard it is to go out with a guy named Wiener?" She frowned when Maggie burst into laughter. "Every time we reserved a table for the Wiener party, I got looks. And I couldn't call him at work and ask for his name without cracking up. Even he seemed embarrassed by it." Feeling guilty about making fun of such a nice guy, Shelby defended him. "Wiener's really not a bad name."

"You're right, Shelby." Maggie bit her lip, but the giggles continued all the same. "Wiener isn't a bad name. Bobby Schlong, that's a bad name."

They both burst into laughter. And like magic, Maggie had lightened her mood.

"Now, Shelby, be honest about Mr. Rude."

"Okay, okay." Shelby curbed her mirth. "I might have noticed he looked pretty solid under that jacket. I might even have noticed that his black hair nicely went with his dark green eyes that stared at me wide with shock."

"And?" Maggie prodded.

"And he was tall," she muttered. The number one standard she and Maggie agreed about their dream man was height. At five-foot nine, Shelby looked down on the average female. But Maggie barely reached her chin. "What's your deal with height, anyway? You're not that tall yourself. What would it matter to you if a guy stood six-foot or five-five?"

Maggie huffed. "We go over this every time you bring up the subject. I don't have to be tall to like tall men. Granted, I'm kind of small, but that just means I'd like somebody larger than myself for protection. Besides, don't all the men in your books stand a head taller than the women?"

"Yeah, they do." Shelby recalled her latest steamy read. Now that hero had been one tall order of hot sex and enduring desire. If only she could find her own hero and shack up for a few days, months, years… "But you'll notice in my books the man always has a tender side around the woman, a touch of chivalry that makes her feel loved and protected."

"I don't know about that." Maggie frowned. "The last book of yours I read had this really hunky cowboy in it that treated the woman like dirt, a real macho type."

"Really? And you liked that?"

"No. I liked the part where the heroine shot at him and roped him. Then she tied him to the bed and screwed him six ways from Sunday. Now *that*, I liked." Maggie grinned and then groaned. "And speaking of restraints, I think it's time I told you what really happened with Michael."

"I knew you were holding out. Tell me."

Maggie had more dates than she knew what to do with, and God bless her, she kept going out, disappointment after disappointment. Shelby sometimes wondered why Maggie bothered, but her friend would tell her that you couldn't win if you never played the game.

"You're not going to believe this." Maggie lowered her voice to a whisper. "I almost don't believe it myself. I have to say he was my worst one yet."

"Boring Dr. Yeats?"

Maggie snorted. "Boring is the last thing I'd use to describe him. So you know it was our fourth or fifth date. I'd decided to maybe let things progress a little further."

"Further?" Shelby's eyes widened. "He'd already hit second. Was he rounding to third or stealing home?"

"Shh, keep your voice down." Maggie glanced around her then said, "I liked the guy, and he seemed so normal."

"What happened?"

"Well, we ate at a really nice restaurant, right on the waterfront. We were having a great time, and then we headed back to his place."

"His place."

"Yeah. He lives on the Hill in a really nice house. Truth is, I was impressed."

"He's a doctor, what did you expect?"

"I expected to play doctor, not participate in some weird S&M games!"

Shelby's jaw dropped.

"I mean, not that I'm averse to that type of thing, I don't think, but I'd just met the guy a few weeks ago. It was really embarrassing."

Shelby pulled Maggie down to a nearby bench and squeezed her arm. "*Tell me.*"

"We'd just gotten back to his place, right? Well, he told me to wait for him, that he had a surprise for me in the bedroom. I knew what he was getting at, or at least I thought I did. I expected some candles, maybe a little mood music, satin sheets, that type of thing."

"And?"

"So I go into his bedroom and find him dressed in a black mask with a zipper where his mouth should be and two slits for eye holes. He's also wearing a studded dog collar around his neck." Maggie's voice lowered. "But this is the real kicker. He was wearing a pair of women's black lace panties and a garter holding up fishnet stockings!"

"I'm getting flashbacks of the *Rocky Horror Picture Show.*"

"Oh yeah. The whole look, but add the ski mask and you have my bizarro evening."

Shelby could only stare when she realized Maggie wasn't lying. Talk about strange. She'd actually met Dr. Michael Yeats and been impressed by his looks, profession, and pleasant demeanor. Maggie typically dated a lot of liberal types that had trouble making ends meet. Yeats had seemed normal, if a little staid.

She tried but couldn't get the image of Yeats in heels from her mind. "I can't see him wearing panties and garters."

"Neither could I until that night," Maggie said dryly. "The worst part about it was that he acted so normal, as if dressing in women's underwear was supposed to turn me on. And then I realized all those questions he'd asked me about my views on sexuality had been leading to that. When I just turned around to leave, he ripped off the mask and wanted to know what was wrong. As if I saw that every day."

"So did you tell him?"

"I didn't stick around long enough to say anything. I

hustled out of there and called a cab from my cell. Who knows what might have happened if I'd stayed?"

"Yeah. He might have demanded you wear a jock while you whipped him for being a naughty little girl."

"Laugh it up. But this just goes to show you that not all guys are the same." Trust Maggie to bring a moral lesson into it. "The last hippie guy I dated was nice, but nowhere near as weird as Michael. They're all a little different."

"Just a little," Shelby joked but gave her friend a sly look. "I notice it's been a few weeks since you've gone out though. Taking a break?"

"Well, a little one." Maggie studied her nails. "I think maybe I'm attracting the wrong type of guys."

"You think?"

Maggie talked over her. "Most of them think if you're an artist, you're easy."

"Speaking of art, have you even started on the present for my birthday yet?" Shelby reminded Maggie at least twice a day about the paper sculpture she'd been promised.

"Your birthday isn't until November. Give it a rest." Maggie stood up from the bench and stretched.

Shelby stood with her and they moved to their cars. "Your sculptures are the best. I want one before you're too famous for me to afford. I just don't want you to forget you promised me one *for free*."

Maggie mumbled something under her breath as they said goodbye, then drove away leaving Shelby with her thoughts. Chuckling at the image of Dr. Yeats in garters, Shelby drove home to clean up before her morning appointment.

Men could be so odd. A vision of male perfection wearing a scowl and a stain of hot coffee lit her mind's eye—black hair cut short to frame a masculine face, deep green eyes the color of shady moss, and a physique that would make a nun drool. A pity he'd been such a jerk. She wondered idly if he'd been having a bad day or if he was normally that aggravating. She smiled grimly to herself and hoped that his bad day got steadily worse until he acted nice to someone, preferably a woman.

CHAPTER TWO

SHANE SMILED AND THANKED JONATHAN GRACE AND HIS wife for their time. The meeting had passed surprisingly well, and he thanked his lucky stars the Graces had gotten stuck in traffic. Mac, true to his word, had dropped Shane at his office with two minutes to spare. And with his clients running late, Shane had straightened up his desk, had their secretary arrange the prepared tray of coffee and pastries to look nicer, and spread out his proposal, acting as if he'd been calmly awaiting their arrival instead of dashing around the office like a madman.

He sighed and sank back into his chair just as Justin Harmon, senior partner at the firm, popped his head in the door. Distinguished looking with dark hair graying slightly at his temples, Justin had an easy disposition and savvy business acumen that made his company one of the best architectural firms in the city. His brother Thomas held the creative side of things together, along with help from Shane and a few others in the wildly successful fourteen-man company.

"How'd things go? Grace seemed happy." Justin leaned in the doorframe, his eyes sharp. "I hear Mrs. Grace *really* likes you."

Shane groaned. "Mr. Grace liked the design, and he's planning to talk to you about it after he consults his board of trustees. I really like him, but his wife…" Gloria Grace had married a much older man, and her roving eye led one to the impression that her nuptials had definitely been for his money.

"I know. I'm just glad we have a younger crowd working here now. I had to deal with her the last time she came in." Justin shuddered, and Shane laughed.

Just then Justin's brother walked by. He frowned. Shane prayed the clock watcher hadn't noticed his hurried entry this morning.

"So you were late again, eh?" Thomas's expression didn't change when he added, "Gloria Grace was in today, wasn't she?"

"About this morning," Shane started, but Justin waved his apology aside.

"Never mind. You arrived before the meeting, and Grace liked him," he said to Thomas. "I meant Jonathan Grace. I think we might need to hide him the next time Gloria wanders in though. He's been limping. Too many pats on the ass, eh, Shane?"

Shane shot his boss the finger, not constrained by the typical employer/employee relationship. The Harmons had a loose working environment, which made Thomas's straight-laced attitude odd in a sea of laid-back architects.

"I've dealt with Gloria in the past. Thank God you're here," Justin said with evident relief.

"I'm glad to be here too." Leaving his uncle's company in Philadelphia three years ago had been hard, but Harmon & Sons allowed him to be near his parents. Not to mention he worked for an outstanding firm.

Thomas shook his head. "If you weren't so good behind the drawing board…" The empty threat joined the others he issued weekly.

"But he is," Justin reminded him. "So cut him some slack. We don't pay by the hour. And it was a known fact before he got here. You remember what Brett said."

"Not this again." Shane sighed.

"Your own uncle told us we wouldn't want you because you were habitually late and had no social skills to speak of," Thomas was quick to reiterate.

Justin added, "But then he explained that despite your lack of punctuality, you always put in more than your fair share of work and could do magic with design. He also said you could charm the pants off a client but that your mother despaired of ever becoming a grandmother, hence the crack about your social skills."

"My mother has wanted to see me married since I turned five, but I'm quite happy being single."

"Hey, you've got no issue from me." Justin held up his hands. "Not all of us long for the marriage noose. I mean, look what happened to Thomas."

Thomas replied with an anatomically impossible suggestion, causing both men to laugh as he walked away.

"So what did happen this morning? I'm curious." Justin handed him a sheet of paper. One of the Cornell idiots in the back had been busy. Shane had attended Syracuse, where he'd had more to do than make stupid charts. He and the guys constantly bickered over which of their universities trumped the other, which made work fun, but at times annoying. Like now.

A graph titled "Shane's Reasons" listed the days of the week on one axis and Shane's past excuses on the other.

"Very funny."

"I thought so."

Good to know he was at least consistent. "Today was strictly legitimate." Shane tried to defend himself. "Okay, so the alarm clock did happen to ring four times before I woke up. Still, I was dressed and ready to go when I noticed my idiot brother had taken my car. I had to run to the coffee shop to meet a buddy of mine for a ride. And when I got there, this ditzy woman spilled coffee all over me." He pulled out his stained shirt from the trashcan beneath his desk.

"Priceless. I'll have to add 'lady throws coffee at me' to the list." Justin laughed as he left the office.

Shane stared at his ruined shirt and wondered how he'd made it to work in one piece. His belly still felt tender and was slightly pink, but he was for the most part unharmed by the hot coffee. The same could not be said for his shirt. His head throbbed from the constant rush of the morning, and his stomach craved something to soothe the acid churning in his belly, courtesy of his caffeine addiction.

He checked his watch and blinked at the late hour. His meeting with the Graces had taken the entire morning. Then he swore when he realized he'd forgotten to grab his frozen entrée from the freezer at home for lunch. Leafing through the phone book until he found a familiar tab, he called downstairs to place an order for takeout.

As he waited on hold, he looked down at the white pages and noticed the name of a massage clinic above the restaurant's name.

That's exactly what I need. In fact, his younger brother had gotten some work done at Bodyworks a few months ago. George had been recovering from knee surgery and at the advice of his physical therapist had gone to the massage clinic for some relief. Recalling his mother's glowing recommendation, Shane knew they not only did clinical work but also the basic feel-good type of massage.

Just what he needed. The more he thought about it, the more he thought about getting one. He placed his lunch order and hung up the phone. He'd just clinched the Grace deal, a nice piece of business that would bring the firm a lot of revenue. And after today's hectic morning, he felt he deserved to give himself a treat.

He called and managed to slip into someone's last minute cancellation for later in the evening. He wrote down the time, address and his therapist's name—six o'clock, Bodyworks on Queen Anne with Denise. Then he returned to work.

The day flew by, and before he knew it the hour had reached five. Thriving on pressure, Shane did his best work when on constant deadline. He knew he was an oddity, enjoying both the creativity Harmon & Sons afforded him as well as the strict guidelines fitting project due dates. Structure and discipline, the foundations of Shane's life. Which explained his venture into the Marine Corps and his need to stay fit. Lately though, between travel, work and too many runs, he'd been pushing himself too hard. The massage would be more than a treat, but a much-needed respite from possible shin splints and muscle strain.

He leaned back in his chair and decided to forego his run tonight in lieu of therapy. No way he'd trade his chance at a massage for a hard race around Green Lake. Oddly enough, his mind drifted back to the clumsy woman from that morning.

She'd knocked into him at Sofa's, which sat directly across from the lake. And she'd worn shorts and a tee-shirt, as if she'd planned on some exercise. He could still see the irritation in her whiskey brown eyes, could feel her soft curves that had jolted him as much as the hot coffee had.

He grimly accepted that the accident had been more his fault than hers. She'd been walking calmly out of Sofa's when he'd plowed into her like a freight train. He must have seemed like a total ass this morning.

Now that he recalled the incident, he realized she'd been more than pretty. Her almond-shaped eyes had widened in outrage, and brown hair streaked with gold had blown across her arresting face in a blast of wind.

He frowned, not liking that he recalled her so clearly. When his body reacted at the reminder of her full breasts against his chest, he knew he needed to get out. A hard-on at work was a sure sign that he suffered from what Mac called the *all-work-no-play* syndrome. Definitely time to get laid again.

God, he just hoped Mac didn't mention the incident to George. Shane's younger brother was a seventeen-year-old walking hormone. Shane loved and respected women. He believed in a serious relationship and felt that good sex was only good if you solidly cared about your partner. Which explained his celibacy for the past eight months, since his breakup.

Mac and George pitied him because he refused to hook up. From Mac he'd expect such nonsense, but from his younger brother, it made him feel old.

Shane glanced at a photo on his desk, a picture of himself and bunch of buddies in camouflage utilities standing knee-deep in sand in Iraq. Back in the day, he'd train hard and play hard when the opportunity arose. But those days seemed like a lifetime ago. Back when he'd been younger and naïve about life and politics. And love.

Not liking the maudlin turn of his thoughts, he took another look at his newest sketches for the Grace project.

Good work deserved a reward. Time to treat himself to some much deserved relaxation. Just imagining the hands of a skilled massage therapist rubbing away his aches and pains urged him to get up and go. He rechecked his penned appointment. He'd been scheduled with Denise. Good. He couldn't picture getting naked under a sheet for some big guy named Bruno.

♥

By six thirty, Shelby had finished with her last client of the day and waved as the kind woman departed. Arching her back, she tried to rub away some of her own tension, knowing her night was far from over. She returned to the front desk to catch up on paperwork.

Massage therapy helped rid the body of contaminants and generally relieved stress. Yet more times than not, Shelby found herself mired in bills and the business side of things rather than dealing with the healing nature of her profession.

The phone rang, breaking into her thoughts. After taking the message, she frowned at the closed door of her massage room, wishing like hell the contractor would finish patching up the wall in Denise's room. She checked the appointment book and noted *Shane Collins* scrawled in Denise's barely legible handwriting. The appointment listed six o'clock, so Denise more than likely had another half hour to go.

Damn, Shelby hated to interrupt the massage, but she knew Denise would need to act on the message right away. She knocked quietly on the closed door and heard a low murmur from the room.

Denise opened the door an inch and peered out. "What's up?"

"I'm sorry, but I've got a message for you that's urgent."

"No problem." Denise called over her shoulder, "Shane? I'm sorry. I have to take this call, but I'll be right back." A low male voice answered before she left the room and closed the door behind her, then moved to the desk. "So who called?"

"Sorry, but it's the man in your life. I'm afraid he's broken his leg." Shelby waited for the worried explosion sure to follow. Denise was fanatical about her man.

"Oh my God! Cupcake! What happened? Was that my mother?"

"Yeah. Your mom said he must have gotten loose somehow and ran out of the yard. A car driving at the speed limit hit him, so he's not too roughed up. I know you'll want to see how he's doing. Why don't you go, and I'll finish up your client?"

Denise had tears in her eyes. Cupcake meant the world to her. A scrawny mutt she'd picked up at the pound, he'd been with her through thick and thin. "Are you sure?" Denise wiped her eyes.

Shelby handed Denise her car keys from the desk and nodded. "Go on home. Give me a call later and let me know how he's doing."

Denise flew out the door, and Shelby shook her head. She prayed, for Denise's peace of mind, that the dog would make it.

Realizing she now had a client to pacify, she quickly moved into the bathroom to wash her hands and returned to her room. She entered to the soothing sounds of new age music and the slight aroma of jasmine from the burning candles in the corner. Dim yet peaceful, the room radiated serenity and relaxation.

"I'm sorry about the interruption," she said quietly to the man lying on his stomach with his head down and resting in the doughnut-shaped pillow, which allowed for ease of breathing.

He appeared almost asleep, his back rising and falling evenly, but he mumbled something she couldn't quite hear. Before she could say anything more, he turned his head to the side, his eyes still closed.

Shelby barely contained her dismay. Upon her table lay the half-naked form of Mr. Tall, Dark, and Rude from that morning. His upper body was bare, a sheet draped over his lower back, buttocks, and legs. She glanced at the clothing rack on the wall to confirm his identity. The same black jacket and dark trousers hung from a hook, along with a blue shirt.

She stared back down at him and resisted the urge to lean into his ear and yell at him to get the hell out of her clinic. That would scare the impoliteness out of him. But her professionalism wouldn't let her. Word of mouth traveled fast, and this guy already didn't like her. She frowned at the thought of him telling people bad things about her business and could almost see the dollar signs flying away.

Grimacing at his unfairly handsome face, she wondered why he'd ventured into her place. Seattle had more than fifty massage clinics open at any given time, yet Mr. Rude managed to pick hers. Some cosmic joke at work, surely. She swore under her breath.

"I'm going to turn your head so you don't strain your neck." She turned his face back into the doughnut-shaped pillow. Frowning at the feel of his skin under her palms, she felt uncomfortable with the heat that raced up her arms. She shook off the strangeness and focused on the rest of the massage.

As she continued to work on his back, she couldn't help noticing the smooth muscles and power in his build. He had a very nice body, she thought with objectivity. As a person comfortable and familiar with human physiology, she was a good judge of such things. And a person would need to be blind and plain oblivious not to see that this man kept in *very* good shape. He had wonderful tone and definition. Working on him was actually very easy due to his fluidity.

As she brought clinical detachment to the forefront of her thoughts, she scrambled to bury the needy woman inside her screaming to see how his ass might feel under her hands.

"Does that feel all right?" she asked softly. She didn't want him to know she wasn't Denise. He needed to get his money's worth and at the same time think positively about Bodyworks. If she gave him a great massage, he'd be too relaxed to be angry with her when he paid her at the session's end and recognized her. She hoped.

"Mmm," he mumbled. "That feels great."

The sexy rasp of his voice made her belly flutter. Her massage wasn't in the least bit sexual, but she couldn't help feeling arousal at contact with his body. *God, I am not getting turned on by this guy. He's a lump of clay, something I can mold into healthy muscles.*

She continued to work on his back. Then she changed position to work on his legs, keeping the sheet in place over his firm, tight ass. *Buttocks, not ass. Ass is sexy. Buttocks is professional.* She felt like a mental patient at odds with herself. Not the best time for slutty Shelby to make an appearance.

"I need to move the sheet so I can get to your legs." Even as she said it she hesitated, waiting for his assent, half hoping he'd insist he didn't need any more of her time, half wishing he'd tell her to get rid of the sheet and hop on.

"Go ahead," he rumbled. "I'm half asleep as it is."

Shelby gritted her teeth and moved the sheet. Then she worked on the muscles of his legs, moving over his hamstrings and calves. They were rock hard and incredibly sexy—*firm, athletic.* Not sexy. Clients were never sexy. Rule number one of massage.

"Are you a runner?" she couldn't help but ask.

"Mmm, hmm. Every day I can."

"Your legs are very toned." She worked a rough section of his hamstrings. Smoothing over the fascia, the connective tissue covering the muscle, she released a build-up of toxins in his body. He sighed, and she moved down toward his calves, then to his feet.

He shifted a bit, and she stopped.

"Does it tickle?"

He mumbled a yes, and she grinned. Maybe she could torture him by tying him down and tickling his feet, demanding an apology for her ruined coffee. Or better yet, she could tie him up and blindfold him, then have her wicked way with him with none the wiser.

Oh hell. Her sexual hiatus had come to a crashing halt. For some stupid reason, this jerk had jumped her libido but good. She hadn't been able to get him out of her mind all day, and she'd tried. Now, after touching him... She glanced down at her nipples, horrified to see them through her shirt, standing at attention.

She'd blame her obvious arousal on the air conditioner if she had to. She might be able to ignore that, but the tingling between her legs and her racing pulse? Not so much.

Why did Mr. Rude have to have the best ass she'd ever *not* seen, the sexiest legs she'd ever felt, and the smoothest muscle she'd ever touched?

She closed her eyes and breathed deeply, calling on every ounce of professionalism and neutrality she could muster. It really wouldn't do to have her client catch her ogling his body. She could lose her license for less.

Shelby opened her eyes and reined in her crazy impulses, determined to give him what he paid for. But she needed him to turn over to finish. Good God, she could all too easily imagine giving him a "happy ending" and turning into the cliché from hell.

Let it go, woman. Finish the massage, then *go find a man.*

"Okay Shane. Now I need you to turn over so I can do your front." *Ignore the innuendo. Ignore the innuendo.*

He visibly tensed, and she held her breath, praying.

CHAPTER THREE

SHANE COULDN'T BELIEVE HOW RELAXED HE FELT, NOT to mention aroused. Denise hadn't done one thing inappropriate or unseemly, yet the minute she'd walked back into the room he'd felt the nerve endings in his body shift to focus between his legs. His cock might well have been made of iron.

Shit. She wanted him to turn over? He opened his eyes and stared through the open pillow at the floor. God, had he ever been in a more embarrassing position? And his *mother* knew these people. Christ, he really needed to end this.

"Uh, that's okay. I just needed some work on my back. I actually have an appointment I just remembered I need to get to. Don't worry about the rest. This was great." Such a lame excuse, but he couldn't think past the pounding in his cock.

"If you're sure." Denise sounded relieved. Or was that his guilty subconscious talking? "I'll be outside while you change."

The door closed behind her, and he breathed out a sigh of relief. He could only imagine her shock had he turned over and showed her how much liked her work. After a moment of silence, he turned onto his back and stared at the tent over his lap. Definitely time to start dating again.

He tried to will away his erection and dressed, concentrating on anything nonsexual. His mother, his brother. Denise? The petite brunette with the sensual hands and large blue eyes hadn't done more than stir a smile from him upon their first meeting. She wasn't exactly his type. Truth to tell, he ran more toward taller women, like the feisty Amazon he'd run into earlier that morning. Denise had been pleasant and professional. But toward the end, something had changed. He wondered if she'd felt any of what he had, or if he was just pent up from going so long without sex.

How pathetic that the most action he'd had in months had been at the hands of a massage therapist who'd done nothing but her job. No doubt Mac would laugh his ass off when Shane told him what happened. The shame of it actually helped calm him down. He felt like a dumbass, but at least he no longer worried about his cock.

He could too easily imagine his mother sitting nearby while a therapist took care of George's leg. Nothing sexual about that massage. Now if Mac had recommended the place, Shane might have expected a masseuse who didn't mind rubbing him *anywhere* he wanted.

He shook his head and exited the room for the front desk. There, he took out his credit card and handed it to…

"You!" He stared in astonishment at the golden-eyed fireball who'd preyed on his mind for the latter half of the day. She stared back at him with a blank look on her face. He was probably the last person she'd expect to see.

Knowing he'd been in the wrong, he tried to apologize. "About this morning, I—"

"Will that be cash or charge?" Seeing the credit card, she plucked it from his hand and ran it through her machine. When she glanced up at him, she gave him a bland if pleasant smile…as if she didn't recognize him. The incident from the morning had been a quick bump, and he now wore a different shirt. But that she might not know him bothered him more than it should have.

"You're not going to pay for my shirt, are you?"

She ignored him and stared at the machine. Her jaw locked as she fiddled with his credit card. Oh yeah, she knew him all right. Apparently she had no intention of forgiving him.

"Don't you remember me? You spilled hot coffee all over me," he reminded her.

She whipped her head up. "*You* ran into *me*, buddy." It didn't escape his notice that even annoyed the woman was damn hot. Her voice turned sugary sweet. "But if *you'd* like to apologize, I'm all ears."

He couldn't stop himself from looking her over when she leaned closer to hand him his card. She had full breasts and a slim waist. The desk hid her legs from view, but he remembered them being long and slender. Just long enough to wrap around his waist while he—

She cleared her throat, and he realized he'd been staring at her breasts. And those tight, hard nipples.

With a grin he couldn't help, he said, "I'd say you're more than just ears."

"God hates me," she muttered.

He laughed. She sounded so annoyed yet pitiful at the same time.

Their gazes met, and a smile curled her lips that she hastily smothered.

"You're beautiful."

She flushed, and he continued before he alienated her once more. "I admit the accident this morning might have been my fault."

"No kidding."

"But I'm willing to let bygones be bygones."

She ripped the paper off the credit card machine and pushed it and a pen at him. "Fine. Let's just forget about this morning. Now would you please sign here?"

"Sure thing." He signed it and handed it to her. "Where'd Denise go? I wanted to thank her."

"Denise had something important she had to take care of." The woman's gaze shifted to the paperwork in front of her, dismissing him. "She said she was sorry to have to cut out but it couldn't wait."

Shane wondered what it was about this woman that appealed to him. He'd never been into looks without the whole package. So far in their short acquaintance, she'd been shrewish, though not without good reason. She seemed as if she really didn't like him, and for some odd reason, that only added to her appeal.

But Denise with those hands… He wasn't a man to juggle two women at the same time. Denise had seemed to like him well enough, so he'd start with her and see where their first date went. Just as soon as he asked her. And if it turned out he'd just imagined their chemistry, he wouldn't be any worse off than he was now.

He continued to stare at the woman now glaring daggers at him, bemused at how much he liked looking at her. Odd how her annoyance only made her sexier.

"Do I even want to know what you're thinking?" she asked slowly, as if each word in his presence pained her.

"I doubt it. Have a great night, and maybe I'll run into you again sometime."

"Good*bye*."

He grinned and left the building. George had dropped his

car off at Harmon & Sons earlier in the day, so Shane had his own transportation once more. Thank God. He loved Mac, but the man drove like he owned a Formula One car. Great when Shane was late, but Mac's jerky steering played hell with his stomach.

He pulled out of the parking lot and headed home, making plans to contact Denise tomorrow. Dinner? A movie maybe? Hell, it had been eight months since his last steady relationship. He frowned. Did he really want that again? Commitment? Cohabitation? Compromise? He liked his life, well, except for the lack of sex. Maybe his buddy was on to something with his fast and loose attitude. Mac could be an ass, but he didn't lie to women. He was straight up about not wanting forever, and he seemed to have no problem finding companionship. Shane could go for that. The more he thought about it, the more he realized he didn't want a relationship right now, just raw, hot sex.

Instead of turning toward his house, he drove past Sunnyside and headed for Jameson's Gym. He hadn't planned on ruining the therapeutic relief from his massage, but Denise hadn't made it all that relaxing, at least, not for the lower half of his body. He had a spare set of workout clothes in the trunk. After his rubdown that left him feeling frustrated, a run on the treadmill tonight seemed in order. Plus he'd get a chance to talk to Mac.

Mac worked for his uncle, biding his time while his body recovered from a blown out knee. Ian Jameson had been threatening to retire ever since Shane had joined the gym two years ago, but the man had yet to step down. Shane wondered if Mac would actually make the move and assume complete control, or if his hard-headed friend would find his own niche and start fresh. With Mac, he never knew.

Shane arrived at the gym, changed and stretched. Then he hopped on the treadmill and ran for three miles without breaking much of a sweat.

"Twenty minutes," a deep voice sounded to his right. A glance showed his muscle-bound buddy studying the treadmill. "Not bad for an old man."

"Please." Shane slowed the machine to a fast walk. "First of all, I'm younger than you are. Second, I could kick your ass in a race even before you tore your knee. Once you heal up, just name the time and place."

Mac snorted. "I'm an injured man. Now if you want a real competition, let's lift some weights." Shane knew it hadn't been easy, but Mac had pretty much accepted his medical retirement from the Marine Corps. The bigger man flexed his impressive muscles, and a small gaggle of women by the elliptical machines eyed him like dessert.

Mac glanced over his shoulder, following Shane's gaze, and grinned. He waved and received several waves back. Then he turned back to Shane. "Come on, hotshot. You're done. Let's hit the office."

They left the main gym and walked down the back hall into a tidy room, furnished sparsely and decorated with Marine Corps regalia.

"Hey man, thanks for the ride this morning." At Mac's look, he held up his hands. "I know. That makes four times this month that you've saved my ass. Thanks."

Mac grunted. "I don't know how you made it in the Corps. You'll probably be late to your own funeral."

"Probably." Shane accepted the water bottle Mac threw at him and gulped down the cool contents. "I need some advice."

Mac's gaze sharpened. "It's that woman from this morning, right?"

"No, but funny you should mention her." He explained the situation at the massage clinic. "She's even better looking the second time. That woman really gets to me."

"Sounds like Denise got to you. Call her up and see what shakes loose."

"Yeah, well, that's what I wanted to talk to you about. I get too involved when it comes to women." Shane wasn't surprised to see Mac's nod. "You on the other hand, are Mr. Love 'em and Leave 'em. So what's the best approach to take to get Denise into bed and then out of it as fast?" Just saying that made him feel like a heel, but he intended to be up front about his needs. If Denise didn't want the same, she'd be free to say no.

Mac leaned back in his chair and laced his fingers behind his head. "Shane, my boy, you've come to the right place for advice. The problem with women is that you have to make them hate you to like you."

"What?"

"For some stupid reason, women love a guy who's a jerk. If you're too nice they ignore you. Or dump you." Mac paused to make his point, rubbing in the fact Shane's ex had done just that, then continued, "But if you pretend you don't care, act like a dick, they're on you like a heat rash."

"That's a great image."

"Thanks, I try." Mac grinned.

"So you're saying I should go abuse some woman then ignore her, and she'll be all over me?" Even Mac couldn't be this obtuse.

"No, no," Mac disagreed. "Obviously roughing up women, like you did this morning, only irritates them."

"That was an accident." Shane scowled. "I don't hurt women, you idiot."

Mac ignored him. "What you need to do is find a girl you like. Take Denise for example. You give her a little attention to show that you're interested, then you back off and watch her flail around trying to get to you. Once she's hooked, you take her out, you both have fun, and you're done. Easy."

Shane didn't think Mac's process had as much to do with getting women as his biceps did. But the man had an impressive track record. Women came at him in droves, and they never seemed unhappy when they parted ways. It was eerie and a little worrisome. Shane had never been good at fucking and flying, as Mac liked to call it. He needed to like his partner to share more.

Mac warmed up to his topic. "For example, did you see that redhead that was staring at us downstairs? Her name's Megan. Not long after I started working here, she started making eyes at me. She's got a great set of tits, a tight ass and nice legs, so I figured, what the hell?"

"Jesus, Mac. I know we're guys, but shit. She's got a brain." He just didn't think he could screw a woman based on her measurements alone.

"As I was saying, *Nancy*, I complimented her body, strictly from a trainer's point of view, mind you. I was pleasant. Then I ignored her for a few days. That woman was all over me like white on rice."

"This really works for you." *Amazing.*

Mac's sly grin spoke for him. "Let's just say that filly gave me one fine ride. My point is that if I'd been complimenting her and taking her out to coffee and dinner and movies, I'd have ended up in some stupid relationship that wouldn't have worked anyway and messed up a perfectly good friendship. Note she was just waving at me downstairs."

"Do you know more than her first name?"

"I think her last name's Wade. Maybe Jessup? No, no, it's Ward."

Shane sighed. "You need help."

"No, *you* do. That 'R' word women love to throw in your face is nothing but trouble. Look at you. Eight months after that witch left you, you're still floundering. Pathetic. Seriously, dude." Mac's ice-blue eyes glowed with sincerity. "A relationship is the last thing you need right now."

"Much as it pains me to admit, I think you're right."

"Of course I am."

"Not about all of it, just that I get too attached. I need a fling, but one that's a little deeper than tits, ass, and an orgasm."

"Not sure what your problem is with the holy trinity, but okay." Mac chuckled, and Shane couldn't help laughing with him.

"Hell, I don't know. Maybe a good fuck will relieve some stress."

"They say people who have sex regularly live longer. I'll live to a hundred and ten. At the rate you're going, I give you maybe two more years."

"Ha ha." Shane drained his water bottle and tossed the empty back to Mac. "So Denise. I'm going to call her. I mean, there was nothing there at first. Totally professional. But then something changed. I swear Mac, that woman's hands were like honey all over me."

Mac sat up. "Oh, so it's *that* kind of place, eh? What's the number?"

"No, no. For God's sake, my mother took George there. I'm just saying Denise and I had some sort of chemistry going on. Or maybe I did since she didn't act like she felt anything."

"At least you're going after this one. Okay, but remember

what I said. Sweeten her up then get the hell out of there before you find yourself joining her at some book reading. Next thing you know it's nonfat lattes or some crap like that."

"I can't wait to see the woman who knocks you on your ass. You'll be wining and dining her with pleasure. Mocha lattes, chick flicks, and the occasional karaoke, just to please the little woman."

Mac groaned.

"Remember this conversation, Major Macho. And when you need help, come to me."

Mac chuckled. "Yeah, right. But you know, you didn't need to come all the way out here for advice. You should have asked your brother. He's a great kid. Got a different girl every week and he's smart enough not to get serious."

"Please. We'll be lucky if he doesn't get some girl pregnant before graduation. He needs to grow up. And whatever you do, *don't* tell him I asked you for advice. He thinks he's the next Casanova and he'd be hurt to think I didn't ask for his help."

"Not to mention it's a little embarrassing to have to ask for advice on women at your age, eh?"

"Kiss my ass, Jameson." Shane swore good-naturedly and left Mac laughing in his office.

After arriving home, Shane showered and ate a quick meal, then settled in for some mindless television. But while he watched, he couldn't stop thinking about his single status and worrying about it. His mother still wanted grandkids, and most of the guys at the office were married. He'd come off a year long relationship, and though he'd been both hurt and somewhat surprised when it ended, a large part of him had also been relieved. Now, in retrospect, he should have seen he and Lisa wouldn't suit. But the breakup had been brutal. He didn't want to commit again, not yet. Though Mac's idea of what could only loosely be called dating left little to be desired, some fun wasn't totally outside the ballpark.

His friends had always told him he was too serious and picky about women. So maybe a few casual flings could fulfill that need for the excitement he craved. A few nights with the woman from this morning would do him just fine, if his erection was anything to go by. Just the thought of her angry eyes and full lips got him full and aching in a heartbeat.

Knowing he had nothing but his hand for company, he sighed and turned off the television. With nothing better to do than jerk off or go to sleep, he chose the less pathetic of his options and sought his bed.

He deliberately set his alarm clock on the dresser across the room so he'd have to get up to turn it off in the morning. As he pulled back the sheets and settled on the bed, he stared at the ceiling and thought of the sensual massage he'd received earlier. An image of the amber-eyed Amazon came to mind, and without wanting to, he reached under his boxers and grabbed himself. Stroking up and down, with firm pressure and a heat that couldn't come close to her mouth, he closed his eyes and pretended he'd run into her again. But this time, she held a glass of water that soaked her white shirt.

Her nipples would show through, and they'd be hard, thick. Excitement spurred him to stroke faster, and he saw her in his mind's eye, kneeling before him, apologizing for being so clumsy. She'd take the blame, and then she'd slip his cock free of his trousers and take him into her mouth. She'd suck him hard, play with his balls, and finger herself while she readied to swallow him down.

He groaned as he climaxed over his hand, making a mess of himself. As he came down off his high, he reminded himself that Denise, not the Amazon, had engaged his interest. With every intent to call Denise in the morning, he moved to the bathroom to clean up then slipped back into bed. And if he dreamed of the Amazon, he'd consider it a form of therapy to rid his subconscious of her once and for all.

CHAPTER FOUR

TUESDAY AFTERNOON, MAGGIE SAT AT THE TABLE entertaining Shelby's mother with tales of Friday morning's run-in. In hindsight, telling her friend she'd met the same guy that night for a massage wasn't well thought out.

"So then she sees him face down on that table. Coincidence or fate, I ask you?" Maggie shrugged. Her perky factor had begun to wear on Shelby's nerves.

"Was he a looker or what?" Mimi Vanzant, Shelby's mother, cut straight to the chase. Her fingers gleamed with turquoise, silver and onyx bands. At fifty-one, she looked ten years younger, with a thick head of dark red hair kept vibrant by a monthly visit to the hairdresser. Her blue eyes gleamed with merriment as she watched Shelby squirm.

Shelby turned to glare at her best friend. Maggie smiled back, all innocence, her head haloed by the delicatessen sign behind her. Today especially, the small booth they occupied felt super tiny, the space taken up by Maggie's big mouth and her mother's loud personality.

She groaned. "We're wasting time talking about this. I only

have a half hour until my next client. And besides, you're missing the point."

"Well, what *is* the point?" Mimi threw up her hands in confusion. The bangles on her wrists clanged and shimmered, causing a few heads to turn in the direction of the noise and brightness sitting in the corner. Her mother's turquoise and magenta tie-dye patterned jumpsuit should have looked outdated. Instead, the silk looked retro-60s and complemented her toned arms and legs. "You haven't had a decent date in six months. Ron told me your sign is blocked."

"Mother, please." Shelby pinched the bridge of her nose. "Would you keep your voice down?"

Her mother should have gone into acting instead of interior design, because she sure as hell liked to be the center of attention. Shelby loved the woman, but just once she'd like to go out and *not* wish she blended into the walls to avoid the scrutiny of a crowd.

She'd specifically avoided any mention of Shane Collins to her mother for this reason. Trust Maggie to blab the whole ordeal. Her mother had no doubt consulted her astrologer, channeler and God knew who else to see how Shelby's nonexistent love life would pan out. Oh man, and she didn't want to think about Ron. Ron Aandeg was her mother's closest friend, confidant, and business partner. Their successful design business catered to the eclectic and unusual. They had similar tastes in everything, from clothes to designs to men. If Shelby hadn't known better, she'd have thought her mother and Ron were twins. Ron had been a part of the family for over twenty years. Her surrogate father also had dreams that talked to him. With her luck, he'd had a nightmare about her over this mess.

Mimi pushed back her sleeves and clanked her bracelets. "Now Shelby, you're a water sign. You need to flow. In order to do that, you have to let go of that anger and resentment over Rick's betrayal."

Again with Rick. "I'm over it, Mom. Maggie." She glared at her friend. "Just because I'm not into dating doesn't mean I'm hurt over one asshole in a sea of swarming men."

"I think that would be schooling men. Like fish. They school," Maggie offered.

"Yes. I'd go with school too." Mimi nodded, and Shelby thought they might finally talk about something else. "But don't you see?" Mimi said excitedly, her voice rising. "Not only have you run into this man once, but twice. It's fate throwing him into your arms. I'm going to talk to Ron again and see what he thinks."

Shelby swore under her breath and lowered her forehead to the tabletop.

Maggie laughed, the little witch.

Her mother placed a kiss on her hair and stood to leave. "I've got to get back to work. We've got a new client coming in today, and Ron told me she promises to be difficult. An Aries. Stubborn and set in her ways."

Shelby raised her head. "Tell Ron I send my love, but nothing else. Please don't mention any of this to him."

Her mother waved her concern away, and Shelby knew she was doomed. When Ron and her mother collaborated—and they loved nothing more than to dissect her love life—the shit always hit the fan. And then she'd be the one cleaning up the mess.

"No worries. He and I will talk, we'll laugh, and we'll forget you by morning."

I should only be so lucky. Shelby watched her mother leave.

Maggie sipped at her water. "What a great lunch. Well, it's time for me to head back to the gallery."

Shelby latched onto her sleeve. "Hold on, you little traitor. *Why* did you tell my mother about rude guy?"

"I thought we were calling him Buns of Steel?"

Shelby groaned, regretting she'd mentioned rude guy's impressive physique. "Do you realize what you've done? Now Mimi Vanzant and Ron Aandeg are on the case. It's like the Hardy Boys on crack."

"Wearing sixties digs. Where the hell does your mother get her clothes? Vintage. I mean, she looks terrific, but wow."

"Focus, blondie," Shelby snarled. "Because of you, my mother will spend the next month making my life miserable. She'll be sending me emails and texts full of astrological readings, planet alignments and spirit walks with Ron over the Ouija board."

"And all to find your soul mate. Very romantic, if you think about it. Your mother loves you enough to go to the other side for help." Maggie's chipper reasoning did nothing but put Shelby into a blacker mood. Mostly because she wished her mother *had* the power to actually find her happiness. But she didn't. And no amount of woo-woo would make Shelby's lack of a significant other easier to bear.

Not that she had to be together with someone else, but damn it, lately she'd been so friggin' lonely.

Maggie shrugged and drew a circle in the water on the table left by her glass. "Come on. Even you have to admit it's pretty weird that the gorgeous guy you spilled coffee all over just happened to be naked in your room Friday night." She blinked. "When I say that out loud, it sounds dirty."

"Yeah, it does." Unfortunately, Buns of Steel hadn't called or said anything after she'd practically driven him from her shop. "So it was weird. Stranger things have happened. And let's be real. He wasn't naked in my bedroom." *Not entirely.*

More's the pity. "He was covered with a sheet and getting a massage, for heaven's sake."

"So tell me again what he looked like au naturel. Was he more muscular than he'd looked like through his wet, white shirt?"

Shelby sighed and chewed on some ice. She'd already dug her grave, might as well get comfortable. "He had a *great* body. Really muscular, but not overly so. He's a runner."

"The thing that gets me about all this is you."

"Me?" Shelby frowned. "What did I do?"

"It's what you didn't do. Why didn't you set him straight about Denise?"

"I didn't want him to get all crabby with me."

"Uh huh. Or maybe you liked him after all, and you think he liked you. But you didn't want to chance it. Better to love from afar than he know you had those magic hands all over his yummy buns. He might have felt taken advantage of."

A few men at a table nearby looked over at them.

"Would you lower your voice?" Shelby hissed.

"Fine." Maggie whispered, "I think you should look him up and use him. Just for sex. Keep it simple."

"You've got to be kidding me." Shelby stared with amazement. "Didn't you learn anything with Yeats? And *he* seemed normal. This guy's clearly obnoxious. He stared at my boobs," she added, careful to keep her voice down.

"I'm staring at them. They're nice boobs."

The guys at the table near them looked more than interested. They were grinning ear to ear.

When Maggie turned and asked them, "Well, aren't they?" Shelby dragged her friend up and away from the table and out of the deli.

Maggie yanked her arm free as they walked toward

Shelby's shop. "Come on, Shel. He's perfect. He's the type who probably won't want a relationship. And you said it yourself that he's got a killer body. Use him and lose him."

Shelby hated that she really liked the idea. "No way. I'm not that desperate."

"Not yet," Maggie muttered. "Oh hell. Fine. Now neither of us has any prospects of a nice weekend. So what's the plan for this Friday night? Funny, sexy or scary? Your call."

"Scary." If Shelby had to watch one more romantic comedy that ended in a happily ever after, she might shoot her TV.

♥

Wednesday afternoon, Shane entered Bodyworks, not sure how seeing Denise would affect him. He'd kept putting it off all weekend, and his workload had made it all too easy to ignore the impulse to call her. Determined to stop avoiding the situation, he'd decided to come down and talk to her in person.

To his good fortune, Denise sat at the front desk with a large smile on her face. She was pretty, petite, and seemed nice enough. He drew closer, looking for that same spark he'd felt a few days ago. Her grin widened upon seeing him, and she finished talking on the phone.

"Hi, Shane. How are you?"

He'd planned to use the excuse that he'd left something behind on Friday, something that would lead him to return. Then he'd apologize for cutting his appointment short and ask her out. But before he could say anything, Denise spoke again.

"I'm so sorry I had to leave you Friday. If it wasn't an emergency I would have stayed. But I left you in good hands with Shelby."

"I'm sorry, I don't follow you."

Denise sighed. "A car hit my dog Friday night, which is the reason I had to leave you after I heard. Sounds silly, but he means the world to me."

"No, I get it. My mom's dog is like part of the family. I swear he's in the will and I'm not."

The shared a grin.

Denise reached over the counter to touch his hand. He felt nothing. No spark, no heat. Just the comfort of another person. "Thanks for understanding. Shelby told me she finished you up with no problem. It felt good, right? The massage? Your calves aren't still hurting, are they?" she asked with concern.

"Shelby?" The only other woman in the place had been the angry Amazon, the one who'd tried to pretend she didn't know him. The same woman he'd been jacking off to for the past three days.

Denise stared at him in puzzlement. "Was there a problem?"

"I thought her name was Shirley." he said, thinking quickly, gratified when the worry left her face. "The tall woman with the light brown hair and eyes?" *And killer hands.*

Denise nodded. "That's her. She owns the place." She handed him a brochure. "I meant to give this to you after the appointment. So it was all good, right? No problems?"

Shane gripped the brochure tightly in his hand and forced a smile. "No problems."

"So what can I do for you?"

"What?"

She gave him an odd look. "Did you want to book an appointment?"

"Oh. No." He sucked at lying. "I think I left something in the back office. Sorry, it's been a long week, and it's only

Wednesday."

She chuckled. "I know just how you feel. Go on back. There's no one in there, but I have to tell you I didn't see anything out of place. What exactly are you looking for?"

"An important business card. Has a contact number I needed for work." Sounded plausible to him. "And since I was in the neighborhood..."

"No problem." The phone rang, and Denise waved him toward the back before taking the call.

He hurried into the back, entered the room where he'd had his massage, and closed the door behind him, not sure what to think.

All his lusting after Miss Annoyed all weekend had been justified. The angry Amazon from the front desk, the woman he'd run into Friday morning, and the sexual dynamo who lit his body on fire were one and the same.

He frowned. She'd acted like she hadn't known who he was. She'd run her hot little hands over his body, gave him the hard-on from hell, and pretended not to know him?

Though aggravated with her, at least he now knew he wasn't losing his mind. Denise hadn't done a thing for him, Shelby had. On some level his body knew her. How else to explain the connection he had every time he saw her?

The realization both complicated and eased matters. He felt attraction for just one woman. No soul searching about dating one woman at a time or being fair and open about a sexual liaison with Denise when he secretly lusted after the Amazon—Shelby.

But how to make Shelby respond to him with anything other than anger? He left the room and said goodbye to Denise while trying to think of a way to get into Shelby's good graces.

Later that night Shane sat in his living room and studied

the brochure for Bodyworks. Shelby's picture stared at him from the inside of the pamphlet, telling him about her experience and qualifications while not giving him the information he really needed. She'd graduated from massage therapy school and specialized in deep muscle work, Swedish and Shiatsu techniques. But what did she do for fun? Did she like to run, to read, to visit museums? Was she a road trip kind of girl? A partier or a homebody?

His gaze continued to shift from her professional qualifications to linger on her physical features.

In the photograph, her eyes smiled at the camera. She looked happy with a genuine smile, not one faked for a picture. Her long hair settled over her shoulders, glints of gold mixed with brown. Her lips were full, her cheekbones and chin framing an intelligent face. She had character, one he'd like to know better.

Hell. There he went again. His quest for sex and a no-strings attached hook up was lost in fantasies of dating. God forbid he told Mac he entertained ideas of getting to know the woman. And after nearly running her over, did he really think Shelby would be excited to sleep with him? The doorbell rang and shook him out of his reverie. He crossed to the backdoor, looked through the window, and seriously considered keeping it closed.

"Come on, Shane. Lemme in."

With a groan, he opened the door and stared into familiar green eyes crinkled in amusement.

"Hey, big brother." George angled past him into the kitchen, turned and smiled. "So what's this I hear about you having woman problems?"

CHAPTER FIVE

SHELBY STUDIED THE BOOK IN FRONT OF HER AND TRIED to stop envisioning herself and Shane Collins as the sexy leads. She tossed the steamy novel to the table and resolved to give up reading for a while. Too bad this particular book revolved around a hero with muscles, dark hair and green eyes. She'd fallen for the hero when she'd first read about him, but now after meeting Shane, she couldn't read about the warrior bent on conquest without envisioning Shane Collins in his place. She could imagine him calling her a slave girl as he tied her to his bed…

She groaned. "I need to get laid."

Life was so unfair. Shelby had a real thing for muscles. And Mr. Tall, Rude and Clumsy had a captivating grin to go with his killer abs and rock hard thighs.

She needed to forget how he'd felt under her hands. Thank God he hadn't turned over and seen her ogling him from head to toe. With her luck, he'd have taken her pert nipples and wide eyes as an invitation. No way would she have said no, and she could have kissed her sterling reputation as a therapist good-bye. Sex and work didn't mix, not in her particular field. But man, for a few moments during that massage, she'd wished she wasn't so moral.

Shelby had to get out of her stupid apartment. She couldn't concentrate on reading, there was nothing on television, and she had that familiar, disquieting sense that her mother would soon make an appearance to talk about destiny again. Inspiration struck, and a half hour later, dressed in workout gear, she met Maggie by Green Lake.

"I'm so glad you called." Funny, Maggie didn't sound happy. "I hope you know I'm missing a brand new Jack the Wonder Mutt for you."

"On the animal channel?" Shelby snorted. "You should be thanking me for saving you from the ravages of boredom."

"Whatever. I just hope my body can take an extra dose of exercise on an unscheduled walk night." Maggie groaned as she bent over to stretch. "Then again, it's not like I'm getting any *other* kind of exercise." She mumbled something else.

"What?"

"I said I'm on the verge of becoming a born-again virgin. Hell, I'm becoming *you*."

"You're so not funny."

"Really? I thought that was clever." Maggie chuckled.

As they started around the lake, Shelby wasn't surprised to find several late night runners and walkers populating the path. Seattle was full of freaks, especially of the fitness variety. "You know, blondie, you're not as loose and exciting as you like to think."

Maggie sighed. "I know. But now *you* know. That means my life is in virtual decline. I wish all of my dates ended in groans, moans, and prayers for more. Unfortunately, it's been more than six months since I've seen any real action."

"Try again, Wonder Woman. If I recall, that action was on stage stripping for Barbara Woodly's engagement party."

"Now I'm really depressed. You remember that night?"

Shelby tried to smother a grin. "I think so."

"Don't dance around it. Fake Conan dragged me up on stage, was bumping and grinding all over me, and dislodged the sock in his shorts. Talk about false advertising. And that's the only excitement I can brag about in nearly a year. Just call me Shelby." She pretended to hang herself.

"Shut up." Shelby grinned, and they ribbed each other as they walked. She thought about confessing her confusing emotions about Shane. She needed to talk about them. Bad enough she couldn't stop thinking about the man. But if she told Maggie, Maggie might run to her mother. The pair of them were determined to get Shelby back on the dating circuit.

They'd gone a short distance before Maggie stopped short of a water fountain marked *Out of order*. "Shoot. I forgot my water bottle. Wait here while I run and get it. Well, I won't really run, but I'll be quick."

"Want me to come with you?" While it had grown darker, twilight still shed pale light across the lake and the trail. Enough people traveled the path to provide a sense of safety, but Shelby always felt protective around her smaller friend. But God forbid she tell Maggie that.

"Nah. Tell you what, I'll meet you at the duck sign farther down." Maggie turned and walked back down the trail toward the parking lot.

Desperate to keep her mind free of Shane Collins, Shelby resorted to running, the one sport in life she really detested. Yet as she settled into a loose jog, the tension seeped out of her by degrees. She skirted a few baby strollers and dog walkers, as well as a couple holding hands. The love between the pair showed through their smiles and the way they walked in step, shoulder to shoulder.

Suddenly annoyed with life in general, she put on a burst of speed, passed the duck sign, and sprinted for the turn-around point which wasn't that much farther past the sign.

Once there, she turned around and readied to go back when she stumbled into what felt like a steel wall.

Large hands steadied her. "Easy there."

Oh hell. She knew that voice.

He pulled her out of oncoming foot traffic into the tree line but didn't let her go.

Sheltered in his arms beneath the awning of a leaning willow above them, Shelby tried to catch her breath and looked up into the bright eyes of Shane Collins. "What are *you* doing here?"

"Well, well." He smirked as he gave her a onceover. "What a pleasant surprise."

"You're not stalking me, are you?" A stupid question, considering she hadn't seen him in days, but still.

He grinned. "I live a few blocks away. You?"

"No, I live in Queen Anne." He lived close. That would explain his presence here tonight and how they'd collided the other day. "And I'm sorry."

"For what?" She couldn't believe he could still look this good, at night, in sweaty clothes. Holy crap, his legs were really, really cut. And his chest looked broader than she remember it being. She curled her fingers and tried to concentrate on his words and not the lips shaping them.

"…sorry for running into you the other morning. It really was my fault, and I blamed you for it unfairly."

An apology was the last thing she'd expected. She opened her mouth to speak but didn't know what to say. She'd been rude to him in her clinic. Should she apologize back? Though it had been his fault, accusing him of starting the mess in the first place sounded awfully third grader-ish.

He was staring at her, waiting for what, she didn't know. An excuse? A rebuttal? A kiss? *Bad, bad thought.*

"Shane—"

He placed his finger over her mouth, and all thought fled. The intense heat of his flesh seared her lips and traveled through her body to center between her legs.

"I might as well apologize again," he rumbled.

"For what?" Shelby stared into mossy green eyes turned dark.

"For doing what I've been thinking about since you first touched me."

His mouth covered hers, and she felt warm all over. She clutched his forearms, aware his hands had crept to circle her waist. He deepened the kiss and groaned, then pulled her against his hard body.

Oh wow. He felt incredible. Firm, warm muscle, so vital, so strong. Yet her reaction to his touch was much more intense. She traced the contours of his chest, slightly damp through the soft shirt he wore.

She didn't know what he'd done to her, and God help her, she didn't want him to stop. When he raised his head and stared down at her, she could only stare back.

To her disappointment, he stepped away, and it was all she could do not to look at the front of his shorts, having missed that part of him during the massage. A good thing, because if he was as large as he'd just felt against her, she might have done the unthinkable and given him a rub-down he'd never forget.

Shelby blushed, grateful to the limbs and leaves that obscured them from view. She heard Shane take a few deep breaths. The same sense of urgency rode her, and she had to work to will it away. After a few moments, he tugged her with him out from under the willow trees.

A devilish glint lit his eyes. "I'm sorry. Again."

"You should be," she muttered. *For making me want you like crazy.*

His gaze traveled from her lips to her breasts and lingered. She crossed her arms over her chest, hiding her nipples that screamed for his attention.

"You're so cute when you're pissed off."

"What a *lovely* thing to say." She couldn't help liking his sense of humor. On top of that kiss, his attitude made him even more attractive. She had to keep remembering his rudeness, spilled coffee, anything except how utterly sexy he was. A man like this could do a lot better than Shelby. She'd learned that the hard way not too long ago.

The sex she could more than go for. The hurt feelings? The lies? Not so much. And unfortunately, she'd never been a one-night stand kind of girl.

"So am I forgiven?" he asked, his voice a low purr.

"For the kiss or the coffee?" Damn. She sounded out of breath.

He grinned. "Either. Both." He paused. "Is it wrong that I want to kiss you again, in a place where we have some privacy and time to…explore?"

"I—"

"Shelby. There you are. I was looking for you." Maggie stared from her to Shane and back again. "Who's your friend?"

As if she didn't know.

"Shane Collins. Nice to meet you." He held his hand out and shook Maggie's. Once done, he immediately turned his attention back to Shelby. She gave him extra points for not fixating on the blond bombshell most men couldn't look past. "I have to be going. I'll see you again soon." He called over his shoulder as he started jogging, "And Shelby? Thanks for the massage Friday. I definitely owe you one." Then he put on a burst of speed and ran off.

Crap. He'd found out.

Maggie grabbed her by the arm and walked with purpose in the direction he'd gone.

"What's your hurry?" Shelby managed, still tongue-tied from Shane.

"That was Mr. Rude. Shane Collins, he of the magnificent thighs and tight, tight buns." Maggie and she craned their necks to watch him disappear out of sight.

Shelby sighed. "I guess he's not that rude."

"What is that *look*? You're flushed and glassy-eyed. What the hell did I miss?"

"He apologized for being a jerk the other day." Shelby let out a deep breath, knowing she shouldn't say anything, but she had to share. "Then he kissed me."

"*Oh my God*."

"Shh. Keep it down." Shelby still swore she could feel his lips over hers, where her mouth tingled.

"What was the kiss like? He looks like a really good kisser," Maggie prodded. "And holy hotcakes, but he has a nice body. You should have thrown coffee on him tonight. We could have gotten a good look at his top *and* bottom." She wiggled her brows.

Shelby chuckled. "Yeah, that would have been a sight. Okay, I'll give you details on one condition."

"Sure, anything. Come on, Shelby. This is the most exciting thing that's happened in your love life for the past six months. Except for my date with the cross dresser, it's the most exciting thing that's happened in mine. Spill it."

"First, promise not to tell my mother. Or Ron," she tacked on for protection.

"Now why would I tell Mimi?"

"Because you think with her help I'll be more social. But the truth is, too much Mimi and I'll need to be institutionalized. No more interference in my lack of a love life. Swear."

Maggie blue eyes swam with guilt. "But—"

"No buts. If—and I do mean *if*—I see Shane again, it'll be because I want to, not because our stars align."

Maggie shrugged. "Okay. Fine. We have progress. At least you're calling him Shane and not Rude Guy."

"Or Buns of Steel, though I kind of like your nicknames."

Maggie snickered. "Yeah, well, they fit. Because those buns were fine."

"Yeah." Shelby sighed.

"I promise not to tell your mother anything. Now talk, woman."

"He has a killer body. Having seen it on my table then massaging him, touching him… All I can say is wow. Really, really, *wow.*"

"I told you he was handsome."

"Yeah, you did. But that kiss blindsided me. I don't think I've ever been kissed like that before. Too bad it was there and gone before I could get into it." She fanned herself as they walked around *another* couple holding hands. *Is it romance night at Green Lake or what?*

"I've never seen you so dazed. Maybe you're human after all."

"Thanks so much, bestest buddy." She knocked Maggie on the arm.

"Ow."

"So if I do see him again, and there's no guarantee I will, what then?"

"What do you mean?"

"He's sexy, handsome, and built. He's also a professional who happens to work downtown at one of the best architectural firms in the city."

"Nice."

Shelby nodded. "Denise mentioned it. Said when she'd met him, she asked him where he worked, and he'd named a place she recognized, because her brother interned there one summer. Bottom line is Shane is handsome and probably well-off. In other words, out of my league."

Maggie scowled. "Says who?"

"He's the type." Just like her ex. "Except I think I might like to see him again, even though I know I shouldn't."

Maggie sighed. "This is about Rick. Man, I hate that guy."

A handsome, wealthy jerk who'd stomped all over her heart. Shelby hadn't cared about his money or his social connections, she'd loved him for himself—or the man she'd thought him to be. But over time, his snipes about her career, her mother, and her job had taken its toll. Then to find him doing a blond knockout in the bed they'd shared for a year... Of course she was still scarred. It hadn't been that long ago that she'd given Rick the keys to her castle, only for him to toss them aside in lieu of some tart with large breasts. She could only be glad she and he had never moved in together.

Their split had been so easy it depressed her all over again.

"You need to forget him," Maggie continued. "Not every guy is like Rick Matinson. Take Shane. He apologized." Maggie took a swig of water.

"Gee, I guess for that I owe him a blowjob."

Maggie choked on her water.

"No?"

"Give me some warning next time," Maggie wheezed between laughter. "Okay, I get it. Just because he had the sense to say he was sorry doesn't mean he's a prince. But he seems decent enough."

"I guess."

"So if you're starting over, you might as well start with him. I'm not advocating a relationship." Maggie lowered her voice. "But it would be nice if at least one of us was getting some, so we don't both turn into the cat lady on the block."

Shelby snorted. "Please, Maggie. We're not even thirty yet. We have time to indulge in some good old celibacy and planning for the next Mr. Wrong."

"See? That's my point. You're so negative."

"I am not."

"Prove it."

"This is ridiculous. I shouldn't have to go out with some guy—"

"—who kissed you."

"Who kissed me." Shelby glared. "Just to prove to you I'm not afraid to go out again."

Maggie just stared at her while they walked, and Shelby finally gave in.

"Okay, fine. I'm sure if I don't give him a shot, you'll tell my mother."

"Exactly."

Somehow, getting Maggie's encouragement loosened that ball of fear Shelby didn't want to acknowledge. She could exploit this physical connection with a hot guy and leave it at that. No point in trying to indulge in a relationship that wouldn't go anywhere. And after that kiss, she knew he wanted her sexually at least.

"So I'll have the power in this—it's not a relationship."

"Nope. Nothing to worry about. Just some harmless flirting, some fun, and if you're lucky, some hot sex. That's it."

When Maggie said it, it sounded so simple. "So I'll have the power in this flingship." Control. Shelby prized power. She could handle Shane Collins.

Maggie blinked. "Flingship as opposed to relationship, I take it?" She nodded. "I like it. Yeah, Shel. And just think, if he's that good with his lips, imagine how good his other parts will be."

Shelby thought about it as they headed back to the parking lot. "Thanks for the walk, Maggie. I'm not sure about the advice, though."

"Don't worry. I won't charge you for it. This time." Maggie winked. "Anything to get one of us out there, moving and shaking again."

"For the record, this isn't a dry spell. I'm not dating anyone on purpose. I'm still not sure I want to hop in bed with some guy I don't know."

Maggie shook her head. "You know where he works and what he looks like naked."

"He wore a sheet."

"He's not an ax-murderer, we don't think, and he has a decent job. You could do a lot worse." She bit her lip then added under her breath, "You have done a lot worse."

"Jerk."

Maggie stuck out her tongue.

"Okay, Rick sucked. I agree. But I do know I don't want anything serious for a while."

"Exactly. You want a flingship."

"Right." The feel of Shane's lips refused to go away. "So where does that leave me?"

"It leaves you at ten o'clock on a Wednesday night in a parking at Green Lake, standing with your best friend after a smokin' hot kiss from Buns of Steel."

"Shane Collins."

"Whatever. I should have your problems." Maggie stretched her arms over her head. "Now go home, stop worrying, and think about the next step in your flingship."

Shelby gave her friend a stern warning, "One call to my mother and I'll get five cats, become a hermit, and tell everyone I've gone gay because of you."

"I swear I won't call her. Cats aren't my thing. But if this bad streak with men keeps up, I just might try my luck at going to bat for the other team."

"So long as I still get to be bridesmaid at your future wedding, I don't care who you marry, so long as he or she isn't a psycho."

"Or a prick like Rick. Same goes, Shel."

Shelby grimaced and left with a wave. But as she drove away, she kept wondering about Shane. Good guy or bad? And would it matter if she only intended to have sex with him?

CHAPTER SIX

WHEN MAGGIE ARRIVED HOME, SHE CALLED HER brother's number, knowing he wouldn't answer while on a job, and left a message checking in. That done, her second call went straight to Mimi. She didn't consider herself disloyal. Helping Shelby required the big guns, and though her best friend didn't think Mimi would help, Maggie knew she was *exactly* what the doctor ordered.

Poor Shelby had been nursing a broken heart for far too long. Rick the Prick, as Maggie liked to think of him, had broken down Shelby's confidence one block at a time. He criticized her looks, her job, her friends and family. But he was subtle, never going straight into an insult so much as he danced around his unflattering comments and jibes, blending them with humor.

Personally, Maggie had always thought Rick suffered from a bad case of jealousy. Shelby was young, had her own business and thrived in a town that had a massage clinic on nearly every corner. Beautiful, smart, and independent, she didn't *need* Rick. And that had bothered him. Ech. The passive aggressive tendencies in that man had made Maggie's head spin. But telling her best friend the truth hadn't been easy, not when she hadn't wanted to alienate Shelby.

Little by little, Shelby had become a shell of her vibrant, outgoing self. Catching Rick cheating had been the best thing about their relationship, because Shelby had finally seen him for the asshole he was.

Maggie clenched her fists, still wanting to belt the creep. She wasn't alone. Mimi and Ron had known all along he wasn't the right man for Shelby.

Maggie had watched Mimi and Ron do their thing for five years. More than designing homes, they worked with energy. Sure, the psychic stuff was out there, but it got results. Mimi and Ron did more than fix houses for folks; they fixed people as well. More than one couple had found each other and stayed together through Vanzant Interiors. Yet Shelby refused to use the help right in front of her.

Mimi finally picked up on the eighth ring. The woman didn't believe in voicemail. "Hello?"

"Hi, Mimi. It's me, Maggie."

"Maggie, how lovely. So what are you and my daughter up to on a school night?" she teased. "It is Wednesday, isn't it?"

"All day."

"Uh huh." A pregnant pause.

Now to ask for help without asking, because Maggie had made a promise. "I just wanted to talk to a friendly voice after my long walk around Green Lake. I have nothing to say about my best friend, who shall remain nameless. I'm also not calling to tell you about her chance meeting with Shane Collins. Or that the man looks incredible in running shorts."

"Not calling to tell me any of that, hmm?" Something chimed in the background. Probably one of Mimi's many bracelets. Or maybe her wind chimes. Or her shrine to an air divinity aligned with Cupid. Who knew?

"Nope. I would never betray my friend's confidence like that. If I told you that he kissed her right there in the park, you might be tempted to interfere. And *my friend* would never forgive me if she knew I'd shared her secrets. I just called to say hello to my favorite other mom."

Mimi chuckled. "I think of you as the grateful daughter I never had. Thanks for sharing, dear. I'll have to mull things over. So tell me about the newest piece you've been working on."

Maggie chatted with Mimi for a few minutes, gave her love to Ron, who was no doubt nearby, then said goodbye. She closed her phone and smiled as she set it down. She'd started the ball rolling. Now fate, ushered by the unstoppable force of Mimi and Ron, could take over while Maggie watched from the sidelines, keeping everyone in play.

♥

When Friday night came to a close, Shane sighed with relief. It had been an exhausting couple of days since he'd been drafted to help on an overdue project at the office. But now his weekend awaited him. He had plans he'd decided to put into motion. He'd thought long and hard about his meeting with Shelby the other night. As he slipped into his house, he knew he'd been right about her. Just one kiss from those sweet lips of hers had sent his pulse skyrocketing.

It had been far too long since he'd obsessed over a woman. Unfortunately, as much as he wanted to follow Mac's plan of attack, he didn't know if he could go through with it. He lusted after Shelby, sure, but he'd started to like her as well.

Low bass thumped through the main hallway, but he didn't remember leaving his stereo on that morning. Then he heard a familiar laugh and groaned. Rounding to the kitchen, he found George and Mac sitting at the table playing cards.

"Geez, Shane. Could you work a little longer on a Friday night? No wonder you're so boring." His brother shook his head.

Mac smirked. "Now, Geo, you know that's no way to talk to your big brother. He's probably working really hard so he can clear his schedule for the golden goddess down at Bodyworks."

Shane shot Mac a look and contained an inner groan when George whipped his head around and stared at him with wide-eyes. "Golden goddess at Bodyworks? You're making a move on my Shelby?"

"Possessive much?" Mac took a swig of his beer.

George frowned. "She worked on my knee for weeks and really helped. I like her. She's nice, and she's got a body that won't quit. I think she works out." He sighed. "She's hot. Older, but sexy. Like, a cougar who's a definite ten."

"A cougar if you're seventeen." Mac snorted. "So she's that great, huh? Because your brother hasn't said much more than that she has great hands."

George gaped.

"I was talking about the massage she gave me. And you know it," he snapped at Mac. He pinched the bridge of his nose. A headache was brewing.

"I flirted with her some." George's gaze was curious. "But she didn't take to it. I think she digs older guys. Too bad, really."

"Maybe I ought to give her a shot," Mac suggested.

"Not your type." He hadn't meant it to come out as a

growl. Mac and George stared at him, then gave each other a look before focusing their attention back on him.

"But she's yours, I take it?" Mac kicked back in his chair and drank more beer. "So George, what's the scoop on Shelby? Anything Big Brother should know?"

George stared at Shane, his gaze considering. "You could do worse."

"Thanks."

"So Shelby." George tapped the table. "Where to begin? She's hot, oh, but you already know that. She's pretty funny too. Her best friend works down the street from her in some art gallery. She's lived here for fifteen years or so and broke up with some jerk six months ago. As of my last appointment, she was free and not looking for entanglements."

Mac sat up straight in his chair. "How the hell did you pick up so much information?"

George shrugged. "It's in the blood." Their father had been career military, specializing in intelligence. George ignored Shane's snort of derision. "I asked her a bunch of questions while she worked. She answered them."

"And told you about her last boyfriend?" Six months ago. Shane could work with that.

"No. Actually, I overheard her talking on the phone. That and I listened when Mom grilled her. And you know Mom. She just about had Shelby's bra size before my sessions ended. I think she wanted to hook you up, Shane."

Mac chuckled. "The kid's good, you have to give him that. Like your mother. Woman should have gone joined the Corps and gone intel instead of your dad."

"No shit." Shane hoped his mother hadn't been too pushy. Not that he minded her choice of woman for him, but he didn't need his mother interfering in his social life. Bad enough he had Mac and now George to deal with.

"Good news is it sounds like your lady is free." Mac nodded. "Coming off a bad relationship. Nice. Means it opens the door for rebound sex."

George studied Mac with interest. "Rebound sex?"

Shane wanted something stronger to drink than beer. "For God's sake, quit talking about rebound sex and my brother's therapist. In fact, stop talking about sex entirely."

"You're such a prude." George made a face at him and turned back to Mac. "He's a lot like Dad. Believe it or not, Mom was the one who gave me the *where babies come from* speech."

Mac laughed. "Your mom is way cool. Your brother, not so much."

Shane shot him the finger.

George snickered. "Not too creative with his insults either."

"*You* should shut up and take note. At the rate you're going, you'll be a father before you graduate high school," Shane said dryly.

"No way, bro. I'm very careful about stuff like that. I may like the ladies, and God knows they love me, but there's no way I'm ready to be a father yet. Hell, you're thirty-one and still single. If anyone's giving Mom and Dad grandkids first, it's you."

"Terrific."

George's eyes brightened. "Mom loved Shelby. Woman was pumping her for information like nobody's business. It bummed her out big time when Shelby dodged her. I'm pretty sure Lorraine was trying to set you up. But Shelby managed to finesse her way out of the interrogation. It was pretty impressive, actually."

"You've hit an all time new low if you need your mom to get you dates," Mac muttered. "That's just embarrassing."

"I didn't ask her to help, asshole." Shane glared at his friend before turning back to his brother. "In fact, I'd appreciate it if you kept quiet about this, George."

"Yeah, seriously." Mac agreed. "Don't get your mom involved. Sex and mothers don't go hand-in-hand."

"So you just want to have sex with Shelby?" George frowned. "I don't know if I like that."

"Christ. You," Shane said, pointing to Mac, "quit talking about sex. And you…" he pointed to George… "keep your mouth shut about this. What I do or don't do with Shelby is my business."

"Not that you have anything *to* do," Mac added. "Not after you ran her over and then stalked her at her place of business."

"What?" George's eyes were the size of half-dollars.

Mac explained, and George started laughing and didn't stop. "Oh man, you are so lame."

"Great. You're a big help, Jameson." Shane would have been more irritated if the events didn't sound funny, even to him. Good thing he hadn't mentioned running into her at Green Lake and kissing her. He'd keep that nugget all to himself.

"Okay." George rubbed his hands together. "So Shane, the king of commitment, wants a hook-up. That right?"

Mac nodded.

"And he wants Shelby for that?"

"Yep."

Shane scowled. "I'm right here."

"I guess I'm okay with that, so long as Shelby knows what he's after. She's nice. I don't want her hurt by a guy who says he'll call but won't. Or some ass who's late all the time or stands her up."

"I'm not late all the time, you little punk." Shane wrapped George in a headlock and gave him a king-sized noogie until his brother cried uncle. "Now let's ditch the topic of my love life for something much more interesting."

"Like what?" Mac asked.

"Pizza." Shane's answer did the trick. Now more concerned with their stomachs than his social agenda, Mac and George argued over pizza toppings while Shane dug for the phone number to call it in. But all the while, he thought about Shelby and what to do about her. A kiss, now what? Where did he go from here?

♥

Shelby rolled her shoulders as she finished her third client for the day. She normally arranged her schedule so that she had her weekends free, but two cancellations earlier in the week had caused her to work an extra day on Saturday. She watched her client leave and started to shut down the shop when a voice came from the back door.

"Hello?"

She turned around and smiled as one of her favorite prior clients walked in with a smile on his face. He had dimples that would make any young girl sigh and smile. If only she were sixteen again. "George Collins! How are you?" she asked as the lanky teenager approached with a familiar swagger.

George flinched. "Shelby, how many times do I have to tell you? It's Geo, like Leo. Not George." He enveloped her in a bone-crushing hug. Shelby hadn't seen George—Geo—in over a month. He'd had knee surgery at the end of the school year and had come into her clinic to speed his recovery. She looked down at the fading scar on his knee.

"How's the leg?" She knew football practice must be near to starting if it hadn't already.

"It's good. I wear that hellacious knee-brace, but it doesn't slow me down."

Shelby had been flattered yet hesitant when Geo had first flirted with her. But his sense of humor, tenacity, and drive to recuperate had made her like him tremendously. With his dark good looks and charming grin, she had no doubt he had girlfriends galore in school. She'd bet her last paycheck Lorraine Collins had her hands full with this one.

"So what brings you around?"

"I was strolling down Queen Anne and thought I'd look in on my favorite therapist. Actually, I was getting a card for my aunt's birthday and saw your door open. I'm surprised to see you working on a Saturday."

"I don't normally, but I had clients needing extra help. So what about you? Are you playing yet?"

George strolled around the large hardwood area at the front of her shop, toying with the exercise balls on the floor that Ann, a fitness coach, used for training. "Practice began last week. So far, so good. It's looking like I should start as quarterback again this year."

"Good for you. So who did you decide to make your number one? The head cheerleader or ex-Student Council president?" Ah, the dilemmas of youth.

George gave her a devilish grin, and Shelby had a sudden case of déjà vu. Weird. "Neither one yet. I decided to ask the captain of the girls' soccer team on a date. We're seeing a movie tonight."

"Wow, George. Just one girl during senior year?"

He smirked. "It's too early to tell. Besides, I'm too young

for monogamy."

"Gimme a break."

"No, really. I can't imagine settling down 'til I'm old, like thirty-one maybe." He smirked. "Or twenty-seven."

"Jerk."

He snickered and hopped onto a nearby stool. "So what's the story with your love life?"

"Nosy guy." When he only stared at her with that engaging grin, she sighed. "Nothing much to tell," she said. "I'm taking it easy for a while. Heck, I'm young like you. I figure I don't need to settle until I'm old and gray. I have four more years until I hit thirty-one, right?"

He hopped off the stool and chuckled. "That's what I'm saying." He wandered into each of the back offices and called out, "Place still looks as good as it did when I was in here."

Shelby managed to refrain from remarking that just because George had moved on didn't mean she'd let her practice go to ruins.

"What's this?" he asked as he came out of her massage room.

He handed Shelby a card.

She took it from him. "Shane Collins, Harmon & Sons Architecture? I could have sworn I'd swept up in there," she murmured to herself, a frown on her face as she studied the card of the man who'd been on her mind all week long.

"Who's the dude?" George asked innocently. "New boyfriend?"

"I don't think so."

"Oh, you're not sure?"

She glanced up from the card to see him looking at her strangely. "I'm not discussing my love life with a seventeen-year-old."

"Love life, eh?"

"And get that smirk off your face. I'm not old and dried up yet."

"Aw, Shelby. I'd never think that of you." The leer on his face looked out of place.

"You're creeping me out. No way I'm even pretending to flirt back with you, Geo. I'm too young and pretty to be carted off to jail for carrying on with an under-aged boy."

He scowled. "I'm not under-aged. I'm seventeen. And I'm not a boy."

"Man, male, boy. You're all the same. You're missing that important leg of the chromosome that includes common sense."

"I think that's an insult, but I'm still processing the fact you might have a love life."

"Shut up, Geo." She chuckled, wishing she'd had a younger brother like him growing up. It would have made her days much less lonely.

"So who's the dude?" He nodded at the business card still in her hand. "A client, huh?"

"Kind of. You want the truth? He ran into me, spilled my coffee, and blamed me for it."

George shook his head. "What an idiot." He paused and remained silent.

"Geo, are you all right?"

"Oh, uh, yeah. Sorry. I just realized Gina is going to be waiting on me if I don't get moving."

"Well, it was good seeing you." She gave him another hug, pleased when he patted her on the shoulder and quickly backed away. She glanced down at the card again, and Geo was forgotten in a rush of memory and heat. That kiss refused to be a distant memory. Damn it.

George left her with a wave. As he walked past the front window, he noticed she stared at his brother's card with a frown. Perfect.

He walked down the street and entered the passenger side of a raggedy blue Wrangler. After slamming the door, he turned and grinned at Gina.

"What was that all about?" she asked as she pulled away from the curb.

"Nothing. Just doing a favor for my brother."

CHAPTER SEVEN

SHELBY READ THE NAME AGAIN FOR THE TENTH TIME. Shane Collins. Obviously no relation to Geo, who hadn't batted an eye at the name. The card confirmed what Denise had overheard. Shane did in fact work as an architect, at least, according to the card she held.

Oddly enough, she could see him sitting behind a drafting board creating things. The notion that he had more in his favor than a hot body registered. A man with an actual job. Now if he didn't live with his mother, he might be a real keeper.

She snickered at the joke Maggie would appreciate and decided why the hell not. Twenty minutes later, after fighting the downtown traffic, she found a parking spot near Eighth and Pine. She left her car and walked to the large corporate offices where Harmon & Sons was located.

She wondered which floor he worked on as her eyes strained to count windows. After standing there craning her neck for several minutes, she felt stupid. Deciding to at least take advantage of her parking spot, she walked down to the market.

After that kiss the other day, Shane had said he'd see her around. What did that mean? He obviously knew where to find her but hadn't given her *his* address.

Maybe he'd left his card on purpose? Yeah, right. A guy like Shane Collins could pretty much have any woman he wanted. He'd probably bragged about that kiss to his friends. Another conquest, and after he'd run her over the other day.

Needing a boost, even if it was from caffeine, Shelby walked down to Pike street and grabbed an iced coffee from Tully's. Sitting on one of the many benches near the market, she watched the crowd, alarmed by her behavior. Hadn't she learned her lesson from the last handsome man in her life?

She reminded herself to relax and took in the scenery. A rotund man carting a nagging wife and two screaming kids passed by two women holding hands and mooning at each other. Mooning. Something Shelby had done once, what seemed like forever ago.

A young man wearing a backpack kept asking for change from passersby, a few cents to make his bus fare. She grimaced but had to give him credit for his novel approach to panhandling. Several couples, young and old, strolled by, laughing and talking and kissing. More reminders that she sat alone, unattached, on a perfectly wonderful Saturday afternoon.

God, what was wrong with her? Why couldn't she have what the lovers passing by had? Her ex had seemed so nice at first. Rick had been handsome, charming, and independent. He'd had a great sense of humor but could be serious too. He liked to make money as much as he liked having fun. Unfortunately for her, Rick's love affair with fun had manifested in an actual affair with a woman named Candy.

Such a cliché, except Candy didn't strip and wasn't a hooker, but his ditzy secretary. Apparently the office romance had been going on for almost as long as they'd been dating. Not wanting to play to type, she hadn't reacted in a dramatic fashion. She'd called him a prick and left him. Period. And with nothing at his house to take back that was hers, their relationship had ended in a flash. Over. Done. And so damn hurtful.

Shelby had always taken pleasure in her lean body and pretty, if not stunning features. Catching Rick having sex with another woman sunk her self-esteem, big time. While the rational part of her knew he was a complete jerk, she couldn't help wondering if she'd pushed him into it. What had been so lacking in Shelby that Rick had been forced to look elsewhere?

Her thoughts grew steadily darker as she thought back to that period of her life. After several years struggling to make ends meet in her clinic, she'd found herself in the black. A profit, finally. Until that point, she hadn't had much time for a social life, let alone the energy to pursue one. A chance encounter with Rick at a downtown festival had blossomed into romance. Now, when she looked back on it, she thought she'd loved him. But his bullying tendencies hadn't allowed her to fall all the way.

Thank God.

Still, she missed him in bed, where she'd had no complaints.

Rick was tall and lean, with dark hair and dark eyes. He'd been polite and charming to her mother and friends, though Ron hadn't liked him from the start. She had spent less and less time with her family and friends and more with Rick and his circle. The jokes at her expense she'd tolerated. The subtle jibes about her mother she'd handled, because she'd often thought the same and they'd never seemed overly cruel, just funny. She tempered her feelings for her mother and Ron with love, but she could understand how they might rub Rick the wrong way.

A few comments he'd made about Maggie had almost ended their relationship early on. No way did she want her boyfriend lusting after her best friend. Maggie hadn't liked him for it either. But Rick had wised up, shut up, and managed to string Shelby along for ten more months of what she'd assumed was a monogamous relationship.

She sighed and put her empty cup aside. Now she had no more intimacy, no more pleasant nights spent cuddling and relieving her of loneliness. No more feeling as if a man could desire her for herself. An entire year wasted on Rick Matinson.

God. Had she ever been with someone she clicked with? Her entire bevy of lovers—all six of them—had been pleasant. Bleh. What a mediocre word. Nothing like the romance books, her sex life had been fun but nothing stellar, earth-shattering or heart-stopping.

Honestly, she didn't think she had it in her.

The kiss with Shane had been a fluke. The more she thought about it, the more she believed it. A woman desperate for sex would feel tingly from attention from anyone. And like it or not, Shane Collins could only be described as handsome.

Her cell phone rang, and she dug around in her purse to find it, glad to be taken from dark thoughts. "Hello?"

"Where are you, Shelby?" her mother asked. "I tried you at your work number but you'd already closed. Have you eaten lunch yet?"

"Not yet. Why? Where are you?" Mimi was nothing if not a bright vision to dispel a bad mood.

"I'm working with Ron on a project. Give us half an hour and meet us at the Pub."

Shelby could count on her mother to turn her world upside-down. Even an astrological reading would be welcome at this point.

"Okay, Mom. See you guys there soon. No rush." She disconnected the call and walked back toward her car. But as she walked past the building where Shane worked, she saw him standing there, staring at her in shock.

"Shelby?"

"Shane?"

His smile widened into a grin big enough to split his face wide open. "Well, now. My weekend is complete."

She felt herself blushing and forced herself to frown. "You are so full of it."

"Of bad lines, yeah. Guilty." He moved faster than she expected and latched onto her arm. He wore a pair of jeans and a tee-shirt and looked good enough to eat. Her heart raced uncontrollably.

Oh man. I am such an idiot. Remember Rick.

"Now before you accuse me of stalking again, I should tell you I work here." He pointed behind him to the building. "Want to see?"

"Yeah. Prove it."

He chuckled and walked her inside. They passed two security guards who nodded at Shane. Once in the elevator, he pulled her close.

She put a hand on his chest when he looked like he might kiss her—because she wanted him to. "Whoa. What's that about?"

"Just a kiss to say hello." He grinned, and a dimple flashed in his cheek.

"Hello." She blew out a breath, quietly, but gasped when he kept her hand on his chest. "Let go."

"Feel my heart racing?" His eyes darkened. "I'm really glad to see you again."

What did a woman say to that? "Uh, okay."

The elevator door opened, saving her from looking like a total fool.

"My floor. Come on." He left the elevator with her in trace. "Harmon & Sons is designing the new sports complex for the Seahawks, you know. An extra training facility near the stadium."

"Nice." Impressive, but she didn't want to seem bowled over.

As they walked down the quiet hallway, she noted the lack of people. "Where is everyone?"

"Gone. We at Harmon & Sons appreciate our down time." He winked at her. "I had some work to catch up on, so I came in to finish up. Here." They entered a spacious room. "My office."

"Nice."

"You said that already. How about, 'Gee Shane. This is so impressive. I'll give you that kiss you wanted earlier.'"

Shelby snorted. "Dream on. It's not that great."

He sank into the couch facing his desk. A leather couch, facing a grand desk that sat across from a drafting table. He had a small refrigerator in the corner and what looked like another door, to maybe a bathroom or a closet. Wooden blinds shuttered the windows on either side of the door. It was more than a nice office. The place smelled like high class and money all rolled into one.

Shane was so out of her league.

The thought annoyed her.

"What's that look?" he asked, seeming fascinated.

Enthralled by a plain Jane with a humble background? Well, why not? Why the hell wasn't Shelby good enough for him, anyway? "Kiss me."

He blinked. "Ah, okay."

"Right here. In your designer office."

He didn't refuse. But instead of coming right to her, he closed the door to his office. It *snicked* shut, and then he was right there in front of her.

"You're quick," she said, impressed despite herself.

"You're sexy."

Flattered but not convinced, she took back control of the situation. Rick the Prick had rejected her. This guy had run her down and appeared to like the look of her. Well, let him prove it. If nothing else, she'd be rid of this dry spell when it came to men.

The excitement of what she considered doing made the circumstances feel unreal.

"Shelby?" Shane asked, his voice hoarse. He stared down at her, his breathing fast, uneven. "I'm going to kiss you."

"You're going to do more than that." She dragged his head down and plastered their mouths together. A rough mating of lips and tongues and teeth that alerted every cell in her body to wake the hell up. *Right now.*

He groaned and yanked her against him, grinding into her body with a massive hard-on. Then he pulled away. "Shit. I'm sorry. I didn't mean to… I want to… *Fuck.*" He licked his lips, and she smiled.

"Yeah, fuck. That's what I want. You have a condom?"

"A condom?" His voice rose. "You want to fuck *here*?"

"Problem?"

He opened and closed his mouth several times, like a fish gasping for water.

The idea made her grin. "Scared?"

"Oh hell. I'm an idiot for hesitating, aren't I?"

"I don't know." She pulled him down by his shirt. "I could

be a stalker. Some psychotic woman who gets her kicks scalding men with hot coffee."

He groaned. "I am so sorry for that."

"So make it up to me."

He nodded fiercely, and his quick turnaround surprised her. "You bet."

Before she could rethink her impulse, question the condom issue again, or wonder about the incredible turn her life had taken—hello, sex with an almost stranger on a whim in his office—he kissed her again.

This time, he took charge. Shelby forgot her own name. She could only moan into his mouth as he devoured her will to do anything but submit. She'd never in her life felt so hot and bothered by a man. She ached to feel him inside her. Though she knew it was crazy, she couldn't help it.

She wrapped a leg around his and tried to ride that hard ridge pressing between her legs.

His lips left her mouth to trail over her cheek to her ear. "I'm gonna fuck you hard, Shelby. Right after I suck those pretty tits."

Not breasts. *Tits.*

His dirty talk turned her into a heaping mass of lust, as if she wasn't needy already.

"Yeah." She couldn't think of anything else to say. Her hands went to her shirt and his covered them.

Together, they whipped her shirt over her head. In seconds, her bra followed. She took a breath, and then his lips were around her nipple, pulling and sucking loud, embarrassing groans of need from her.

He grunted and continued to use those magical hands to ease her jeans open and push them down her legs. She hadn't realized she'd lost her sandals until she felt her jeans over her ankles, followed by her panties.

A large, blunt finger parted her legs and delved between her slick thighs, rubbing through her cream.

He left her breasts and stared at her. "Christ. You're wet for me."

Why had she thought his eyes were green? They appeared black, his pupils large and wide and focused on her. He didn't give her time to answer before shoving the whole of his finger inside her while he kissed her again.

The sensation of fulfillment made her gasp, and his tongue intruded. Taking and tasting and plunging in time with his finger *inside her.* She had a hard time believing any of this to be real. Excitement blazed through her, her orgasm rising like the shriek that built at the base of her throat.

He left her mouth and murmured against her neck, "Come for me, baby. I want to feel you soak my fingers."

Finger? He only had one— He added another, stretching her wider. It burned and soothed that need for more. His mouth surrounded her nipple again, and he nipped her as he fucked her with his fingers.

She came apart without warning. One moment reveling in his touch, the next going off like a rocket.

"Yeah, clamp around me. That's good." His voice sounded gravelly, and as she grew aware of her surroundings once more, she realized she'd been lowered onto his desk. She lay flat against it, her ass hanging over the edge, perfectly positioned for him.

He pulled back from her, and she saw a thick, hard cock jutting out at her.

She couldn't look away as he hurriedly removed a condom from his wallet. He ripped it open and rolled it down an impressive length.

Then he looked down at her, his face drawn, his eyes blazing with need. "Open your legs," he growled and leaned over her.

She did without question and cried out his name when he slammed inside her. He fucked her hard, ruthlessly, and kissed her while he hammered home. Though thick, he fit without a problem, gliding through her slick walls in a race to the finish she hadn't intended to join.

He reared back, and each time, his pelvis grazed her sensitized clit. God, he felt so big inside her.

"Yes, oh fuck. I'm coming. *Fuck*." Shane gritted his teeth as he plowed her harder then stilled.

The damage had been done. His jerky movements rushed another climax out of her, and she squeezed his orgasm while she experienced her own a second time.

She loosed her grip on his forearms and stared up at a more than satisfied male.

"You okay?" he asked and brushed her hair from her face.

The tender action sparked something inside her, something gentle and warm and affectionate, putting waste to her idea to be spontaneous and physical without emotional entanglement.

"Yeah. Thanks." She felt suddenly awkward and would have darted for the door if she hadn't been stuffed full of his semi-hard cock.

"Shelby…" He kissed her again and shocked her by moving. Small, short thrusts that he shouldn't have been making. Rick had never been up for more than one go, and not after an explosive orgasm like Shane appeared to have felt.

"Shane—"

"Sorry, wait. Just let me…" He continued to push in and out of her, and the motion felt more than pleasant. Arousing and soothing, surprisingly enough. She wanted to come again but couldn't yet. It was too soon after his rousing command of her body, but apparently not too soon for him. He jerked inside her as he threw his head back and moaned her name.

She watched him, taken with his beauty, that agonized pleasure that he wore so well.

After some time, he withdrew and discreetly disposed of the condom. They dressed in quiet, gazing at each another, confused, wary, and on Shelby's part at least, wanting to know when they could do this again.

"It was just sex," she blurted, alarmed at her need to be with Shane in the future. *Again?* Try never. A one-shot deal, she told herself. Or tried to tell herself.

He finished pulling his shirt over his head, and she missed seeing his glorious chest, so smooth and tan. He nodded. "Right. Just sex. On my desk."

"In your office."

They slowly smiled at each other.

"Pretty hot," she said.

"Damn hot. Scorching." He licked his lips and focused on her mouth.

"But tame." She wished she'd been more creative with her one-time only deal. Maybe a handjob while she watched him, or a daring sixty-nine. But with a condom? Something sexier than…sex on his desk? Who was she kidding? Shelby had gone wild for the first time in her life, and she loved it.

"Tame?" Shane seemed to consider her words. "Maybe next time we'll get creative."

The silence built between them.

"Next time. Hmm." Shelby wanted a next time more than she wanted to breathe. But she'd been down that road before. Though Rick had played havoc with her self-esteem, today had helped a ton. But another time was a step closer to a relationship. Yet a shot at Shane's killer body beckoned. Should she or shouldn't she?

"Yeah, bad idea," Shane said with a sigh before she could actually make a decision. "Another time would ruin the spontaneity, I guess. All that excitement about a romp in the office would fade if we did it again."

"True." Sad but true.

He walked her out of his office, and she noted all his papers scattered to the floor that she'd missed earlier.

He followed her gaze. "I'll clean that up. But hell, it was worth it."

She nodded, in total agreement. He said good-bye to her on the first floor and watched her walk out of the building. But he didn't walk her outside. Instead he went back into the elevator, presumably back to his floor to clean up the mess they'd made.

Shelby walked in a daze back to her car. She'd had sex. With a man. No planning, not a steady boyfriend, but an orgasmic experience during the day in his office. She felt like the star in an adult rated movie and broke into laughter.

Holy shit. She'd had sex with Shane Collins, the hottie with a huge cock. The sexy architect hadn't been able to keep his hands off her. "I did the architect," she said aloud, just to hear it.

Part of her wanted to rush to Maggie and share the juicy details, but Shelby wouldn't. Today had been an important turning point for her. She could now have meaningless sex and not attach meaning to every look, wink, or kiss.

So then, why did she feel something more for Shane? Why did she have an urge to see him smile again, or wish he hadn't been so quick to agree with her only-once disclaimer?

The buzz of her cell phone nearly gave her a heart attack. "H-hello?"

"Shelby! Where are you? Ron and I have been waiting for ten minutes. Are you coming?"

Oh God. Her mother. Shelby thought about cancelling, but that would attribute more importance to her lovemaking than it merited. *Lovemaking.* She scoffed at the term. It was fucking, nothing more, nothing less.

"I'll be there soon. Sorry, got to window shopping and lost track of time."

Her mother huffed and hung up.

Shelby tucked her phone into her purse and sought the nearest rest room, which happened to be in the marketplace. After doing her best to clean herself up and appear normal, she met her mother and Ron with a smile.

Nothing like sex in the afternoon to brighten a girl's day. Now to rid herself of thoughts about seeing Shane again.

CHAPTER EIGHT

SHELBY STUDIED HER MOTHER AND RON ACROSS the table. Ron wore jeans and dark blue shirt with the logo *Vanzant Interiors*. He was the perfect foil to her mother's flamboyancy. A handsome older man with cropped dark hair and Native American ancestry evident in his reddish brown skin, Ron Aandeg would have made any woman proud to hang on his arm. Unfortunately for her gender, Ron preferred men.

"Tell me again, sweetie," he drawled. "You're not coming to our quarterly gala for what insane reason? You're playing cards with Maggie? You're dog sitting Denise's pooch? Oh wait, I know. You're washing your hair that night, is that it?"

"No, Ron." Shelby ignored her mother's titter of laughter. "I'm not coming because every time I show up to one of your professional events, you and Mom try to fix me up with a date."

"That's not true," he denied then paused to flirt with the waiter for another slice of lemon. "He is so cute," he said under his breath before turning his attention back to her. "We simply want to share our lives with you. Is it so wrong that we're proud of your accomplishments?"

"No, but—"

"Or that we're in effect networking? Our clients could be your clients, and vice versa?"

"Well, no, but—"

"Or that we want our friends to know how fabulous Mimi looks considering she has a daughter your age?"

"There is that." Mimi fluffed her hair.

"Okay, okay. Maybe I'm a little too sensitive about my social life." *I just had sex with a man I barely know in his office. Oh my God. I'm a slut, a hot slut, because Shane totally came hard. Twice. Take that, Rick!*

"...Shelby?"

She coughed and took a quick sip of water. "What's that?"

Ron and her mother stared at her. "Is it me, Mimi? Or does her aura look a little different to you?"

Her mother leaned in and frowned. "You know, I think I see it."

Being a slut was one thing, having her mother know about it another. "Oh gee. Look at the time." She reached into her purse and grabbed her wallet. After digging out a few bills, she tossed them to Ron. "Use this toward lunch. I just remembered I have a client coming in. Gotta go!"

She gave her mother and Ron a kiss on the cheek, trying like hell to forget whom she'd been kissing not too long ago and how it had felt. *Ew.* Mother. Sex. Together, not good.

"Bye." She flew out of the restaurant like the hounds of hell were on her heels. But if she knew her mother and Ron, they likely were.

"That girl had sex." Ron didn't mince words.

Mimi choked on her iced tea. "Good God, Ron. That's my

daughter."

"Mine too."

She wished that were literally true. Ron had been a better friend, man, and all around human being than Shelby's sperm donor, or as Mimi liked to think of him, the inspiration for her inarticulate years. Unlike David, her daughter's MIA father, Ron had attended the girl's school events, oversaw her prom, and celebrated her graduations, from both high school, college and massage therapy school. He was loyal, handsome, and creative. Everything she'd always wanted in a man, except for the sex of course. Which brought her back to the discussion.

"Yes, you're right. I'm sorry, she is yours."

"Thank you."

"Don't pout." She frowned at him. "I don't see how you can use the words *Shelby* and *sex* in the same sentence. She's been in a man-hating phase for months because of that imbecile."

They refused to say his name.

"Normally I'd agree. But her horoscope today said she'd find love if she looked for it. I'd say she found it."

Mimi frowned. "Love and sex don't go hand-in-hand."

"With Shelby they do."

He had a point. Her daughter made her proud in so many ways, except when it came to relationships. The poor girl picked disappointing men and committed her whole heart, only to have it stomped on time and time again. Rick Matinson was the latest in a string of losers. A surface ten, an under the skin zero.

"But who does Shelby know, that's male, to have sex with?" she asked.

"Indoor voice, Mimi," Ron muttered when the couple next to them gasped in shock.

She turned to them and huffed. "Please. You people know what sex is, don't you? You're both old enough to have gone a few rounds in the sack." She wasn't surprised when they protested and left. "Seattle used to be filled with free thinkers, now they're all prudes," she complained.

"I know, honey," Ron commiserated. "But really. Focus. Who does Shelby know that—"

Mimi snapped. "Buns of Steel."

"What?"

"Not a what, a who." She reminded him of Shelby's run-in the other day. "The girl is starry-eyed over him, from what Maggie *didn't* say. And she's already seen him naked. Technically she felt him naked too."

Ron sighed. "Tell me again why I didn't become a massage therapist?"

"You tried it, but the frequent police raids didn't help business. Remember?"

"Oh. Right."

They shared a smile.

Mimi continued, "So Shelby is in a tizzy over this man. Shane Collins." That was the name Maggie had passed on a few days ago. A good girl, that one. They needed to help her find happiness too, just as soon as Mimi nabbed the right man for Shelby. If her daughter had any sense, she'd eschew marriage, the way Mimi had. But Shelby had too much of her father in her. The girl needed permanence and babies and a white picket fence. Which wouldn't be too bad if Mimi could have the grandchildren she'd been hungering for without an idiot for a son-in-law. Ah well, sacrifices had to be made if she wanted precious babies to cuddle.

"Do we check him out?"

"We do." She gathered her purse and bags and eased the

check to Ron. "Pay this, then let's head to my place. We have some charts to gather and some numbers to crunch."

"I'm on it, honey." Ron whisked the check away, and Mimi soon joined him, eager to pave the way to her daughter's future. Of course, it would help if they had something personal of Shane's to use in their readings. Something Ron might use when he worked that magic he'd learned during his New Orleans years.

Once back at her house, she made a call to Maggie, frowned, then tucked her cell phone back away.

"Well?" Ron asked as he lit a few candles and herb bundles to clear the energy in the room.

"She's not happy about it, but she'll do it. Now let's begin…"

♥

Shane spent the rest of his weekend doing chores and cleaning up the mess his brother and Mac had left. He couldn't get Saturday afternoon out of his mind. He'd had sex. Mr. Vanilla, as he'd been labeled, the plain, uninteresting guy Lisa had thrown over for some schmuck with piercings and covered in tattoos, had fucked a woman in his office on his desk. And he'd come not once, but twice inside the tightest pussy he'd had in a long, long time.

Just thinking about it made him feel dirty…and turned on. Though proud of his quickies in his office, the emotion attached to the act didn't jibe with the idea of a one-night stand.

God, he wanted her again. Not some faceless woman in a scene straight out of any guy's fantasy, but Shelby Vanzant. Talking dirty to her, shoving into her on his desk, where he worked, made him feel like a real man. Stupid, but true. He wanted to be able to leave it as an incredible experience, to be more like Mac and fuck and forget her. But he couldn't. Shane *liked* Shelby. He'd loved seeing the expression on her face when she came. Learning what pleased her, how she felt around him.

He glared down at his constant erection, wishing he could find one of Mac's many admirers, several of whom had made overtures in his direction, and relieve this ache. But he didn't want any of them. He wanted Shelby. But this time he'd bend her over while they fucked. Or he'd tie her up. He'd always wanted to do that. Or he'd fuck those beautiful breasts…

"Stop. Let it go." He tried to thwart his impulse to build a relationship. He didn't want commitment again, not yet. He knew that. But he couldn't convince himself he wanted sex with no strings attached either. *Damn it.* He liked the woman he'd fucked, and he felt bad because of it?

I am so not normal.

Sunday blurred into the next week. He worked hard on the Grace project, but he accomplished more at home than at the office. The desk gave him too many reminders that he wasn't yet the man he wanted to be. Not a lighthearted Romeo like Mac, or even George. Shane was a stick-in-the-mud serial dater. God, he needed to do more casual sex and let himself enjoy it without getting so attached.

Didn't he?

Thursday night, his brother swung by to drop off the movies he'd "borrowed."

"Thief." Shane snatched his Lord of the Rings trilogy from his sticky-fingered brother the moment he walked in the door.

"Dude, relax. I'm sure your Aragorn fan club buddies will forgive you for lending them out." George rolled his eyes. The kid did exasperated better than anyone, even Mac.

"Don't be a jerk. Next time ask before you take."

"Yeah, whatever." George hopped onto Shane's kitchen counter, despite being told a million times to use a chair. "So what's going on?"

"Nothing. Work. Why?"

George shrugged, but he had that look in his eye, the one he wore when he was up to something.

"What did you do?"

"Me? Nothing." George fiddled with the magazine next to him. "So, you talk to Lisa lately?"

Shane just stared. "Lisa?" He hadn't heard from that woman in eight blessed months, since she'd dumped him for Mr. Tattoo. Yet hadn't he been thinking about her just now? "Why ask about her?"

"I know she broke your heart, man." George looked into his eyes with an odd determination. "And I want you to be over it."

"Uh, I am." *I'm getting there, at least.* "It's obvious she and I would have been a bad mix."

"So if she came to you tomorrow, begging you to take her back, you wouldn't?"

An image of Shelby, on her knees, begging to suck his cock, appeared in his mind's eye. He hurried to replace it with thoughts of his mother and cut off the erection before it could manifest fully. Jesus, he had issues if just the idea of Shelby could get him hard.

"Dude?" George looked worried.

"No way. Nope. I'm over Lisa. Permanently." Disloyalty, and the things she'd said about him while trying to steal half his shit when she moved out, had killed whatever tenderness he might have felt toward her.

"Good. That's great, man." George hopped down to the

floor. After a moment, his knee buckled, and he groaned.

"Are you okay?" Shane hoped like hell his brother hadn't damaged his knee again. Though he'd healed fast, it wouldn't take much to set him back, not with football season coming into swing.

"I think so. Just a twinge." George sighed. "Too bad Shelby isn't seeing me anymore."

Shane jerked to a stop, his mind and now George talking about the woman. "Huh?"

"Shelby, my massage therapist? The woman you're so hot over?"

Shane frowned. "I am not."

"Whatever, dude. I just came by to drop off those discs." He limped to the door. "Don't tell Mom about this, okay? In fact, maybe you could do me a favor."

"Here it comes."

"Could you let me see Shelby here this weekend, if I can get her to see me? I swear I'll pay you back. If Mom knows my knee hurts, she'll make me quit the team. And it's my last year. Dad will be so disappointed. The scholarship…" Tears glistened in George's eyes.

Shane nearly bought into it before he remembered who he was talking to. "Emotional blackmail. Creative. The tears are a nice touch."

"I thought so." George blinked and his sadness vanished. "But seriously, bro. I'm gonna ask her to meet me here Saturday. Could you make sure you clean the place up? And maybe wear something nice and act less pathetic than usual so she can get those healing hands on me without feeling awkward around you."

How much more awkward would she feel to see the man she'd had sex with alongside his brother? Yet it was the perfect way to see her again. He could justify bringing her to his house to heal George. It wasn't at all needy to want help for his brother.

"Okay, George. You set it up, and I'll host."

"Great." George hurried to the door. "But you can't tell Mom."

"Trust me. I won't."

"Thanks, man. You're the best." George turned back to hug him, then hustled out the front door so fast Shane suspected foul play. If his brother could move like that, how the hell did the little faker think he could fool Shelby into fixing his knee?

For some reason, George wanted Shane and Shelby together. Shane didn't know why, but he'd find out. *After* he had a taste of his Amazon again.

♥

"Did he buy it?" Mac asked as he drove George away from his brother's.

"I think so." George kicked his feet up on the dash before Mac shoved them to the floor.

"Respect the car, nimrod."

"Sorry, sorry."

The kid was a natural around women, but still a kid. All the Collinses were decent people. Shane's old man had been a Marine, the inspiration for Shane's service to the Corps. And probably Geo's. That's if the kid wasn't drafted to play pro out of college. He already had a bead on a full scholarship to Washington next fall, after he graduated high school.

"So what did he say?"

"He's not giving anything away, but I'm telling you,

something went down. At dinner Sunday night, he zoned out. Shane never zones. And he's been goofy. Grinning for no reason. It's a woman, I swear."

"But he hasn't mentioned anyone to me." Not that Shane had to, but he and Mac were tight. Best buds for years. They had the Corps in common, as well as a basic decency too many civilians lacked.

"I didn't know you two girls shared everything." George batted his eyelashes, and Mac grinned.

Then he cuffed the kid in the back of the head.

"Ow. Okay, so he didn't share."

Which was Shane's MO when it came to a woman he liked. Mac had to pry the information from him. Unless there was no woman, and Shane had zoned for some other reason.

"Tell me again about Shelby. Don't leave anything out."

As George described the woman, Mac's curiosity grew. She sounded too good to be true. And if she had his buddy's dick in a knot, she needed to be investigated. He'd be damned if he'd watch Shane go through the hell of a bad relationship with some bitch again. Lisa had been more than enough.

The next morning in the gym he was busy doing paperwork when one of his trainers entered with a confused expression on his face.

"Yeah?"

Ed shook his head. "This is gonna sound weird, but there's some woman here who needs to see you."

Not so weird. "So?"

"Oh. Not like that. This one says she needs to get into Shane Collins's locker."

"Why?"

"Says she's his ex girlfriend, and he has something of hers. I thought I'd bring it to you."

Lisa was here? "Good. Bring her in." Mac wanted nothing more than to give the bitch a piece of his mind.

But the woman who entered his office wasn't the cheating redhead his buddy had once fallen for. This chick was a platinum blonde with a petite frame and beautiful breasts. Just his type. And man, those cornflower eyes were killer blue.

He had a hard time remembering his manners when she entered and glared at him. No way Shane had tagged this babe and Mac didn't know about it. Or had he? If Mac had been with her, he'd have been zoning and goofy for days. Weeks. Hell, years.

"I want in Shane Collins's locker. He has my old hairbrush, and he told me I could grab it. Your trainer didn't believe me, but I'm not lying. You can get it for me if you want. I'll wait here. I'm not out to steal from him, just to find what's mine."

Mac stood and moved from behind his desk, pleased when the woman's mouth opened and she looked up. Way up when he loomed over her.

"Okay, honey. Try again. Who are you, and why are you really here?"

"First off, my name is Maggie, not honey. Second, it's not your business, He-Man. Just point me to Shane's locker, or better yet, get my brush. And if you think I'm making all this up, think again. I know all about his brother George, his mother Lorraine, his father Colonel Collins, Harmon & Sons, his time in the Marine Corps, all of it."

So she had information. How did she know Shane? Because he sure as shit hadn't mentioned her.

"So then you've seen his tattoo." Mac crossed his arms over his chest, amused at the flare of panic that lit her eyes.

"Ah, right. His tattoo."

Shane, the pussy, would never desecrate his body with ink.

The woman zeroed in on the snake on Mac's bicep, as well as the eagle globe and anchor on his opposite forearm. She swallowed audibly. "How tall are you?"

"Me?" He narrowed his eyes. "Who the hell are you?"

"Damn it. I knew this was stupid. Get the hair from his brush. It'll be easy. Ha!" She drew in a deep breath and let it out in a rush. "Look, isn't Shane your best friend?"

"He is. And I won't let anyone screw with him, no matter how hot and stacked she might be."

"I'm all aflutter with your compliments," she said dryly, then moved around him to sit in a chair across from his desk. "Sit down and we'll talk."

Intrigued and turned on by the woman who didn't appear cowed or enamored, he sat and listened. And smiled.

CHAPTER NINE

SHELBY SPENT THE REST OF THE WEEKEND CLEANING HER apartment and hanging out with Maggie. Anything to fill her time so she'd stop thinking about Shane. Not about his body or the demanding and thrilling way they'd had sex, but about his smile. That dimple added to the joy reflected in his beautiful eyes.

So much for her new resolve to tramp the night fantastic. She hadn't seen one man all week who made her feel even a tenth of what Shane had. The days passed by in blessed normalcy, and Shelby thanked her good fortune that her mother and Maggie seemed to have forgotten all about Shane Collins. She wished she could do the same.

Her dreams about him grew more graphic each night. She wouldn't have minded trying a few of the things her brain came up with, but he hadn't approached her since their freakishly good sex on Saturday. And really, did she want to jinx it? Why not remember him fondly without all the drama of a relationship—one that didn't exist?

The weekend rolled around after what felt like forever.

The first part of her Friday passed by in relative quiet. She worked with several repeat clients and had one walk-in. When administrative needs pressed, she headed into the back, where she kept her records, some office supplies and the main computer. She was in the middle of updating her files when Denise interrupted.

"Phone call for you." Denise nodded to the front of the clinic. "I'm not sure who it is. Want me to transfer it in here or take a message?"

"Um…" Where the heck was the power bill for this month? She'd just had her hands on it.

"Riiight. I'll transfer." Denise ducked out while Shelby sought her garbage bill. Being her own boss was terrific, but a hassle when it came to the books. The phone rang and she answered and tucked it against her chin and shoulder as she kept looking through her stacks of papers.

"This is Shelby at Bodyworks. How may I help you?"

"Shelby? It's Geo."

"Who?"

A huff. Then, "George Collins."

"Oh hey, Geo. How are you?"

"I need your help." He didn't sound right.

Shelby immediately put down the power bill she'd just found and focused on the call. "What's wrong?"

"I think I may have strained my knee earlier today at practice, and I wondered if you could take a look at it."

Now she understood his worry. The kid lived for two things: girls and football. "Sure thing. Do you want to come down here today? I have time after four." After her last client of the day.

"No." He lowered his voice. "Actually, I need a big favor. I don't want my mom to know about this." He continued over her objections. "I'll tell her if it's a problem, but I'm not sure if it's just sore or if I did real damage. If she even thinks I'm hurt, she'll pull me from the team. Scholarship, Shelby. I can't lose it."

"But I don't want to lie to your mother." Technically, George was seventeen and still a minor. Shelby liked Lorraine Collins. The woman only wanted what was best for her son. Unfortunately, she hated his participation on the football team. George had a right to be worried.

"Come on, Shelby, please? It was all I could do to get back on the team this season. And I think I just strained it. Nothing major. I hate to worry her for no reason. I'll pay you, I swear."

"It's not about the money, Geo." And it wasn't. She genuinely cared about him and his promising future.

"Look, my older brother will be with me. He's thirty-one. An adult," he bit out. "It's not like I'm asking you to do anything unethical."

"It's not that I don't want to help you, it's just that—"

"Shelby, please." He sounded desperate.

"Okay, fine." She didn't have to treat him if in her estimation he needed serious medical help. She'd give him her opinion. "But if I find anything wrong with you other than some normal wear and tear, I'm calling your mother and you promise to see a doctor. This is an unofficial visit, one you're not paying for, because I'm not really seeing you. Understand?"

She heard a sigh of relief on the other end. "Great, I knew I could count on you. Uh, Shelby? One other thing… I can't come down there without her knowing. I was wondering if you could meet me at my brother's house? I'll give you the address."

Shelby frowned. She didn't normally make house calls. "Can't your brother bring you here?"

"No. He's working, and Dad's still out of town. I'd have to use Mom as my ride, which won't work. Tomorrow would be best to meet, if you can make it. My brother's already going out on a limb for me with Mom. You met her, so you get me, right?"

She did. Lorraine was friendly and loving, but a powerhouse. "I get you. But I won't lie. If she asks me about this, I'll tell her the truth."

"Sure. Don't lie. Just see if it's something to worry about first. If it is, I swear, I'll tell her myself. You can watch me dial her number from my brother's."

"Okay."

"Great. Saturday."

"Give me the address. It'll have to be after six though, since I'm working the weekend again. Bills to pay, you know?" Especially since she'd found the power bill.

"Whatever you can do. Perfect. Thanks, Shelby. You're a lifesaver."

So why did she feel like a doormat, instead?

She took a closer look at the address and frowned. His brother lived in the Green Lake area. Just like Shane Collins.

The next day, Shelby arrived at just after six after a rough eight hours of work. If she had to sacrifice a weekend, she'd rather be busy than sitting around waiting for clients to walk in, so she couldn't complain. Pleased at the amount she'd accomplished, she showed up at the address George had given her in a good mood.

She'd take a look at his knee and head home for a long soak in the tub. A book and a glass of wine, then she'd hit the bed hard. She rang the doorbell of an attractive Craftsman. Dark red wooden siding covered the house, set off by bright white trim and black piping. A nice place and one worth a good bit this close to the lake.

George opened the door with a wide grin. "You made it." He looked boyishly cute in athletic shorts and a Seahawks tee-shirt.

"You did tell me you needed my help. Weren't you crying and wheedling for my expertise?"

"Yeah, I was." He looked nervous, and she had the odd feeling he wasn't being completely honest about the knee, well, more than she knew. His last name continued to bother her. What were the odds George and Shane both had Collins as a surname? George's brother happened to live close to Green Lake. And they both had similar facial features she started to notice the closer she looked at him.

"George—"

He grabbed her by the arm and dragged her inside. "Come on in, Shelby. I really appreciate this."

She followed his growing limp into the living room of a tastefully decorated house. Lots of oak built-ins with a masculine taste that wasn't overdone or bachelor pad-like, but comfortable. But it was the picture on the mantle of the fireplace that drew her gaze. One of a handsome, smiling family: Lorraine and Chad Collins, George, and their older son—Shane.

She turned around to glare at George and instead stared at the broad chest of a man she couldn't stop thinking about, no matter how hard she tried.

"Shelby. What a surprise." Shane cocked his head, studying her. "Are you stalking me?"

She snorted. "You're kidding me, right?" Moaning drew her attention to George, who sat on a plush leather chair rubbing his knee. "Okay, champ. Let me take a look." Focusing on George made it easier to breathe. Good God, but Shane looked better to her each time she saw him.

Tonight he wore faded jeans and a tee-shirt molded to his powerful upper body. She loved that he didn't look like he ate steroids for breakfast, but that his muscle looked sculpted, bunches of strength and nothing in excess.

As she sat on the ottoman at the foot of the chair and took George's knee in her hands, she had to wonder if he'd colluded with his older brother to bring her here. The little sneak hadn't said one thing about being related to the owner of the business card he'd just happened to find in her massage room last week.

"Sorry about the secrecy. My little brother is freaked about our mother finding out he's screwed up his knee again. She didn't want him to play football this year, not after what he did to himself during baseball season the past spring."

"The perfect slide into home, Shelby. You should have seen it," George bragged. He didn't show any signs of swelling around his patella, nor did he flinch when she gently rotated his knee, looking for any trouble or strain.

"Mom has never liked us playing football," Shane continued. His deep voice stroked over her senses like a feather down her spine.

She concentrated on George's leg to dull the sensation, with no effect. "Right. Lorraine mentioned that when she first brought George to see me."

"Geo," the teen murmured and stared down at her hand on his knee. "You have nice hands."

She yanked them from his knee and sat up straight. "I'm not seeing any trauma." She glanced back at Shane, who grinned.

"Great. I was worried about the idiot." At her look, his grin faded. "What's wrong?"

"I mean, I don't see anything that would account for his

extreme limping the other day or even now."

Shane's expression darkened. "Is that so?"

They turned as one to stare at George.

"Gee, guys. This has been fun and all, but it's Saturday night. Gina and I have things to do." He sprang from the chair and darted to the front door with the grace and speed of a gazelle. After grabbing a backpack from the closet and slipping into flip-flops, he yelled a goodbye and slammed out the door.

After a few moments, Shelby broke the silence. "I should have realized. Same last name, and you guys look alike. But he never mentioned any relation. Funny he didn't mention he was your brother when he found your business card at my office last week."

Shane shook his head. "I'm sorry for the trouble he put you through. I had nothing to do with it, honestly." He took a step back when she stood but didn't give her enough space to be polite. "But I have to admit, I wouldn't have argued if he'd clued me into his plan to get you over here."

"Oh?"

"Yeah. Last week was incredible." He glanced down at her mouth. "I've thought about it. A lot."

Oh hell. "Me too." She hated that she sounded so breathless. She cleared her throat and tried again. "It was really hot. But different. I don't normally do stuff like that." Would he believe it? And what should she care if he didn't?

His wide grin surprised her. "We have that in common then, because I don't either. That condom I happened to have on me was a gift from a buddy who thinks I'm like two steps from being too pathetic to hang out with."

"Yeah, right."

"Seriously." Shane stepped closer and started to lower his head toward hers, then stopped. He let out a deep breath and moved back. "Want something to drink?"

"God yes."

He chuckled.

She followed him into a spacious kitchen designed for someone who liked to cook with wide counters, a triangulated work space for the refrigerator, stove, and sink, and beautiful wooden cabinetry. "My mother would love your place. She's an interior designer. She says you can tell a lot about a person by the way they use their space."

"Beer okay?" he asked. When she nodded, he handed her one. "So what would she say about me after seeing the house?" Before she could answer, he stopped her. "But you haven't seen the whole thing. Want a tour?"

"This isn't one of those *wanna see my etchings* lines, is it?"

His grin made her feel tingly inside. Shane had such a warm smile. It made his eyes appear impossibly green. "Why? Would that work?"

She gave him a look and he laughed again. They spent the next half hour going through his rooms looking at things. He showed off a few of his collector baseballs, answered questions about the many pictures of family in his study and living room, and shared with her the projects he was working on with a confidence that didn't come across as arrogant at all, but sure of himself.

She found herself comparing his attitude and personality to Rick's. Shane came off looking like a rock star with little effort.

"My mom bugged the shit, I mean, the hell out of me about paint colors before I moved in." He made a face as they went up the stairs. "I couldn't have cared less. I mean, I like great architecture and design. But furnishings and decorating? I'm a practical guy more into comfort than flash."

And maybe that's why he hadn't minded having sex with her last week.

As if he'd read her mind, he winked. "Although I'm not opposed to flash on occasion. Like on top of my desk, or in the middle of a running trail."

She couldn't help the flush that warmed her cheeks. "Stop it."

"You are so pretty when you turn pink."

"Jerk."

"And so complimentary."

They looked into his spare bedrooms, one he used more as a room for storage and workout equipment.

"Sometimes I don't have time to hit the lake. I bought that treadmill a few years ago before I joined my buddy's gym."

"Which one?"

"Jameson's, a few miles from here."

"Oh right." She'd been by it a few times and wondered about joining, but she barely had time to walk around the lake with Maggie each week. "So you seem really into exercise."

"All kinds." The look he gave her couldn't be mistaken for anything but a leer.

Idiot that she was, she liked it.

"Yeah, if I don't get to do something each day, I go a little crazy," he added.

I could give you a workout. The sudden images swirling through her mind belonged in a *Penthouse* letter. This despite the fact that he couldn't have been too gaga over their time together or he'd have called her before now.

She glanced at the door they stood outside.

He looked from the door to her. "My bedroom."

She refused to give in to the dark voice whispering all kinds of tempting things they might do in there. She'd be firm.

Just because they'd had smokin' hot sex once didn't mean it had to happen again. Except he seemed more than interested, if that lingering gaze on her breasts was anything to go by.

"Not scared to go in with me, are you?" he dared.

"Unless you have frightened virgins tied down to your bedposts for sacrifice, I think I'll manage."

He chuckled. "Good thing I tidied up before you came, then."

He opened the door and stood there in the doorway, forcing her to brush against him to enter.

The feel of his body heat warmed her from the inside out. Her breasts brushed his chest as she passed, and she swore she heard his indrawn breath.

"Hmm. Nice." A king-size bed, one that had been made, took center stage in the large room. A small desk and chair stood on one wall, while a dresser and bureau fitted the rest of the room. The requisite man-size TV had been mounted to the wall above the dresser, and a few prints of military scenes decorated the walls.

Seeing her attention, he said, "Marines. I served in the Corps, like my dad. Good times."

"So why did you get out?"

"It was time." He shrugged.

She didn't want to pry, but she could too easily envision him in uniform. God, he would have been the star of her nightly fantasies forever if she'd seen him in Dress Blues. She was such a sucker for a man in uniform.

"You seem like the type to go for order and discipline." She took another good look around. "You're way too neat for a guy. Not normal."

His eyes glittered, and he slowly drew closer to her. She took a few steps back before she realized he'd neatly cornered her by the bed.

"Order and discipline, hmm." He closed the remaining distance between them. "Two things I'm pretty damn good at." He leaned down and kissed her so softly she might have imagined it. "Shelby, last week was amazing. Unplanned, and totally unlike me."

"We went through this already, remember?"

"But I think we could do more. You and me."

"More?"

"You mentioned the sex was tame."

She was surprised he'd remembered that. "Um, did I say that?"

He kissed her again, his mouth whisper-light over her lips. The sparse contact and heat of his breath made her shiver.

"I've been thinking about it. Wanting to try a few things. You game?"

"M-maybe." She stood on tiptoe as he sucked her earlobe and nipped before letting go. His hands had found her waist, and he rubbed circles into her skin with his thumbs.

"Guess what?"

"What?"

He answered with another kiss, one that wasn't gentle or light, but firm, hot, and sexy. He thrust his tongue between her lips and took without asking. He plundered and delved, stealing her willpower with that talented mouth.

"I have a lot more than one condom this time. What do you say?"

CHAPTER TEN

WHAT COULD SHE SAY BUT YES? SHANE KISSED HER UNTIL HE couldn't breathe. Their coming together on Saturday hadn't been a fluke at all. The chemistry between them stunned him. Just the touch of her skin, the feel of her smooth lips under his, and the knowledge that her nipples stood on end for *him* made him dizzy with lust. Everything about her appealed to the sexual beast inside him wanting to fuck her raw, while the romantic within wanted to drown in her soft brown eyes that looked up at him with fogged desire.

"Shelby?" he asked, out of breath. "Yes or no, baby?"

Baby. He liked calling her that, because everything he'd noticed about the stubborn female told him she was a woman of independence. He found her hints of aggression sexy. She was no one's idea of a meek woman, or one who'd tolerate a pet name like *baby*. Yet it fit her, especially now. He could see a kernel of vulnerability there in her eyes, and it felt like looking into himself.

"What do you want to do?" The throaty question took him for a loop.

What *didn't* he want to do? He had no plans for the evening. No visitors, no agenda. And he'd been hard and aching for her for a fucking week.

"I want a lot."

"Tell me," she insisted, and he saw her desire. She liked the dirty talk, as much as he did.

"I want to suck that clit until you come. I want to eat you out and then fuck you. I want to come inside you, to watch myself spill out of you when we're done. And then I want to fuck you again." He paused. "But I'll have to settle for a condom." *Until we know each other better.* "And some creative ways to make you scream."

Her hands clenched on his waist, her grip tight.

He stroked her sides, over her hips. "I know last week was supposed to be a one-time thing, but maybe we could shoot for a few more rounds. I don't want to pressure you or anything, but I—"

She grabbed his head and kissed him before he could finish. Apparently her way of saying yes, which he didn't mind at all.

When they finally parted, they were both breathing heavily. He tore off his shirt at the same time she tossed hers over her head. Her sandals and jeans came next. Then his jeans. They stared at one another, her lacy bra and matching panties so fucking sexy he couldn't contain a groan.

"You're big." She licked her lips and stared at his cock, even now leaving a wet spot on his boxer briefs.

"So are you." He moved closer and placed his hands on her breasts. "Your tits are big. And those nipples are so tight and sexy. I want to suck them, Shelby. Into my mouth while I fuck you."

She groaned and pushed against him. "I don't know why,

but you really turn me on."

He gave a pained laugh. "Thanks."

She blushed. "I mean, I know why."

She gasped when he tweaked a nipple then continued rubbing the stiff point against his palm. The silk of her bra might not have been there for all that he could feel.

"You just…" She moaned. "I can't help myself around you."

"Good," he growled. "Because you've turned me into a walking hard-on."

She watched him watching her. His touch grew more frantic, the need to suckle her flesh all-consuming. He reached behind her, his gaze on hers while he moved with deliberation.

She bit her lower lip, and he couldn't help himself. He kissed her while he removed her bra. It dropped to the ground as his tongue stroked hers. She stepped closer, and her tits rubbed his chest.

He needed to fuck her in the worst way. And the damn condoms were on the other side of the bed in the night stand. *Shit.*

Shane reached between them, more than eager to feel those breasts in his hands. Two handfuls, and he had large palms. She sighed into his mouth while he massaged her and pulled on her nipples. Her squirming did the most incredible things to his cock. He didn't think he'd ever been so hard in his life. Each gyration of her hips pressed against his erection. The rhythm she picked up nearly had him coming in his underwear, and he hadn't gone down on her yet.

Shane pulled away and found it hard to breathe. More, he found it hard to concentrate when he glanced down and saw Shelby in nothing but pink lace panties. "Christ. Shelby, I, uh…"

He started when her hand grazed his abdomen. Then her fingers toyed with the waistband of his boxer briefs. Those skilled little fingers continued to trail under his clothing to the hard heat of him.

"*Oh fuck*. Be gentle."

"Afraid, big guy?" she asked with a husky laugh.

"Of coming in two seconds, yeah." He groaned when she trailed a finger up and down his length. "You're so sexy. God, I need to get inside you in the worst way." And that should have led to a discussion he wanted to have about protection. But then she pushed down his underwear and grabbed his ass, pulling him against her belly.

"You are so big and wet. I like that," she teased and licked his nipple.

He jerked against her, ready to come.

"Wait, wait." He had a hard time breathing. The ache at the base of his spine, the tension in his balls, his rock-hard dick… He needed relief. And if she kept that up, he'd get it all too soon. "I just...wanted you to know…" He groaned. "I haven't been with anyone but you in a…while."

She paused, her hand now around his cock, and looked up at him. "How long?"

"Eight months." He should have lied, because now he looked desperate and horny. Maybe she'd give him a pity fuck, at least.

"Six for me," she said shyly.

He wanted the full story, but not now. Not when he wanted her like crazy.

"I'm clean," he rasped. "I'll wear the rubber, okay? But I'm clean."

"Yeah. Me too." She let his dick go and cupped his sac, and Shane lost it.

He tossed her back on the bed. She landed with a squeal while he took of his underwear and then joined her. "These have to go, sexy as they are." He removed her wet panties and spread her thighs wide. The glistening dew of desire didn't lie. Shelby wanted him, almost as much as he wanted her.

Without thinking anymore, he scooted between her thighs, placed his mouth over her, and indulged. She cried out his name and grabbed his hair, but he couldn't stop. He had to absorb the essence of this incredible woman and know her, in the truest sense of the word.

It didn't take much before she cried out and came all over his tongue. He sucked her clit and ate her up, excited that he'd brought her to climax and needing to feel her around him. But he had to reach over her for the condom.

He hurried from between her legs and leaned over her for the dresser drawer. But the shifty woman scuttled under him when he crawled toward the dresser. "God. Wait. Don't move—*shit.*" Shane groaned when she took him in her mouth, fully under him and laving his cockhead with her tongue.

The heat and suction of her mouth made him lose his concentration. And then he was pumping, and she was sucking, her clever hands scratching his inner thighs, cupping his balls, and running around his ass to tease his crack with her nails. "Fuck. I'm there, baby. Gonna fill up that fucking mouth. Oh yeah."

He couldn't stop. And she wouldn't let him. Her fingers came in contact with the rim of his asshole just as she shoved her tongue into his slit, lapping up his seed. Shane held himself up on trembling elbows as he groaned and poured into her mouth.

He washed her mouth and throat with plenty of happy little guys wishing for nothing more than a shot at her hot pussy again. Holy hell, but he couldn't stop jerking, loving that fact that she swallowed.

After sucking him dry, she moved away.

He fell to the bed beside her, breathing hard. "Jesus, Shelby. I think you killed me." He rolled to his side and blinked at her, pleased to see her smiling.

"You did the same to me." She ran a finger over his chest and traced the line of muscle.

His gaze trailed from her sleepy eyes to her pouting lips and lower, to her pretty, pretty breasts. "I need to fuck those tits."

She froze, and he couldn't believe he'd said that out loud.

"What else to you want to do?" she asked as she stroked him again.

"You really want to know?" Because he was going to lay it out on the line for her. "I want to do all the things to you I fantasize about. The things I was too afraid or *vanilla* to do before." He hated that fucking word.

She frowned. "You mean last week?"

"I mean in my last relationship." Hearing himself say it out loud, he groaned. "Man, you tied not only my dick in a knot, Shelby, but my brain too. Sorry to bring up the past."

She shrugged. "Hey, I'm fine with it. My ex tossed me over for a hot blond that would do all the things I apparently was too *vanilla* to do with him." She blinked up at him. "I want in."

"In?"

"In. We start this new sexual relationship. No feelings or dating stuff. Just hot sex any way we want it."

Shane rose up one elbow. "So we get together to have sex, but I can't call you. You can't move in or nag me to clean up after myself."

They looked around his spotless bedroom and shared a

glance.

"Okay," he relented with a grin, excited about this potential future. "So you wouldn't have anything to nag about."

"I don't nag." She frowned. "Or at least, I didn't think asking someone to let me know not to make dinner when he planned to eat out was nagging."

"It's not. It's called consideration for someone else's feelings." He commiserated, having been in that same spot once or twice himself. "And it's not wrong to expect each of us to remain faithful to each other while we do this." Whatever *this* turned out to be.

"Not at all. I'm big on fidelity."

"Me too."

They stared at one another. Shane felt relaxed and pleasantly aroused again.

"So." Shelby cleared her throat. "Maybe some games? Kinky stuff."

He nodded, stiffening as his fantasies intruded. "Role play?"

"Yeah." She reached between them and stroked his cock. "I'll get a physical next week. And I'm on birth control already. You know, just in case I ever needed it. Though I haven't until you."

The thought of fucking her with nothing between them gave his libido the equivalent of a B12 shot.

She held his stiff rod between her hands. "Yeah, you like that, don't you?"

He moaned. "I do. I'll get a physical set up right away. Like, tomorrow," he said, not caring what day it was.

She laughed. "Good." She leaned closer and whispered, "Then you can come inside me and watch it trickle out of my pussy. No condom, just that big cock stroking into my cunt."

He shivered. "I love when you talk dirty."

"Mmm."

He reached over her and opened the nightstand drawer. After taking out a condom, he handed it to her. "How about we try this? I give you orders, you do what I say."

Her eyes narrowed and her breath hitched. "Okay."

Seemed like his Amazon liked the thought of not being in charge. Oh man, were they going to have fun with that. He rolled onto his back and scooted to the middle of the bed. He watched her rip open the packet and straddle him, her breasts so full, her nipples so erect he wondered how long he could hold off without fucking those large mounds. Maybe next time. He wanted to come inside her pussy.

Shelby held him by the root and rolled the condom over his tip. She watched his eyes as she smoothed the rubber over him, and he was glad of his size, hoping to impress her. Women might worry about their breasts and weight, but men definitely worried about dick size.

"How's that?" She held him firm with one hand while she massaged his balls with the other.

"Good. Now quit playing and hop on. Good girl." He helped her sit over him and forced himself not to thrust up when she gloved him with moist warmth. "I love your cunt," he said bluntly, wanting to shock and arouse her. "That thin strip of hair over your pussy is pretty. But nothing is as tasty as the cream between your legs."

She moaned and moved. Up and down, she rocked over him while she planted her hands on either side of his shoulder.

"Yeah, that's good, baby. Let me watch those tits bounce while you ride me." She had a killer body. So firm yet curvy. Soft and hard. And he wanted to suck her again.

"Come here." He stilled her movements and sat up. "Wrap

your legs around me."

She did without question, and he loved her response.

"Now put your tit in my mouth. All of the nipple. That's it." He opened his mouth and waited, enthralled with the way she guided herself between his lips.

He sucked the hard bud while she pressed his head to her. Shelby definitely liked her tits sucked, and a breast man like Shane was perfect for the job. He played with her while he ground her over him. The close contact rubbed her wet clit against his pelvis and made her wetter for him.

He wished to God he didn't need the condom, but he respected her limits and wanted to go the extra mile for safety at least. Going down on her hadn't been exactly smart earlier, but man, it had been worth it.

Her excitement bled through to him, and their motion became frenzied. In this close position, he couldn't slam into her, and the challenge of getting as deep as he wanted enhanced their pleasure. Shane let go of her breast and kissed her lips, aching to come again. But not until she did first.

When her pussy clamped hard against him and she moaned into his mouth, he let himself go. Shoving her back to the bed, he pounded into the wet suction of her pussy and found his orgasm moments later.

Sweating, panting, and pleasantly exhausted, they curled up together, somehow ending up with her head on his chest. Mesmerized didn't begin to describe his feelings. And like that, he tensed. *Sexual fling, my ass. You like her. You want to date her. To get to know her.* He could almost hear Mac's disappointment, could almost feel himself redoing his time with Lisa once more. Why the hell couldn't he have meaningless sex with a beautiful woman without wanting it to be so much more?

She must have felt his tension, because Shelby stirred. She

smiled down at him, looking relaxed. "I'd love to stay, but I need to get home. I'm sweaty and probably sticky."

He glanced down at the condom now covering his flagging erection. "Yeah. I need to clean up too."

As one they rose and took care of their respective messes. It felt a little awkward, but nowhere near as uncomfortable as he might have imagined. Shelby seemed happy with their arrangement, and as he escorted her to the stairwell, he started to think that maybe this would work. That they could have a sexual relationship devoid of hurt feelings and emotional minefields.

"Um, there's one thing." Shelby stopped him. "I hope you don't take this the wrong way, but we have to keep this quiet."

"Oh?"

She let out a frustrated breath. "It's my mother. It's complicated, but she, Ron—my surrogate dad, you could say, and my best friend are always all over me to get back into dating. They don't care that I'm happy now, they just want to see me with some guy. And if they know about you, they'll be all over you about marriage and kids." At his stunned look, she nodded. "Seriously. My mother runs astrological charts on men she thinks I should date. She needs to be committed. I love her, but it's hell having a quiet, normal social life around her."

He liked the fact that she loved her crazy mother. Shane loved his family too. "So you won't feel bad when I tell you I agree, wholeheartedly. My mother is nuts about the idea of grandkids. Hell, you met her."

"Oh yeah." Shelby's smile grew.

"And my buddy, Mac? He's totally into women being…let's just say Mac is a great guy, but I don't want his input on this relationship between us, or whatever you want to call it," he hurried to add, not wanting to scare her away. First the sex, now this? Was this woman real? Sex without strings. And she wanted to keep it quiet.

"And let's not forget George."

He groaned. "You see my problems? After my last big break up, they all think I'm scarred for life."

She laughed. "Like you can't manage on your own. You need everyone else's help to have fun."

He nodded. "You totally get where I'm coming from."

"Do I ever. Trust me, if you ever run into Mimi Vanzant, of Vanzant Interiors, you'll know exactly what I mean."

"You already met George and Lorraine."

She laughed with him. "Yeah. It's not that I don't want help, it's that I don't need it, and no one seems to understand that. I just want to live my life, alone or with someone, on *my* terms. Not to show my friend that I'm healed over my jerk of an ex, or to give my mom grandkids."

"Exactly."

The moment seemed to linger, the satisfaction of clear understanding and empathy for similar situations a bond between them. Shane felt another push, a need to turn their simple relationship into something deeper. He shrugged it away and started with her down the stairs once more.

All finally seemed right with his world. And then the doorbell rang.

He and Shelby froze.

"Why don't you go—"

"I'll wait upstairs," she whispered and darted back up into his bedroom. He heard the door quietly latch and continued toward the front door.

Who the hell would come visiting at… A glance at the clock on the mantle showed the hour had reached nine. Man, he'd been making love to—*having sex with*—Shelby for hours.

And it wasn't nearly enough.

He threw open the front door with a disgruntled curse and stared at retired Colonel Chad Collins.

"What took you so long?" his father asked and stomped past him into the living room.

"Dad, what are you doing here?" His father rarely visited even though he and his mother lived a mile down the road. It wasn't for lack of affection, but Shane was usually busy rushing somewhere between his job and the gym, and family get-togethers took place at his parents' home.

"Your mother sent me to find your errant brother. He didn't come to dinner and he's not answering his cell phone, though he did text that he'll be home on time. Some girl showed up at the house looking for him an hour ago. What's up?"

"I have no idea." Why did his father think it was Shane's place to keep tabs on his younger brother?

"Hmm." Chad gave him the stare that had broken many men down in interrogation chambers. It looked odd coming from a face that might just be his own in another twenty-five years. "Did you see him at all today?"

"Dad, I'm busy."

"Doing what?" Chad looked around him with suspicion.

Shane read him easily. "I was relaxing." *Oh man, was I ever.* "He's not here, Dad. He showed up around six, ate my food and begged a beer—which I *didn't* give him."

Chad chuckled.

"Then he said he had a date with Gina and took off. I think they went to a movie."

His father nodded. "Ah well. Then that explains it. The girl who showed up said her name was Amber. And she didn't seem pleased not to find the boy home. If you hear from him before I do, tell him to call me. I won't worry unless he misses curfew."

"Sure thing." Shane walked to the door, inwardly groaning when his father didn't budge from the middle of the living room. "Dad?"

"You seem awfully eager to get rid of your old man. I thought we could watch a movie or something." His father shrugged. "We don't spend enough time together."

"Ah, right." They'd just gone golfing last weekend. "Tell you what, I'll grab a shower, then we'll—"

Something upstairs fell over.

They both stared at one another. Shane, to his embarrassment, felt his cheeks heat.

"So, he *is* upstairs." His father scowled and started for the stairwell. "I know you love your brother, Shane, but he has responsibilities too. He's old enough to—"

"Dad. It's not George." Why he felt protective of this new relationship with Shelby he couldn't fathom. Not like his dad would ruin things for him, not like his mother, George, or Mac might. But Shane didn't want to share her. It made little sense, but there it was. "I have a friend over."

His father blinked. "A friend?" Then he grinned. "Oh. A *friend*." His father left the stairs and hustled to the door, laughing. "Why didn't you say so? Okay. I see you're busy. I'll catch you tomorrow."

"Don't tell Mom. I'm having fun, not planning to start a new line of the family tree. Okay?"

His father nodded. "Roger that. Have fun. But if you're not wanting little Marines, make sure you wear a raincoat, Son."

His father had not just warned him to wear a condom. "Shit, Dad. I'm thirty-one years old." *Please tell me Shelby can't hear this.*

"I know. I'm just saying. More than one Marine I knew found himself tricked into marriage, led by his dick."

"Thanks, Colonel. You're inspiring. I can't wait to get back to my date now."

Chad chuckled and left with an order to meet tomorrow for coffee.

After making sure his father drove away, Shane raced back upstairs and opened the bedroom door. Shelby sat on his bed biting back a grin.

"Oh man. You heard him."

In a deep voice, she mimicked, "Wear a raincoat, Son." She laughed. "I like your dad. Sounds as bossy as Ron, just less flamboyant." At Shane's confusion, she explained. "Ron's gay and proud of it."

"Gotcha." Shane sighed. "I was loving that post-coital afterglow. And then my friggin' father showed up."

She laughed with him as they walked down the stairs to the front door. "Well, hey. At least he didn't ask for your sign and do a cold read with tarot cards. Trust me. My mother is atypical, to say the least."

"She sounds fun."

"She is, but she's loud. And I kind of like living a quieter life." They reached the door. She stopped and gave him a lingering kiss that raised his temperature. "But not too quiet."

When he could catch his breath, he answered, "Right. No more vanilla for us."

"No more vanilla." She rubbed his cock through his jeans and grinned. "Call me and we'll meet next week at my place."

"You got it."

Shane shut the door behind her and watched her drive away. He could still taste her kiss, and the sight of her wearing nothing but him refused to fade away. He couldn't wait until next week.

CHAPTER ELEVEN

THE NEXT WEEK PASSED BY IN A BLUR. SHELBY HAD ENOUGH to do to keep her busy, but the phone calls from Shane had kept her on cloud nine, enough that Maggie had asked her about her upbeat attitude.

Lying to her best friend hadn't been as difficult as she'd have thought. Shelby wanted to keep Shane to herself for a while. Who knew men actually gave women orgasms without having to beg or even ask?

She blushed crimson when she remembered all they'd done. Shane, vanilla? He was anything but. Sexy, hung, and so ripped. How could any woman turn him aside, unless he turned out to be some macho creep when in a relationship. Yet he didn't give off those vibes. If she trusted what he'd said, and she did, he hadn't been with a woman in eight months. A guy like that, going without. It wasn't for lack of a sex drive.

The messages he'd left her on her cell phone had been creative, and the exact opposite of tame. She hadn't recognized the unlisted number, but she'd known his voice. The things he talked about doing to her made her hot and bothered and eager. Hell, yes, *eager.*

She wanted to go down on him again. She'd never been into oral, because with Rick, he never reciprocated. And she hadn't cared for his taste. Just thinking about him like that made her ill. But Shane didn't bother her at all. And then there was his mouth… He'd known exactly how to pleasure her. Not once, but twice in one night. Shelby hadn't left a man's bed still hungry for sex. Shane had tired her out. Score one for the record books.

So why couldn't she be satisfied with the sex alone? The stupid part of her, the girlie part, wanted to hold hands. She'd almost fallen asleep on his chest after that last orgasm. Had he not stiffened up underneath her, she might have. But he'd come to his senses and brought her to hers.

After Rick, she wanted to play. No more being tied down to one man and one man's ideas about being a couple. Shelby wanted raw, dirty, mind-blowing sex. She wanted to try different things, to feel sexy and powerful and free, the way she'd been with Shane.

Until his father had shown up.

At the thought, she laughed. She liked Colonel Collins. The one time he'd met him she'd known where George got his charm. Hearing him with Shane had made her like him all the more. *Wear a raincoat.* It had been all she could do to stifle the giggles when Shane had groaned at the advice. To see a man as hot as Shane getting girl advice from his father was priceless. It made her feel less of a loser to get constant, unasked for counsel from her mother and Ron.

Just this week Ron had called asking about Shane's sign and birth year. As if she knew. And if she did, did he really think she'd tell him?

Although she didn't think Shane would mind. He seemed

to have a decent sense of humor and an easy way about him. She wondered what he'd be like as a boyfriend. Would he like to go out to movies? Catch dinner? Would he ask about her day and she ask about his? His messages had been sexy but brief. She'd deleted them after hearing them, horrified to think of her mother finding them by accident. But to hear them and know he'd called meant he thought about her. She liked it. She liked *him.*

And like that, she sensed a crazy infatuation developing. *Use him for sex and get on with your life. Do you really want to connect and give him everything, only to walk in on him getting blown by his secretary?*

Did he even have a secretary? She'd seen his office and the main entryway of the building, but little else. *And why do you need to know? So long as he keeps his dick out of everyone but you, you're golden.*

Her inner voice had a point, and she called her doctor to schedule a physical. Just her luck, Dr. Conn had an opening the following morning, when Shelby intended to get proof of her clean bill of health.

That afternoon she closed early, glad to have cleared herself for a break. She cleaned up the areas and did some laundry, basking in her ability to just relax. Someone knocked at the backdoor, which startled her. *Probably Denise forgetting her keys.*

But when she moved to the back of her shop, she saw Shane standing outside on the patio wearing a suit and tie. He looked good enough to eat. Literally.

She forced herself to calm down and unlocked the backdoor. "Shane. Hi."

He nodded but didn't say anything. He locked the door behind him and walked around her into her massage room, where she'd first touched that fit body and wished she could do more. He put a piece of paper down on the table.

She leaned over and read his medical checkup. "Clean as a whistle, I see." Her pulse rate jumped. From the look on his face, the man had more than information sharing on his mind.

"You?"

She liked his abrupt manner. Something about the firm set to his jaw made him seem determined. Aggressive. Sexy.

"Um, my appointment is tomorrow."

He just stared at her. Then he closed the door to the small massage room behind her and locked it. After taking off his coat, he rolled up his sleeves, removed his tie and unbuttoned the top of his shirt. "Good thing I'm a doctor then. Go ahead and undress and get on the exam table." He nodded to her massage table, where she'd already changed the sheets in preparation for her first client tomorrow.

She glanced from him to the table, not sure she'd heard him right.

"Is there a problem, Miss Vanzant?" Shane asked, all seriousness.

Role playing. He'd said he wanted to do it. She thought it ironic he chose to portray a doctor when six months ago she'd been dating one, and they'd never once tried this game. Even if they had, she doubted she'd have been this turned on. Something about Shane really got her motor running. She liked that he wanted to play with her. *Very much.*

She toed off her shoes and socks, jeans and tee-shirt. "Should I strip all the way down, Doctor?"

His eyes gleamed as he studied her. In a low voice, he answered, "Yes, Miss Vanzant. I need you completely naked for your exam."

She stepped out of her underwear and bra, self-conscious.

The last time she'd been with Shane naked, she'd been under him and too aroused to care what she looked like. But now, he was dressed and she wasn't, and he took his time looking at all of her.

Rick had hinted she'd look wonderful if she'd lose more weight. But Shelby had always felt anorexic when she dropped the ten pounds he insisted weighed her down. She wasn't a small woman, and if Shane didn't like that, he could—

"Hmm. Very nice. You look healthy." He moved close but didn't touch her. "Turn around and bend over."

"Um…"

"Touch your toes, so I can check your spine."

She bit her lip but did as he said. His hands roamed from her neck to her back and down over her ass.

"Nice and firm. I wonder if you'll need a rectal exam as well?"

She'd always wondered what it might feel like to have anal sex, but she didn't know about doing it now, today. "I don't think that's necessary. That area is pretty much, ah, clean. Unused."

"Miss Vanzant, I'm a doctor." He sounded amused. His fingers prodded her ass cheeks apart and she felt warm breath over her hole. The sensation shook her, because the tingle between her legs blazed into an inferno. Moisture flooded her pussy, and she wanted more.

"Spread your legs, Shelby."

She did and moaned when his hands found her. He toyed with her, sliding his fingers along her labia, not penetrating, but rubbing. He teased her clit into a taut bud then ordered her to stand.

She did and turned, only to see him watching her with hunger. His hard-on appeared enormous behind the silky black trousers he wore.

"Hop on the table and spread your legs. Make sure you scoot to the end."

Where he could fuck her easily.

She hurried to obey, amazed at how much she enjoyed this. She hadn't thought to see him until the weekend, assuming they'd be weekend fun-buddies. Role playing had seemed like something she'd tolerate to make him happy. She'd thought she'd have to control her laughter through it, but she had no urge to giggle, just to do whatever he asked.

"You seem nice and wet." At the foot of the table, Shane crouched between her legs. He set his mouth over her clit and licked her until she thought she'd explode.

She couldn't help moaning and begging him to fuck her. "I need you inside me."

He moved back and stood. After wiping his mouth, he smiled. "You taste healthy. Creamy." He walked around the table to her side and massaged her breasts. "But we haven't finished your exam." When he leaned closer, his cock pushed through the opening in his pants, though she hadn't seen him unzip. She didn't see any evidence of underwear. He looked huge, the swollen head of his shaft glistening with precum.

Seeing her attention, he murmured, "Feel free to suck it. It has medicinal value."

She snorted. "I'll bet."

He coughed to cover laughter and continued to fondle her breasts.

She wasn't laughing anymore when he pinched her nipples and tugged on her breasts with enough pressure to push her toward orgasm. Shelby turned her head and opened her mouth. When his cock neared, she licked or sucked what she could reach, but he always pulled back before she could truly get started.

Shane left her breasts and moved to the foot of the table. He pulled her closer and placed her ankles on his shoulders.

Then she felt a hand graze her ass. "Shane?"

"That's Dr. Collins to you."

She felt him brush her slit and bit back a groan. "Dr. Collins, what are you—"

"I'll explain the procedure as I go." His voice had turned gritty. He pushed, and his cockhead penetrated her channel.

With her legs raised, she provided a tighter seal, and as he slid inside her, he felt larger and thicker than he had before. "Oh God, yes."

"I should wait until you see your doctor, but I don't doubt you're as clean as I am. You also mentioned that you're on birth control." He seated himself fully inside her and stilled. "*Fuck.*" He took a few deep breaths. "I'm going to make sure you're as tight as you should be. I need to fill you up, Miss Vanzant." Hunger shone in his eyes, and his jaw clenched as he began to fuck her while keeping his hands on her ankles to hold her in place.

"Yes, Doctor. Give me my medicine," she pleaded, feeling like a bad actress in an X-rated flick and loving it. So naughty, so sexy. So unlike Shelby in her everyday life.

He kept one hand around her legs while his other moved to her clit. And as he pounded inside her with longer, measured strokes, he rubbed her nub, increasing the stimulation.

"Shane, yes, *yes.*" She couldn't stop her orgasm, and she didn't want to. Knowing he'd soon come inside her was a huge turn-on, though she couldn't have said why.

"You have no idea how good you feel coming around me." He moaned and hammered into her, his thrusts growing choppier as he neared his end. "I'm going to come inside you.

Fuck, Shelby. You feel so good. So hot." He stared down at her and came, his agony one she wanted to see more of.

He wore that fancy suit while he fucked her. He remained dressed while she was naked. The reality of their fantasy was so much better than she ever would have imagined.

"There we go," he said in a rough voice as he pumped a few last times before withdrawing. "Now you're full of what you needed." He didn't stop there. Shane pushed a finger inside her and pulled it out, only to run it down her ass to her anus. He rimmed her with his own seed and toyed with her ass, inserting the tip of his finger.

"I've never done this with a patient before." Shane's thick voice attested to his excitement. "We're going to try this later. Not today, not now, but soon. I'm going to slide my dick inside this hole. Stretch it out and fill it up. Maybe when we have a better prep room for the doctor, hmm?"

He watched her as he pushed his finger deeper, and she tensed at the unfamiliar burn. He stopped, and she let out a breath. Then he pulled it out and wiped his hand on her sheets. He used another towel to clean off his cock and put himself to rights. "Don't move."

Like she could process past the intense pleasure still thrumming through her body.

Shane grabbed his suit jacket, unlocked the door and left. She heard water running briefly before he returned smelling of lavender—the hand soap from the bathroom. He carried a wet washcloth in one hand and a towel in the other.

"You're the best doctor I've ever had." Shelby stretched out on the table feeling limp, relaxed and totally at peace for the first time in forever.

"And you're the best patient I've ever had." He winked and proceeded to clean her up. When finished, he set the towels aside and handed over her clothing. "I wasn't sure what you'd think of today, but I haven't been able to stop envisioning fucking you on that table."

She finished dressing and laughed.

"Come on," he protested. "You thought about it too, admit it."

"Yeah, but I was trying to be professional when I filled in for Denise. I don't lust after my clients. Or at least I didn't before I met you."

Shane groaned. "Do you know how confusing that was for me? I was relaxing and enjoying my massage. Denise leaves, comes back in, and gets my cock hard enough to split nails."

"So that's why you didn't turn over." Shelby decided to take a chance. He seemed in the mood to want more. And God knew, she did. "Next time we do this in here, we'll have to play naughty masseuse and her poor client instead of doctor."

"I'm definitely in." Shane hauled her into his arms for a kiss. It didn't feel sexual to Shelby, but affectionate, almost loving. Carnal need vibrated on a lower hum, while the connection between them seemed to deepen. Or was that just the emotional nutball in her wishing for more despite knowing it would be a mistake?

Shane released her from the embrace and sighed. "I have to get back to work. I only had a short window of time, sorry to say."

"Yeah, well, you made the most of it."

"I did. But so did you."

Then she realized something else. "You're going back to work without underwear?"

"Actually I put them back on when I cleaned up. And a good thing. The Graces are in today."

"The Graces?"

He grimaced. "Mr. Grace is terrific. He's older, has a real thing for quality architecture, and can afford to indulge. Problem is, he married a much younger woman with a roving eye, if you know what I mean."

"Oh wow. Has she sexually harassed you?"

He grunted. "Is the sky blue? But they're big clients. And frankly, any man who claims sexual harassment from a woman is asking to get his ass kicked. Not PC, I know, but come on. I'm a former Marine. If my dad or Mac heard I'd lodged a complaint, I'd never hear the end of it."

She shook her head. He had to do what he felt right, but she didn't like the thought of some skank trying to hook her claws into him.

"Sorry, Shelby."

"For what?"

"I'm supposed to keep this light, right? Just hotter than hell sex. And here I am yakking about my job. Ignore me." He gave her a peck on the lips.

"No, it's okay." She felt suddenly shy and had no idea why. "I like you talking to me. About work, I mean. It's not a problem."

He frowned but nodded. "Well, if you're sure. I don't want to screw this up, what you and I are doing." He stared at her breasts and grinned. "Man, I should have been a doctor."

She laughed, and for the first time in months didn't inwardly flinch when someone mentioned Rick the Prick's profession. "I agree. You'd have a ton of repeat clients, I can tell you that."

"Long as you're one of them, I'm good."

The smiled at each other, the mood intimate.

Shelby cleared her throat. "Next time, I pick the place."

"Anytime, anywhere. Although my office will never be the

same. It's tough to concentrate in there now. I'll be in the middle of work and remember you splayed out on my desk."

"Well it's not going to be easy forgetting what we did in here. Thank God my doctor is a woman. I couldn't handle putting my feet in stirrups for a man after what you just did. He'd be down at that end and I'd keep wondering what was going into me."

He chuckled and adjusted himself in his pants. "Damn. Cut that out. I have to go back to work. I really don't need to be showing off my package."

"But it's such a nice package." One that Grace woman needed to keep her hands off of.

He kissed her once more. "Back to work." He paused. "I have some family stuff to do Saturday, but I'm free Sunday. To get together again, I mean."

Later tonight sounded even better, but she didn't want to appear greedy. Or needy. "That works for me. How about Sunday afternoon, my place?"

"Perfect." He looked relieved. He couldn't possibly believe she'd say no to more sex from him, could he? "Text me the details. Bye, Shelby."

She watched him go. The minute he left, she sagged to the table and wondered what she'd gotten herself into. He was dangerous. The first time with him had been bad enough, but after playing doctor, she wanted him even more. *Again.* But trust her dumb psyche not to be content with just the sex. Her emotions started spider-webbing all over the place, wanting bits of him to linger with every thought and breath.

She made a mental note to be early for her doctor's appointment tomorrow. She liked that Shane trusted her and didn't want him to think his faith misplaced. That warm fuzzy feeling blossomed into affection. What if sex between them proved him to not only be an outstanding lover, which she could verify, but boyfriend material as well?

"Shut up, romantic Shelby." And this was why she'd had her heart broken before. She'd seen Rick's problems but had overlooked them because he had looks, a decent profession, and seemed to like her. Now she had Shane, who had looks, a decent profession, and seemed to like her. Except unlike Rick, Shane had been bluntly honest from the beginning. They would have sex and nothing else. A friendly relationship centered on orgasms and naughtiness.

She could handle that. She prized honesty above all things. But that didn't mean she had to be honest with herself. Not yet. Because she had a feeling the sex with Shane was turning into a crush she might not be able to stop. She didn't look forward to heartache again, but damn if she could resist him. Not good, not good at all.

CHAPTER TWELVE

SHELBY TOYED WITH HER FOOD SATURDAY NIGHT. SHE'D met Maggie at Maggie's house, due for a good girl's night out. Which with Maggie, amounted to a pot of buckwheat spaghetti, Maggie's killer pesto sauce, and a healthy salad, followed by some decadent chocolate dessert and a movie on TV.

"What did I do?" Maggie asked.

Shelby started. "What?"

"You're not eating my famous noodles. And you've barely commented on my hair." Maggie twirled her shorter locks. The more severe cut made her look even more like the model she insisted she would never be again.

"I'm sorry. Work this week was tough. Denise and Ann did their thing, but I'm feeling burned out." And frazzled because she couldn't stop thinking about Shane. It was killing her not to tell Maggie, but she really didn't want her mother and Ron bothering her about him.

"Tell me what's wrong. I can help." Maggie blinked at her with those big blue eyes, and Shelby weakened.

"It's just…" The notion of her mother cornering Shane and scaring him away before Shelby could make sense of what he might mean in her life scared her straight. "I feel bad that I'm manless. Does that make sense?"

"Join the friggin' club."

"But you're manless because you choose to be, not because you can't find one. You're different than I am."

"Well, I'm smarter, sure."

Shelby ignored the smartass comment. "I mean, I've never been sure when it comes to guys. Before Rick, there weren't that many interested in me."

"That's because you don't see yourself the way others do. You call yourself average, but you're beautiful. You're built like a real woman, with curves. But you're toned too. You know what I wouldn't give to be taller than five-four?"

"Five-three."

"And a half. But the point is, you're closed off because you're insecure."

The insight surprised Shelby.

"You definitely fit the profile."

"What profile?"

Maggie looked so earnest as she leaned over the kitchen table. "The one about beautiful but insecure women that Dr. Phil talked about yesterday on television."

Shelby groaned. "Not the relationship special. I thought I told you not to watch that?" Maggie had a bad habit of following talk show advice.

Maggie shrugged. "Say what you want, but I need as much help as you do. I seem to go for losers. You refuse to see that guys want to date you. Remember Todd what's-his-face from last month?"

"No."

Maggie huffed. "You know, the dark-haired guy hanging around your office all the time? I ran into him by accident, and he knocked me over Denise."

"Oh, that guy." Shelby grinned. "Now I remember."

"He liked you."

"He was a client. He hung around because he was booking an appointment."

"So he could date you. Hell, I was right there. He danced around your availability for like ten minutes. It was embarrassing to watch you ignore him."

"I didn't ignore him." Shelby frowned. "I don't remember it like that. He wanted to know where to go out in town since he was new to Queen Anne. I gave him a few ideas, booked him an appointment which he never showed up for, and that was that."

"You are so clueless." Maggie shook her head. "He wanted to go out with *you*. He asked you to go to dinner with him."

"He did not!"

"He almost asked it. Until you bluntly asked why he was staring at you. You're kind of intimidating, you know? You sounded mean."

Shane didn't seem to mind her being mean. Even when she'd been rude to him, he'd laughed it off.

"And Bob?" Maggie continued.

"Bob was an idiot." A contractor who had spent way too much time fixing her pipes when he should have gotten the job done right the first time. "Only thing I can't fault him for is that he didn't charge me for all those follow-up visits."

Maggie smacked herself in the head.

"What?"

"You are so clueless." She stuffed her face full of noodles and washed it down with wine.

"What movie do you have for us tonight?" Shelby asked to change the subject.

"It'll keep." Maggie paused. "So I'm thinking of joining a new gym."

"Okay."

"Not to get fit, but to get paid. I'll be working there. You should come to my class."

Shelby groaned. "Didn't I tell you when we first met? I'm a walker, and on bad days, a runner under protest. Aerobics is for more coordinated people. I felt off a step once, in the middle of my one and only class. It was embarrassing."

"But I'm teaching. The place is a step up from the other gyms I worked. You have to go and tell my new boss how great I am."

Maggie sounded desperate, and Shelby wondered if her friend had been having money problems again. Though Maggie seemed to do well with her hours at the gallery, teaching aerobics helped fill in the gaps while her artwork started to sell. Lately she'd been doing better on her commissions, selling more through Shantell than she'd thought she might. But Maggie would be the last person to ask for financial help, even if she needed it.

"It means that much to you to keep this new job? What if your boss is a loser? Or the gym is for steroid abusers and catty women?"

Maggie got that stubborn look on her face. "It's a nice place. I don't want to lose the job."

"Fine, fine." Shelby held up her hands and pushed her half-eaten plate away. "I'll come. Just tell me when and where." *As long as it's not tomorrow.*

She couldn't stop thinking about Shane and what they'd do during his visit. It was her turn to come up with something sexy. She had to top his doctor fantasy. With so much she wanted to do, she didn't know what he might consider off limits or what he might really be into.

"Hey, Maggie." She joined her friend in the living room to watch the movie.

"Yeah?"

"Ever wonder what it would be like to have a man cater to your fantasies? I mean, to have a guy who would do whatever you wanted in bed? What would you make him do?"

"Ooh, I love these kinds of conversations." Maggie muted the television and faced Shelby on the couch. "Well, not to get too involved, but I kind of like the idea of being overtaken by someone stronger, you know? I mean, I'm smaller than most men, but I have a tendency to be kind of aggressive."

"You think?"

"Please. Pot calling kettle, hello? Except you look as tough as I really am. Every guy treats me like glass when we date, like I'll break because I'm not huge. Dominance sounds like fun, but not the kind where the guy wears leather and makes me call him Master. Something a little tamer, I think. What about you?"

"I don't know. I read a lot of books with sexy storylines. Slave girl sounds fun. So does roping my own cowboy."

"What about a threesome? I've read a few of those. Thought about doing it too."

Shelby shook her head. "No way. I have a hard enough time with one guy."

"But just for the sex, not a relationship."

"Nope. Just one man for me. But I wouldn't mind trying a lot of other stuff. Bondage, maybe." She flushed, suddenly knowing what she and Shane should do tomorrow.

"Hmm, that does sound like fun." Maggie laughed. "Now if we had a few guys on hand, we could make some magic happen." She turned and grabbed a bag of chocolate covered pretzels. "But since we don't, how about some fun food, a scary movie, and more wine?"

"Sounds good. What's tonight's entertainment?"

"The original *Nightmare on Elm Street.* One of my personal favorites."

"You just like Freddy's glove."

"Yep. And I'm wearing it this Halloween. I look good in red and green stripes, don't I?"

The woman looked good in everything. But it was funny how much Maggie enjoyed being scary, considering she looked so soft and feminine. The opposite of terrifying.

"Don't say it," Maggie warned, expecting what Shelby so often told her.

"Fine." She paused. "But beauty is not a curse."

"You would know."

"Yeah right."

"You're pretty," Maggie stated in as insulting a tone as possible.

"No, I'm not." Shelby was okay, not ugly, but nothing like Maggie.

"Are too. Beautiful with a capital B. Now shut up and watch while Freddy gets ready to rip into Johnny Depp."

"Loudmouth."

"One, two, Freddy's coming for you…"

♥

Shane couldn't wait to see Shelby again. Though they'd had sex just three days ago, it felt like forever since he'd been with her. Mac would have called him a pussy for wanting to see the woman's smile so much, but Shane couldn't help it. He had a bad feeling he could really fall for her, and though it had a lot to do with their natural chemistry, more of it had to do with the woman he sensed hiding behind sexual need.

He arrived on her doorstep at two on Sunday afternoon. He knocked on the door of a cute townhouse a few blocks from her work. The door opened, and he entered into a contemporary living room done in bright colors. Unlike his house, she had clutter, and a lot of it. But she also had a sense of organization, so that her myriad crystal figurines, artwork, and eclectic furniture seemed cozy and not crazy.

The door shut behind him, and he turned to face her. The blood rushed from his head and centered between his legs. The woman wore a red lace teddy that cupped her breasts yet left a hint of her nipples exposed. It also showed off her tapered waist and rounded thighs. And when she turned, Christ, he saw a thong between those luscious cheeks.

She turned back around and smiled at him. "I've been waiting for you." He saw she wore a bit of make-up. He liked her face without it, but right now she looked like a siren out to seduce him. Dark black lined her eyes, and her lips shone a glossy pink. Man, he couldn't wait to feel those lips around his cock.

Any ideas he'd had about getting to know her better before sinking his dick into her again disappeared.

"You're in my house. My rules," she whispered before stepping closer and looking him over.

He wore jeans and a button down shirt, casual clothing he'd planned to discard the moment she said so. He had no problem following her lead, because he was curious to know what she fantasized about. The teddy, now that was something he might have asked her to wear. To know she wanted to wear it only made her that much hotter.

Her long hair draped over toned shoulders and curled over the exposed slopes of her breasts. He couldn't quite see her pussy past the red silk covering her, but he saw snaps and knew he could have easy access when needed.

His cock pressed uncomfortably against his jeans. He'd gone without underwear, wanting to give *her* easy access to him whenever she wanted it. God, he still had a hard time believing he'd really fucked Shelby Vanzant. The Amazon who'd captivated him from the first kept getting better and better.

"What do you want me to do?" he asked, his voice thick.

"Everything I tell you to. At first…"

At first? He couldn't wait to see what she had in mind.

"Come into the back room."

He followed her into her bedroom. Pale blue walls framed the centerpiece, a large brass bed that had scarves tied to the corner posts. Oh hell yeah, he was going to love letting her have the lead. He almost wished Lisa was here to see him behaving in a thoroughly non-vanilla way. But then again, he couldn't imagine doing anything outside of missionary with her. The few times he'd tried, she'd given him so many instructions he'd lost the will to carry on.

Interesting how his few times with Shelby beat anything he and Lisa had done, and he'd thought himself in love with his ex. Maybe he was more like Mac than he thought. Because he didn't know Shelby all that well, but he felt connected to her from a few sexual romps. Or maybe—

"You're thinking too hard." She shoved him forward and he landed face down on the bed.

Before he could move, she lay on his back, and he stilled.

"That's better," she practically purred. "Now let me take off these clothes of yours." She left him to remove his shoes and socks.

He wondered if she could hear his heart beat, because it sounded like banging war drums to him. He was really hard, stirred up because he had no idea of what she might do next. It was like telling secrets to a stranger. The ability to be anyone and do anything with Shelby was a freedom all in itself.

"I'm yours." He cleared his throat, alarmed at how much he liked that simple phrase and the implications that went with it. "I mean, whatever you want to do, I'm good. Nothing is off limits for me, nothing too kinky for us to try. You're completely in charge."

She leaned up over him and whispered in his ear, "I'm *so* glad you said that."

Her breasts pressed against his back, and he swore he could feel the points of her nipples against his shoulder blade. Wishful thinking, but the mental image had a huge effect on his erection.

She leaned up and tugged at his shirt. He helped her take it off him. Then he felt her hands reach around him to the snap of his pants. Her fingers brushed his abdomen, caught between his flesh and the bed, and he shuddered.

"Have I told you how sexy you are? That belly is so tight." She kissed his neck and he arched his hips to give her easier access to his fly. Reading his actions, she pried open his jeans. The button first, then the slow glide of the zipper over his cock.

Once the denim parted, she reached inside and gripped him tight, running her fingers over his slick cockhead. "Oh yeah. My big boy is ready for me."

He groaned and pushed into her hand, ready to come right now.

"But not yet." She let him go and stepped back. He helped her take off his jeans, careful to positioned himself belly down over her bed. He didn't know how keen she'd be if he came all over her pretty blue comforter.

"Shelby, your bed is—"

"Hold that thought." She moved away and returned, then slid something near his head. He glanced at a copy of her medical report. Touched that she'd gone through with her physical even though he'd pretty much made health issues a moot point by going down on her last time, he read over it and handed it back when finished.

"Thanks." He turned onto his back and smiled up at her.

"No, thank you." She placed the paper on her dresser. Then she closed the door, lit a few candles, and just stared down at him.

Long dark fabric covered the windows, the candlelight the only thing illuminating the space around them, with the exception of what little light filtered past her heavy drapes. Shelby in a red teddy and Shane completely naked made the scene feel like something out of a fantasy. *Her* fantasy, from the way she smiled at him.

"You are so cut. I love looking at you." She bit her bottom lip. "Get in the middle of the bed and put your hands behind your head. Spread your legs. I want to see all of you."

He liked letting her have a look. Shane had never been self-conscious about his body. About a lot of other things, yes, but his appearance? No.

She knelt on the bed next to him and ran a hand over his foot. She continued to trail her fingers up his leg to his knee, over his thigh and across his groin. His cock jumped, and she caressed him with the lightest of touches.

"Fuck. That's good, baby." He wanted never to leave her hand, his hunger building when she began pumping him with a grip too light by half. "Harder. Hold me tight."

She let go.

A frown turned those pretty eyes a darker brown. "You do what I say, not the other way around." She paused. "Not this time."

Oh shit. "Sure, right. Lost myself there." He definitely was going to come more than once today. Thank God. Sleeping with Shelby had opened the door on his libido, and now he couldn't go through the day without a few hard-ons thinking about the sexy brunette.

"Be a good boy." She leaned down and licked his shaft from root to crown.

He bucked up, unable to control himself. But he kept his hands behind his neck.

"Mmm." She put her mouth over him and sucked hard, licking up the fluid that pooled at his tip. "Yummy," she added, her voice husky, arousing him to no end.

It was so much better to know she wanted this, that her fantasy included seducing him. She could have done anything, asked him to make her come in any way possible. Yet she chose this.

She played with him until he thought he'd burst, then completely let him go.

"Not now," he moaned and heard an evil laugh.

"Now it's my turn."

She straddled his waist, rose up on her knees, and slowly moved her hand between her legs. Shelby unsnapped the teddy and took the crotch piece away, leaving a wet, bare pussy open to view.

"Christ. You shaved it all. Let me fuck you, please."

"There's more." She reached up and pulled down her top, revealing all of her breasts, so that the fabric acted like a bustier, plumping up her already full breasts. "I know how much you like these."

He gripped the back of his neck so hard he feared giving himself a headache. If the woman would just lower herself a little, he could angle his cock up and let her slide down his pole one inch at a time.

Shelby slowly eased a bit of herself over him, setting her hot, wet cream over his cock. She slid forward, pulling away, and he nearly lost it.

"Easy," she warned and lifted her breast. "See my nipple? How hard and tight it is for you?"

He groaned.

"Suck me. I want you to get me wetter, so that when you slide inside me, I'll come all over you."

He didn't have to be told twice. He opened his mouth and took that tasty nipple inside. He sucked and licked, nipped and teased as she writhed over him, coming closer and closer to his dick.

She pulled away and offered her other breast, and Shane couldn't stop himself from letting go of his neck to reach for her hips while he sucked her hard. Hell, if he didn't fuck her soon, he'd lose his mind.

"No, not yet," she rasped and stopped him.

It all but killed him, but he froze under her and let her slip from his lips, breathing so hard it sounded as if he'd just finished a marathon.

"Please. I'm dying to fuck you."

She scooted up and walked on her knees up his body.

Understanding what she wanted next, he waited with barely concealed patience.

"I want to come over your lips." She settled her knees on either side of his head. "Make me come."

He'd never wanted anything more. Shane drew her down

and sucked her sweet juice into his mouth. Giving oral to a woman ranked in his top sexual favorites, but Lisa hadn't been that into it. Shelby, it appeared, was nothing like his ex, and he couldn't be more grateful.

He ate her out, loving the taste of her, the essence of the sultry woman needing a good hard fuck. It wasn't going to take her long, not with her breathy cries and all the grinding over his mouth. He added one finger, then two into her cunt, stretching her for him.

His dick throbbed, wanting in that sweet heaven that tasted like candy.

"Shane, oh yeah. Baby, please. God, I'm coming," she cried as she ground her face over his mouth.

He swallowed her juice, enthralled with the tight bud under his tongue. Man, her clit was hard, and the shocks of her vaginal walls gripping his fingers tight made waiting to take her unbearable. And thrilling, because waiting had never been so difficult.

After she calmed down enough to lever off him, she lay back over him like a blanket. She had to feel his arousal, because her belly rolled over his prick. But she made no move to ease him.

After a moment, she chuckled low. "Hard and hurting, hmm?"

He groaned. "You're such a cock tease. After letting me eat that sweet cunt, you get me rock hard, then nothing?" He rubbed himself against her belly, needing to be inside her.

"I want you to fuck me doggie style," she said against his chest. "Take me hard, be wild. I want—"

She squealed when he exploded into action. He rolled her over and moved to his knees in one breath, then flipped her to her hands and knees and pulled her up to a bent over position in the next.

"I'm fucking you right now. No more waiting," he growled and speared her in one hard thrust.

She cried out, but he didn't stop. Shane was like a madman possessed. He slid inside her with ease. The friction over his already sensitive cock made everything brighter, more intense. Despite the dim light of the candles around him, her skin seemed to glow. A peachy silk that was perfect against his darker, tanner flesh.

He looked down and forced himself to slow, so that he could watch himself disappear into her before he pulled all the way out. He punctuated each thrust with a snap of his hips, hitting as deep inside her as he could.

"Oh God. Yes, please," Shelby moaned and rocked back with each shove, meeting him halfway.

Shane had just about neared his end when she reached under them and grazed his balls.

"*Fuck me.* Here it comes. All in you." He held her tight as he pounded inside her once more and stilled, jetting into her in a burst as she tightened around him once more, lost in her own orgasm.

The rush of pleasure overwhelmed him, and he could only kneel there and ride the wave as jolt after jolt of pure adrenaline washed over them both.

When he finished, he felt weak with repletion.

Shane slowly withdrew, already regretting the loss of her warmth. He slumped to the bed beside her and welcomed her into his arms when she crawled over him.

"I'm messy," she murmured as she kissed his chest.

Emotional entanglement threatened to undo his peace. As much as he'd hoped to remain unaffected by the feelings sex often engendered, he opened to her. He couldn't help reveling in her kiss, as caught by her tenderness as he'd been by her seduction. She leaned over and looked down at him with an uncertain expression, one that made him want to hug her and tell her everything would be all right now that they had each other.

Time seemed to freeze.

Oh hell. He'd gone and done it again. Fallen for a woman after trying so fucking hard not to.

"You okay?" she asked.

He nodded and forced himself to relax. He kept telling himself the affection was merely the result of one hell of an orgasm. Bliss, endorphins, sexual satisfaction, that's all it was.

"I'm better than okay," he said back, his voice embarrassingly hoarse.

Her grin eased his discomfort. "If it makes you feel better, I don't think I can move, and I know I'm getting you all wet."

He felt moisture over his belly but for once didn't cringe. He'd never been a big fan of the cleanup after, despite the fact that most of the mess came from him. But he didn't mind knowing he'd come in her, that his seed now stained her legs and his belly.

"We should shower." He rubbed her back.

"We should. Together." She kissed him, a slow leisurely merging of mouths that soon morphed into a need for more.

"You're in charge." Shane followed her off the bed and into her bathroom. The shower stall looked big enough to fit three comfortably. "Nice. We could have a party in here."

She winked at him as she took off her teddy. When she stood naked, he just looked at her.

"Call me a sex-drunk fool, but you are the sexiest thing I've ever seen." He couldn't look away from her breasts. Until he spied her smooth mound. "And shaving… I admit, you hooked me. Now I can see what I've been eating."

She blushed, and he thought the reaction both surprising and sweet considering what they'd just done.

"So you mentioned something earlier about you being in charge—at first." He followed her into the shower after she adjusted the water. "What does that mean?"

He watched her clean herself, knowing he'd replay this scene over in his mind again and again.

After she cleaned herself, she turned to him with the soap and ran it over his body. She paid a lot of attention to his arms and chest, then played with his balls and cock until he threatened to come again.

She let him go with a smirk. "You're hard, I see."

"I wonder why."

She laughed. "I wanted you ready for round two."

"I'm hoping we'll eventually get to round six, but that may be reaching."

They grinned at each other, and something suspiciously like the beginning of love fluttered in his chest.

Her grin faded. "I liked being in charge, but I also want to be taken." She looked away from him, and he nudged her chin with his finger, so he could see her eyes.

"Why are you looking away?"

"This is a little embarrassing."

"Considering what we just did, I'd think you'd be over any embarrassment." What the hell did she want him to do with her?

"I want you to take charge. It's weird. I mean, not just be domineering, but to make me totally helpless."

He thought he understood. "So the scarves in there are for you, not me?"

She nodded, the flush high on her cheeks. "I don't want

you to rape me or anything. But I want to feel powerless, you know?"

He thought he did. A common fantasy among many independent women, or so his girlfriend before Lisa had told him, was to be dominated. He empathized. Being in charge all the time grew wearying. Hell, having Shelby take the lead had been a welcome relief. But commanding her would be a treat as well.

"So I get to tie you up and do whatever I want to?"

She nodded. "And be a little rough. Not too rough, just—"

"Forceful. I get it." He grinned, liking their next adventure already. He glanced down at himself. "I'm good for it. You?"

"Almost. I need to get back in the mood."

He frowned. "Really? Because…" he tapered off as she lowered to her knees between his legs. He widened his stance when she tapped his inner thighs. "Because… Oh fuck it. You're going to…" He groaned and gripped her wet hair. Talk about a wet dream. Literally.

CHAPTER THIRTEEN

MAGGIE DIDN'T KNOW WHY MAC JAMESON CONTINUED to harass her. She did everything the big lout said. Her aerobics class had drawn more people than the other instructors normally did, or so the jealous bimbo with a tight ass and fake breasts had mentioned while gawking at Mac as he walked by.

"Doran, in my office." He breezed by her without waiting.

The jerk.

She took her time chatting with a few women who had come back after taking her first class last Tuesday. Thursdays at six was a popular time, but with Shantell amenable to giving Maggie the hours she wanted, Maggie would do whatever she could to not only make ends meet, but help her absent best friend snag a decent man.

Everything she'd learned about Shane Collins pointed to a guy Shelby might click with. He was good looking, as Maggie had seen for herself, and he had that same health fixation going on that Shelby did. Her friend could bitch about running 'til the cows came home, but she still used it as her go-to measure for taking off the pounds. Maggie only resorted to jogging to nab a sale item before another shopper could get to it.

She waved goodbye to her new friends, passed by the catty airheads dreaming about Mac, and grabbed her water bottle. She refilled it at the water fountain and turned to see two men looking right at her, or right where her ass had been before she turned around.

"Hello?" She glared, giving them her man-hater stare, the one Shelby had perfected.

They smiled at her.

She sighed.

"Not getting any younger, Doran." Mac's warm breath in her ear startled a shriek out of her, and she jerked around and accidentally spilled water over his shirt.

He grunted and grabbed her by the arm. "I need to talk to you. In my office. Today, short stuff."

She discreetly tried to yank her arm out of his meaty hand as they left the main gym. But he wouldn't budge. So like a kid being dragged to the principal's office, she walked next to Mac on her tiptoes, trying to keep up with his longer stride.

In his office, he finally let her go, and she rubbed her arm and scowled. "Nice, Jameson. I'm not a piece of meat, you know."

He turned to regard her and settled his fine ass on the edge of his desk. Then he grinned, and she lost her train of thought. For a man who acted like a Neanderthal half the time, he could be a charming guy. That combination of black hair, ice blue eyes and a body Hercules would envy packed a one-two punch.

"You're so cute when you're angry."

Cute. She was so tired of *cute*. She'd much rather be likened to an Amazon, as she'd overheard Mac call her best friend. Or a goddess, or maybe a Marilyn Monroe type instead of petite Barbie.

"You wanted something, slave master?"

His eyes narrowed. "Yeah, I wanted something." He paused, and she couldn't for the life of her read the look he gave her.

"What?" She slammed her hands on her hips, glad she'd worn a shirt over her sport bra and more conservative tights today. Whenever he turned his assessing gaze in her direction, she felt half naked. And she didn't like it. Mac seemed to fit her type a little too much. He had sex with tons of women, acted way too macho for this day and age, and had too many muscles. She liked men bigger than her, but with Mac, she felt dwarfed. It wasn't so much his height as his brawn. He could crush her with his pinkie before she could even think of fighting back.

"Never mind." Mac circled his desk and sat behind it. He continued to study her.

"If you have nothing better to do than stare, I'm out of here. I'm working here to do Shelby—and *you*—a favor, remember?"

"Shelby, right." He nodded, and the unreadable expression on his face faded. "It's been almost three weeks already. When am I going to meet her? I want to see what she's all about. Shane seems a bit too evasive lately." He shook his head. "I think the dick is holding out on me."

"I can't get through to Shelby either. I've been busy at work myself, you know. Between the gallery, here, and my work at home, I'm tapped for time."

"Work at home?"

"I'm a sculptor." It still made her heart race to say the words out loud, to admit she created art, not as a hobby, but as a career.

"Oh right. You mentioned that." Mac seemed interested, which surprised her. "You got anything downtown in any of the galleries?"

"Not yet. Well, kind of. Shantell…" Before she could get started, she stopped herself. Mac didn't care about her artwork. "I'll check on Shelby again."

He frowned at her. "Fine. Do it. I want to meet this chick who has my friend so interested. I get the feeling he's avoiding me."

"Gee, I wonder why?"

He surprised her by laughing. "You know, I like you, Maggie Doran. You aren't afraid of me, you don't seem to care about impressing me—"

"Because I don't. Care that is."

"—and you don't seem to want in my pants."

"Good God. Your ego could stand a few knocks." She shook her head and moved to leave.

Mac met her by the door to his office. He stood so close she could feel his body heat, and once again she was reminded of how much bigger than her he was. "Maybe I should keep you around, so you can make sure I remember my place."

Was it her, or did his voice sound huskier than normal? She reached for the door handle to the office, and he put his hand over hers. The flutter in her belly returned, the one she got when she stood too close to Mr. God's Gift to Women. Hell, she was attracted to him. Not that she liked the feeling, but she recognized it at least.

"Maggie?"

"I'll show you your place. At the bottom of the barrel," she muttered and refused to look past his chest, now wet thanks to the water she'd splashed over him. "You might want to change your shirt."

He didn't move. "Yeah. I will."

They stood in awkward silence, his hand on top of hers,

their bodies so close they might as well be dancing.

He stepped back and coughed. "So. Shelby. Swing her by. I'll check her out."

Maggie had agreed to look into Shane's background, at Mimi's behest. Now she was stuck with Mac. He wanted to know more about Shelby, fine. Because Maggie would do whatever it took to help her find love again.

"I'll try to get with her today. I teach again Friday at four. Make sure you're here."

Mac blinked. "I'm sorry. Who's the boss?"

She chuckled. "That's supposed to be, 'you're not the boss of me.' And well, big guy, you're not. I can quit at any time, so watch your tone."

His eyes widened, a comical sight, and she left him sputtering before he could ruin her exit. She left the gym whistling, determined to find out what Shelby had been up to so she could leave the gym and Mac Jameson behind before she did something really stupid.

Like sleep with the man.

♥

Thursday afternoon, Shelby hung up the phone, bemused and not sure what to do about it. Shane had asked her to lunch on Saturday. Not as a euphemism for oral sex, not at his place as a prelude to steamy sex, or in any manner which led her to believe he'd expect sex. They were having lunch this weekend at Pike's Place Market. And it felt like a date.

Denise interrupted her worry. She left her newly renovated massage room with her client in tow.

Shelby rang the woman up and watched her leave with a smile on her face. To Denise she said, "Hiring you was a great decision."

"Yeah, well, letting me have Mrs. Meyers was a boon. She's a great tipper."

Shelby made a face. "I know."

Denise laughed. "Hey, it's time to go. Five o'clock on a Thursday means the weekend is almost here. You don't have anyone else, do you?"

Shelby shook her head. "Just cleaning up."

"I'll help."

"Nah. Go home to Cupcake. I've got this."

"Actually, I have a date." Denise's grin lit up her face. "Our contractor, Greg?"

"You mean Mr. Slow?"

Denise flushed. "He's not that slow." She bit her lip, then confessed in a rush, "He was taking so long on the work because he was trying to get the courage to ask me out. He told me so yesterday. And he's not charging for any overtime or anything."

That sounded familiar. Maybe this guy knew Bob, her other slow contractor. "There's that at least." Shelby nodded. "Good luck on your date, but if he turns out to be a jerk, I'm coming after him with a bat."

"Yes, ma'am." Denise gave her a mock salute, giggled, and took off like schoolgirl.

"Did she just skip?" Shelby watched her friend race out the door.

Grumbling to herself, she locked up and did her daily cleaning. Just as she finished, she glanced up to see Maggie cupping her eyes against the outside glass, looking in.

Hell. She pasted a smile and let her friend inside before locking up again. "Maggie. Just the person I was hoping to see."

Maggie scowled "Yeah, right. Why are you avoiding me?"

"I'm not avoiding you. I'm busy."

"Yeah. Busy avoiding me. But that's okay. I realize your aversion is to the aerobics class you *swore* you'd come to, not to me exactly."

Shelby groaned. "I've been busy."

"Me too. But I talked to Denise, and she told me you're free tomorrow." Maggie smiled, her spry attitude grating yet charming at the same time.

"Terrific."

"Yep. You and me, honey. Four o'clock at Jameson's Gym."

Shelby frowned. "That sounds familiar."

"Yeah. It's the place I go to work now. Remember me telling you about my new job, the one I want *to keep?*" Maggie looked hurt. "I know life gets in the way, but I could really use your support."

Shelby sighed. "Of course I'll be there tomorrow. I'll swear up and down that your class is the best I've ever had."

Maggie nodded. "And you'll pretend not to know me and tell my boss how great I am, right?"

A game they'd played before, to benefit them clients. Shelby grinned. "You bet."

"Great. I'd stay to chat, but I have to go. I'm behind on your birthday present." Maggie darted away before Shelby could yell at her to hurry. September had rolled around pretty quickly, and before they both knew it, Shelby would be twenty-eight.

The next day, at five o'clock, Shelby felt all of her almost-twenty-eight years and then some. Her calves ached, her ass felt like one giant throbbing pain, and she'd tripped twice on her step but hadn't fallen, thank God. The class had been packed.

Shelby had to hand it Maggie, though. The music was stellar, and the beat had kept her moving long past her body telling her to quit. Because her friend took the time to introduce new sequences, Shelby hadn't gotten too lost, either.

She left the water fountain and headed back to Maggie, only to see her best bud dwarfed by some testosterone-laden giant. He was handsome in a blunt, hard way, and he seemed to hang on Maggie's every word. She heard them arguing as she drew closer, which surprised her. Maggie was usually peaches-and-cream nice to everyone she met. Was this guy giving her a hard time?

Determined to defend her friend, she moved as fast as her aching body would let her and joined them.

They both stopped talking mid-sentence.

"Shelby, isn't it?" Maggie's grin was a bit worrisome, definitely forced. "Shelby is new to the class," she explained to Muscle Man. "Mac Jameson, my boss."

Ah, that explained the tension.

"I'll be right back. I have some things to straighten before Jane's class." Maggie left, giving Shelby the opportunity to plug her friend.

She turned to Mac to see him studying her from head to toe. "Um, Maggie. She's great."

"Uh huh."

"Her class was really easy to follow, and for a klutz like me, that's saying something."

His grin was unexpected, especially because it transformed his face from fierce to devastatingly handsome. If she hadn't been so consumed with Shane, she might have given Mac a try. But still, even under his bright smile, Shelby couldn't forget Shane's kiss.

"You don't look clumsy, Shelby."

She grinned back at him. "Thanks. But don't let the workout gear fool you. I don't like exercise."

"So what do you do to stay in shape?" he murmured, the compliment there in the way he looked over her curves.

"I like to walk and hike. The elliptical is great, and I use hand weights to tone." She decided she might as well network while she was at it. "I'm a massage therapist, so I'm into good health and staying fit. Promotes strong muscles."

He nodded. "Yeah, there is that. It helps you live longer too." His subtle grin told her she'd missed the joke, but he changed the subject. "So Maggie did a good job?"

"Terrific."

"Good to know. She's new, but from what I hear and see, her class is fast becoming a favorite." He glanced back at her friend talking with some guy behind the glass walled studio and frowned. "I'll have to see if we can work more of her classes into the schedule."

Shelby had the impression he didn't like Maggie talking to the guy. "That would be great," she said, glad when he looked at her once more and stopped glaring at Maggie. Oh man, was this guy into her friend?

She studied him, taking in his looks, his height, and the way the gym-goers smiled his way.

"You seem pretty popular." Especially among the women. Not a good sign for her friend. A playboy would only break hearts.

"I own the place. Correction, my uncle owns it," he said with a self-deprecating grin. "I run it for now."

"Ah. So you're Maggie's head boss. Not just the manager." Which Maggie hadn't mentioned.

He shrugged. "I guess. Want some water? I have a few extra bottles in my office."

She wondered if that was a line he used to get women, but the way he continued to look over his shoulder at Maggie told her not to worry about his attention. "Sure."

She followed him down a hallway and entered a masculine office filled with Marine Corps pictures and placards. "You served?"

"Yep. Retired a few years ago."

He didn't look old enough to have retired, but she didn't ask any questions. She accepted the water bottle he handed her from a small fridge and drank. That he hadn't closed the office door behind them eased her worries.

"You new to the gym? I don't remember seeing you here before."

She nodded. "A friend told me about your new instructor. I'd been meaning to check this place out a while ago and thought, why not?"

"Good. Glad you're here." He smiled, but the way he looked at her gave her the idea he had a secret agenda. Maybe he wanted to pump her for information about Maggie.

"Maggie's great," she said again.

"Yeah." He sat on his desk and crossed huge arms over his chest. Oh man, if Maggie saw that on a daily basis, her friend would be well and truly hooked. Maggie liked height, and she liked a nice body. Or was he too big for her friend?

He frowned when he saw her staring at his arms.

"Didn't mean to stare. I was looking at the tattoo."

He relaxed. "Oh." He flexed and showed off his snake. "I have an EGA too."

"A what?"

"Eagle, globe and anchor. It's a Marine Corps thing."

Nice. Shane didn't have any tattoos. Then again, he didn't need them to decorate that sexy body.

"So your massage place. What's it called? We get folks in here all the time needing a place to go. Or do you only do that feel good crap?"

If she had, she wouldn't tell him now. "No feel good crap. I'm all about deep tissue. More clinical stuff."

He nodded. "Had a knee problem when I left the Corps. Surgery helped, but my PT recommended I see a good massage therapist."

"Did you?" She looked at the knee he rubbed. He wore athletic shorts, and she could see a few scars over his knee.

"Yeah. He didn't help much, though."

"Too bad. Scar tissue builds, and therapy would help."

He brightened. "Great idea."

"What?"

"Can I make an appointment with you?"

"I wasn't angling for work." Now she felt awkward. "I just meant—"

"No, no. I always put this shit off. Give me your number and I'll make an appointment."

"I, um, okay." She wrote down her number with the pen and yellow sticky note he handed her.

He looked pleased. "Great. Maybe I'll be up and running again after a visit."

"It takes more than one," she warned. "You have to continue to work the area and over time retrain the muscle."

"Hey, if you can work your magic, I'm in." Mac grinned. "Oh hell. I need to talk to Maggie again. Want to take this outside?" He walked her to the door and back into the gym, his hand at her waist. Nothing sexual about his touch, oddly enough.

He was gruff, liked to swear, and seemed interested in becoming a client. According to Maggie, that meant he wanted her. She stopped him before he could nudge her any farther.

"You okay?" he asked.

"You aren't hitting on me, are you?"

She could tell her bluntness had shocked him, because he blinked at her.

"No, should I be?" He seemed interested.

Great. Now she'd created a problem for herself. "No. I just wanted to be clear about that. I've been told I'm as dense as a brick when it comes to understanding men."

He chuckled. "Who told you that?"

"My best friend," she grumbled.

"So if I was interested in more than therapy, you'd say…"

"Nope."

"Because?"

"I'm seeing someone."

"Ah. My loss."

They smiled at one another.

Shelby liked the guy. They made more small talk before he called Maggie over to discuss scheduling.

Shelby left them and mouthed to her friend, *"You owe me big."*

Maggie nodded absently, frowning at whatever Mac said. Shelby didn't know if he'd call her or not about the appointment, but she'd left her number. With any luck, he'd pass it on to needy gym patrons. But at least she could put a check in the box—she'd finally shut Maggie up by coming to support her.

Now if she could just get past her worry that accepting Shane's invitation tomorrow hadn't been a colossal mistake.

CHAPTER FOURTEEN

SHANE WAITED AT THE FRONT OF THE RESTAURANT, CURSING the fact that he'd been late. Fifteen minutes after he'd said to meet her at the café, he saw no sign of her in the lobby or inside the bistro. He wondered if he'd annoyed her by not calling ahead of time, but she hadn't answered her phone when he'd realized how late he'd be. And he couldn't blame George this time. It was his own fault for losing his friggin' keys.

After another ten minutes, he decided she wasn't going to show and turned to leave, swallowing his disappointment.

He'd just exited when she ran up to him.

"I am so sorry I'm late," she apologized, breathing hard. "My mom needed a ride since her car broke down. And then I couldn't find my phone to let you know I was running behind. I think I left it with her by accident."

The relief he felt that she hadn't ditched him made him smile. "Hey, no problem. I was a little late myself." A lot late. But hell, he'd let her wallow and be magnanimous.

They were seated right away, having come at just the right time. The cozy seating area inside more than made up for their near miss.

After they were handed their menus, he just looked at her, wondering what it was about this woman that got to him so completely. The sex was too obvious. Great sex would have been easy to enjoy then forget. He didn't have to wine and dine her for physical gratification. But he wanted to talk to her, to know her.

"This feels like a date," she said, staring back at him.

"Call it whatever you want. We're honest about not wanting relationships, right?" Actually, he didn't think that was the case anymore, on his part.

"True." She seemed uncertain, and he took that as a good sign.

"So we have a nice thing going. And we're going to talk and get to know each other better. As friends," he quantified, which seemed to make her feel better.

"Yeah. Friends with benefits." She smiled at him, and her grin made him feel ten feet tall.

His heart pounded and he lost any appetite for food.

"No reason we can't do what we want. Besides, I like this place. They have great juice."

He agreed. They spent the next half hour eating and drinking and enjoying one another.

"Your mom sounds terrific. I'd love her to meet mine." Shane chuckled. "My mother runs the house like a general. My father is retired military, but she orders everyone around. I swear, I have to remind her on a daily basis that she's not my commanding officer. And that I'm thirty-one, not seven."

Shelby grinned. "Well, my mother thinks she's God's gift to the lovelorn. She keeps setting up her clients."

"A matchmaker, eh?"

"Yeah. The problem is, most of the people she's interfered

with are still together." She frowned. "She didn't like my ex at all, or so she told me after we broke up."

She sounded confused, but not bitter, so he asked, "Why did you break up again? Because he cheated, right?"

She nodded. "He and I met at one of the many festivals around this town. I forget which one now. It was fun while it lasted, but looking back, nothing I did was ever right for the guy, who was, and this still makes me laugh, a doctor."

Their eyes met, and Shane clearly recalled their sexual encounter in her massage room. "Oh hell."

She laughed. "Trust me. That was the best thing that's happened to me in months. And I've never thought about the word *doctor* since then without a mental image of Dr. Collins giving me my medicine."

He saw the irony of it. "I'm surprised you didn't laugh my ass out of the room."

She leaned closer and whispered, "You mean, before you licked me to orgasm or after?"

"Shit. Don't talk like that in public." He groaned. "It's too hard to hide what you do to me. You're lucky. When you're turned on, it doesn't show."

She smirked. "My nipples get hard."

"Stop, please."

She laughed again.

"So, your doctor?"

"He's not mine anymore. Thank God. The guy had the nerve to constantly criticize everything about me. He was subtle, but when I look back, I see how much I changed for him."

"If he wanted change, he should have had someone else."

"Exactly what I ended up telling him. But the kicker was finding him in bed with his secretary." She grimaced. "She was on her knees and… well, you get the picture."

"Ouch." He hurt for her.

"Yeah. A pretty blond with big boobs and no brains."

He gave a mock sigh. "The perfect woman."

She grimaced. "Jerk."

"Yeah, well, I learned that not only was my ex cheating on me with some tattooed bastard, she tried cleaning me out when she moved out of my place."

"No way."

"Yep. The cheating was a big problem. I'm big on loyalty. Like you." She nodded, and he felt that closeness with her deepen. "Then stealing from me? Hell no. I kicked her ass out and haven't seen her since. The hard part was that I thought I loved her."

She didn't say anything for a moment, then asked in a softer voice, "Did you?"

"I thought I did. The good times we had were nice. I liked being part of a couple." Hearing himself out loud, he knew the time had come to change the subject. He sounded like a sap. "But that's the past."

"And the past should stay buried. I've heard it all before." She took a large swallow of water and continued, "But trust me, it rises up to bite you in the ass when you least expect it. The hardest part for me was that I trusted the creep."

"I should have seen Lisa for who she was." He nodded. "We both had lapses in judgment."

"Kind of makes it hard to trust again, you know?"

He did know. "Which is why you and I are friends. We know each other, well, carnally, but this. I like this, us having lunch. I'm not trying to impress you or anything." Okay, that was a lie. "And I don't need to make up stories to get into your pants."

She choked on her water. "True. I'm not after your money or an engagement ring, and I have no reason to lead you on about anything. We have a good thing going." They nodded at each other. "So let's not screw it up." She lifted her glass. "Here's to keeping everyone else out of our business."

He knew she referred to their mothers, his brother, and their friends. "Hear, hear."

Shane hadn't bothered mentioned Mac to her, because he didn't want her to worry about him, or possibly be attracted to him. Mac's track record with women could be intimidating, and considering Shelby's quest to have sex and nothing more meaningful, his friend would be the perfect candidate to try if Shane fizzled. Not that he intended to fizzle…ever.

They ordered coffee and told each other more stories. The ones about George had them both amused.

"I swear the kid is my mother in a seventeen-year-old body. He's mature for his age and really open about life. You have no idea what it's like to get dating advice from a high school senior, especially when his words mirror my mother's. It's eerie," he said over her laughter.

"I like Geo. Rhymes with Leo."

He chuckled with her. "What about Ron? He sounds like a character."

She raised a brow while the waiter cleared their plates. "You were military, but you don't have a problem with gays? Good to know."

"I'm in Seattle."

"So? Lots of haters everywhere."

"Yeah, well, I'm not one of them. Just because I served in the military doesn't mean I agree with policy, and in case you missed it, they repealed Don't Ask Don't Tell."

"Finally."

He agreed. "I don't care what people do in their spare time, as long as they aren't hurting each other and it's consensual."

They spoke about his time overseas in generalities and about her business.

After a pause, Shelby changed the subject. "I'm sorry, but I have to ask this. So you broke up a while ago too. My relationship was a total loss, but I didn't see the end until he cheated. Did you see it coming?" As soon as she said it, she looked like she wanted to take the words back.

Should he take it as a good sign she wanted to know about Lisa? He hoped so. "Lisa and I were together for a year." He didn't want to lie, and the thing Shelby definitely wanted him for was the sex, so he confessed the ugly truth. "She said she started up with the tattoo guy because I was too *vanilla*," he ended in air quotes.

Shelby gaped. "You're kidding me. You? Vanilla? *Doctor* Collins?" She blushed.

"Yep. Lisa thought I was boring. Too domestic I guess, because I liked monogamy."

"Sounds like a bit—ah, witch."

He grinned. "Yeah. She left me for a tattooed guy who thought piercing his genitals meant he was the coolest of the cool."

"Ew." She cringed. "I'm not against tattoos, I guess, but piercings? Ouch."

"My friend thinks I'm a lightweight because I don't have a tattoo. I just don't want one."

"Why mar such a fine body?"

"That's what I'm saying." He flexed his arm, and she laughed with him.

The lunch crowd left the restaurant, and only when the

waiter kept shooting him looks did Shane realize they'd overstayed their welcome.

He paid for their lunch over Shelby's protests—yet another reason he liked her. She didn't expect him to foot the bill for everything. They left and stood on the sidewalk.

Though he didn't want their afternoon to end, he also didn't want to have sex with her. Well, he did, but not today. Being physical now would water down their time as a prelude to sex, and he wanted to remember today as something special.

"I guess I should get going." To his surprise, she didn't sound in a hurry to leave. Maybe she'd enjoyed their time as much as he did. "Would you like to walk around a little? I don't have anything pressing."

He grinned. "Yeah. Long as you don't try pulling me into any clothing stores while you try stuff on. That's a real date, and one that tortures us poor male creatures. Shoe shopping, purse shopping, and clothes shopping. A trio of horrors."

"Yeah? Well try hanging out at a tool warehouse or car detailer. Bo-ring."

As they walked and argued, the afternoon turned into evening. Shane left her at her car and promised to call her next week, for another nonsexual get-together. Or as normal people called it, a date.

He smiled to himself as he walked back to his vehicle. Not dating had never been so fun.

♥

Late Wednesday afternoon, Shelby couldn't believe Mac had actually shown for an appointment. She'd thought his interest one that he'd later regret. Instead, the man had booked her for an hour and a half.

He lay on her massage table on his back, naked from the waist up and from the knees down. A large blanket covered his groin and upper thighs. He had a broad chest with a sprinkle of dark hair and was thickly muscled all over. An obviously handsome man, any way you looked at him.

And her best friend hadn't said one word about the man other than that he was her boss. Interesting.

"Thanks for fitting me in," he murmured in a deep voice. He lay with his eyes closed, seeming half asleep.

"No problem." She started at his feet and worked her way up his legs. Carefully dealing with his knee, she felt for problem areas. "You know, you muscle types are actually harder to work on than out of shape people."

"Really?"

She gently massaged the area around his tibia and eased under his knee. "Yeah. Your connective tissue is so thick it makes it hard to break through to release the toxins. But I'm stubborn. I'll work it out of you. Might hurt a little though."

He sighed. "I'm used to the pain. But if I can regain more mobility, I'm all for it. Hurt me, Shelby."

She smiled to herself and got to work. An hour and a half later, Mac lay on his stomach, snoring.

She eased out of the room and quietly shut the door behind her. She'd give the guy a few minutes, because she'd really worked him through his paces. He'd tried engaging her in conversation, prodding her about dating and men. Not quite leading to Maggie, but she had a feeling he'd been on the road there. And then she'd started working deeper into his tissue and he'd shut up and let her concentrate.

Flexing her fingers, she tried to work the cramps out of her hands. Maggie happened to stop in and saw her.

"Hey neighbor." Maggie smiled and shook blond bangs

from her perfect forehead.

“Hey there yourself, you old hag.”

“Wuss.”

“Cat lady.”

Maggie laughed at that one. “Tough client? Your hands seem to be gnarled up, like an old, dried up prune.”

“Prune this.” Shelby shot her the finger. “Hold on, I’ll be right back.” She knocked on the door of her massage room and finding no answer, entered.

Mac was still sound asleep. Sexy in a huge, big as a bear and mean as a grizzly kind of way. She liked him for that. “Hey Mac. Wake up.”

He grumbled, turned his head to the side and blinked his eyes open. “Shit, I fell asleep?” he asked groggily.

“Apparently my vast powers of seduction failed. Get up and come on out and pay me.”

“Yeah, yeah.” He yawned and started to rise.

“Hold on. I don’t want to see more than I have to.”

“But there’s so much of me.” He snickered as she made a hasty escape.

She returned to the main office, where Maggie waited with a strange look on her face. Maggie. *Oh hell.*

“You have to go,” Shelby shoved her friend to the door and whispered, “Your boss is here.”

“Here?” Maggie squeaked. “What’s he doing here?”

“He’s here for a quickie in the back.” Shelby huffed. “I was working on his knee, Maggie. What do you think he’d be doing here?”

“Hell if I know. You’re never around to talk to anymore. Working or gone all the time. Rumor has it you’re seeing some guy I know *nothing* about, and you refuse to take my advice about men.”

"Yours or Dr. Phil's?"

"It's all good."

"Wait. Who told you I was seeing someone?"

"Crap. I gotta go." Maggie tore out the front door just as Mac emerged from the massage room.

He rolled his neck and shrugged those massive shoulders into a stretch. "I feel like a new man. You have killer hands."

"Thanks."

"But my knee aches." He walked slowly, his limp noticeable.

"You need to take it easy for a few days." Shelby moved around her front desk and took a bottle of water out of her mini fridge, tucked away under the counter. "Drink this. And drink more when you get home."

"Back to work, actually."

"Dedicated. I like that."

"So why not go out with me?"

This again? She shook her head. "We covered this. I'm seeing someone."

"Yeah, right."

She frowned at his persistence. He hadn't seemed very interested in her before. "I am. He's a really nice guy."

Mac snorted. "That explains it."

"What?"

"Your secret misery. He's nice. I'm so sorry." His sneer actually made her laugh.

"Nice is not a bad thing." She grinned. "Besides, he's not nice when it counts."

"Oh. So you do like a bad boy? Not as quiet and collected as you seem." Mac dug out his wallet and handed her a credit card. "I knew it."

"Shut up." She handed him back his card and had him

sign, and realized she'd told a client to "shut up."

But he only smiled. "Right. I'll see you next week. Same time okay?"

She checked her book and seeing the slot open, wrote his name down. "Sounds good. And keep off that knee, Marine."

He waved away her concern and left. It was only after he'd gone that she saw he'd given her a *fifty percent tip*.

"What a strange, strange man. But nice." She chuckled, recalling what she'd said about Shane being *nice*. They had an encounter scheduled for later that night. She couldn't wait to see him in mean mode.

♥

Mac returned to work after ordering—*calling*—Maggie to meet him in his office. And again he found himself waiting on the woman. Twenty minutes later, she arrived wearing a sexy gray wool business suit, pink blouse, and high heels that made her look fragile, fuckable, and downright tempting.

"There's that look again. What did I do now?" She huffed and threw herself into the seat across from his desk. She raised her hands skyward and moaned, arching her neck, and his blood pressure shot through the roof. If the woman had a lick of sense, she'd stop enticing him with motions that brought attention to those surprisingly full breasts on such a petite frame. If he hadn't heard her bitching about what a pain her breasts were to one of the girls a few days ago and how she'd been thinking about having a reduction—God forbid—he'd have assumed they were fake.

Knowing they weren't only whetted his appetite to see them up close, without the shirt and bra in the way. He wondered what color her nipples would be. Rosy? Red? Maybe a peachy brown?

"Hello? Earth to Conan?"

He forced himself to ignore his sexual fantasies and growled, "Well, Tinker Bell. We have a problem."

"Oh boy. What now? I brought Shelby to the gym."

"Gee, good work. Just a few weeks late."

She rolled her eyes.

"The woman is seeing someone. And I have a feeling Shane is too."

Maggie sat up straighter. "Think they're seeing each other?"

"No way. I'd know if he was into her. We talked about her, but he's not making a move. I think he's up to something though."

"Well, Shelby has been pretty quiet lately. We still get together on the weekends, but she's been happier than I've seen her in a while. I have a feeling you may be right."

"She flat out told me she had a guy on the side, one who knows how to not be *nice* when it counts." He snorted. "That's not Shane. I love the guy, but he's almost like a woman when it comes to sex and dating."

She frowned. "What exactly does that mean?"

"You know. He's all about relationships and feelings." Mac made a face. "He's way too Lifetime-channel when it comes to broads."

"Tell me you did not just say broads and mean that in reference to women."

He grinned. "I did." *On purpose.* He liked to tease her, because her eyes had a fire to them he liked seeing directed his way.

"You're such a jerk, especially when you're trying to be." But her lips quirked. "Well, my best friend is like Shane. She doesn't want to be, but she needs emotional stability."

He groaned. "There you go with the touchy-feely bullshit again."

"She and Shane sound perfect for each other. But I think Shelby needs to sow her oats. She was with Rick too long."

From what Maggie had told him, the guy sounded like a dickhead. "Great, but my boy needs her to break his dry spell. And no, I'm not just talking about sex," he said before she could argue. "I think he really likes her. George sings her praises, you know. And Lorraine and Chad liked her a lot after what she did for their youngest. They'd love her."

"Everyone loves Shelby but Shelby," Maggie muttered.

He didn't understand, exactly, so he asked her again, "So what do we do about this?"

"We?"

"Hey, I'm a paying client. But you have the inside track with your girl. Get her to notice Shane again, would you? I can show up someplace with him. We'll get them together, then leave."

"Us?"

He frowned. "Who the hell do you think I mean? You want Mimi or Ron to get involved?" The pair sounded like a trip, but Maggie violently shook her head no.

"Remember, it was Mimi's idea to grab a lock of hair from Shane's brush. She planned to do something with it I'm better off not knowing."

"Oh, right. And leaving this to George isn't a question. He's a great kid, but hell, he's seventeen. His idea of foreplay is probably taking the gum out of his mouth before he kisses his date."

She laughed. "That's not fair. He's cute."

"Yeah, and he likes blondes. My advice? Don't wear that

purple getup around him again."

She'd worn the sexiest shorts/tank outfit the other day at the gym, and his young friend had seen her in it and walked into a wall. It would have been funny if Mac hadn't also noticed several of the male patrons eyeing her like a stick of candy. Friends of his who would like nothing better than to try Maggie on for size. The jealousy had stunned him, especially because it hadn't gone away.

"What are you talking about?"

He cleared his throat. "Let's get back on track. One option we haven't discussed—we could always leave Shane and Shelby alone, let them fend for themselves. Maybe they'd get together on a date before they turned fifty."

They stared at each other.

"I didn't think so." Mac sighed. "They need our help. And hell, if it goes south after all our efforts, at least we tried."

Maggie cocked her head and studied him.

"What?"

"You actually have a heart under all that bluster."

"Gee, thanks."

"Hey, you're welcome. Trust me, it's not easy to see past the muscle and that fat ego of yours." She shook her head and stood. She wore her hair down, and when she moved, it framed her face perfectly. The woman looked like a walking advertisement for shampoo or sex, and he wondered how long he'd be able to resist putting the two together—Maggie naked in a shower while he washed her hair. That would work for him.

He met her by the door of his office and forced himself not to imagine her naked. "So we're on then? Let's have them meet up this Friday. Dinner at that new steak joint on Queen Anne Avenue. Say seven? I know the owner, and he'll hook us up."

"Okay. But let's keep this simple. In my experience, when it gets too complicated, everything goes to hell in a hand basket."

He blinked at her. "Hell in a what? What did you just say?" Didn't his grandmother used to say something like that?

She blushed. "Never mind. Seven, Friday. Don't be late."

He watched her flaunt that ass down the hallway. Too complicated, she'd said. As he thought about what he'd like to do to her, he knew just what she meant.

CHAPTER FIFTEEN

SHELBY FOLLOWED SHANE'S DIRECTIONS. SHE WALKED through the front door of his house, which he'd left unlocked, and locked it behind her. Darkness had fallen outside, so the candles lit provided enough light to see by. She followed them upstairs to his bedroom but still didn't see him.

She was about to turn around and go back downstairs when he grabbed her from behind and startled a shriek out of her.

He chuckled against her ear and held her tightly, caging her back to his front with a strong hold around her waist. "What do we have here? A burglar?"

"Shane, you told me to—"

"No talking." His hands reached up to cup her breasts, and he squeezed with a roughness that excited her. He shoved himself against her, and she felt his erection poking into her lower back. "Move."

He forced her up against the wall and put her hands up above her head. "Keep them there."

She shivered, totally turned on. The last time in her house, he'd made her orgasm until she couldn't any more. She hadn't realized she'd had a thing for being tied up, but Shane had exploited her surprising kink to his advantage.

Tonight, he didn't bother undressing her. Instead he reached under her shirt and released the catch on her bra. Then he unbuttoned and unzipped her jeans. He slid them and her panties down to her knees.

"What are you—"

He smacked her hard on the ass. "Shut up. Thieves don't get to talk. They get punished." When he shoved his finger between her legs, inside her, she moaned, caught.

"Oh yeah. You're wet. You want this, don't you? You want me to punish you."

"No, wait," she said feebly, her protest a token and no more. They'd agreed during their last sexual encounter that if anything ever grew too intense, she should shout out a safe word. She'd chosen *vanilla*, and she had no intention of saying it anytime soon.

Shane nudged her legs wider before she felt the tip of him squeezed between her legs. He yanked her hips back, bending her over. She couldn't widen her stance enough because of the jeans down around her knees. But he didn't seem to care.

"Keep those hands against the wall," he ordered as he worked his way inside her.

He felt huge because of her position, and when he began fucking her, it burned until he lubricated himself using her cream. His complete disregard for anything but his own hunger aroused her like crazy.

Shane fucked her like he owned her, and she was afraid that might be closer to the truth than she liked. His absolute control, the concentration he dedicated to her when they were together, made her feel more than special.

Even now as he pounded into her, she felt cherished. He gave her the fantasy she wanted, and he got off on it. His cock was thick and bruising as he hammered home. When his hands left her hips and palmed her breasts, she moaned.

"Nice tits." He squeezed her nipples and bit down on her neck, still thrusting in an out of her, his pace escalating. "I'm going to come inside you, and there's nothing you can do about it." He rubbed her breasts and grunted while he took her.

Her moans and pleas for mercy turned into cries of desperation. She was so close to coming. She just needed a bit of stimulation to her clit…

He must have known what she needed, because one hand left her breasts and trailed down her belly, seeking her pussy. He pinched the bud and then rubbed it as he slammed into her and stilled. "Fuck me. Oh yeah." He came inside her and groaned again when she shrieked and came with him.

"Squeeze me. Oh fuck. I love that cunt." He gripped her hips and shoved deeper inside her, his pelvis crushed to her backside while he emptied into her.

After a few moments, he withdrew. "No, don't move. Let it drip down your leg, thief."

She shivered, bare from her ass to her knees, her breasts free but still draped in her tee-shirt and unfastened bra.

"Man, if I had a camera on me. This is totally a scene out of one of my fantasies, and it's even better because I know how much you love it." He caressed her left buttock, where the sting from his slap had faded. "Too hard?"

"No," she said, breathless. "I liked it."

He groaned. "You make me hard all the time. I know that sex is more exciting when it's new and fresh. But seriously, it's never been like this for me with anyone. Ever."

"I know." She did, and she didn't know what to do about

it. They met in secret. They had amazing, dirty, non-vanilla sex. And they'd had their first date just a few days ago. How could she be falling for him so quickly when it had taken Rick months to get this close to her? And look at how that had turned out.

He pulled her from the wall and turned her in his arms. Then he kissed her, and the heat from their embrace aroused her again.

"Let's clean you up, hmm?" He smiled, his green eyes so rich, she couldn't look away.

They stared at each other in the shower, and as they fell into bed again, something was different.

Shane rolled her onto her back and covered her with his body. "Let's try something vanilla."

She smiled at up at him, but her grin faded when his expression changed from amused to intense.

He kissed her slowly, with a tenderness he'd never before employed. His lips coaxed an answering sigh from her, and when his tongue met hers, it was with an inviting glide, no forceful entry.

He kissed her like he had all the time in the world. With each press of his lips, she grew more aroused. Her breasts brushed his chest and his firm nipples. Her belly felt moist from the wetness at his cock—his very thick, very large cock. Knowing he wanted her so much made her frantic to have him.

But Shane wouldn't be budged. He patiently kissed her until she couldn't do anything but follow his lead, fully under his spell. She ran her hands through his hair and tightened her grip when his lips trailed from her mouth to her neck and lower. He worshipped her breasts, plumping them with his hands before drawing each nipple into his mouth, where he'd suck and bite gently as she thrashed under him.

"God, I want you," she moaned when he left her breasts

and kissed his way to her pussy.

He licked her. He sucked her. He nipped her flesh and slid his thumbs through her folds. While he feasted, he eased his pinkie finger into her channel before withdrawing the slick digit. Then he eased it around the rim of her anus while he sucked her clit.

She arched into him. "Shane. Please. Fuck me, baby." She was barely aware of what she said, drawn to him in a way she'd never been to anyone else. This was more than sex. More than a playful need to be exciting and sexy and wanted.

He penetrated her ass and sucked harder on her clit, and she came in a rush. Still climaxing, she didn't want him to leave her. But he shimmied over her body in a flash and slid his thick shaft inside her while they made love.

Leaning up on his elbows, he watched her as he thrust inside her, his rhythm fast and furious as he reached his end. It didn't take him long, and then they both experienced the joy of true togetherness, coming with each other face-to-face. *And heart to heart*, the romantic inside her added.

Shane didn't know what to think. He couldn't stop kissing her once he finished coming. *Oh fuck*. He loved her. He knew it. He'd hoped not to feel this again, because Shelby was so much more than Lisa had been. That date last week had sealed it, as much as he'd hoped he'd idealized their time together.

Taking her earlier had been incredible. He was able to play the domineering male to her submissive female, and fucking her had been amazing. But this…

He kissed her lips again and sighed into her mouth when she kissed him back.

This tenderness was new to them both. It added a definite emotional aspect to their weekly get-together's he wasn't sure she'd accept. And though he didn't want to scare her away, he couldn't stop himself from showing her how he felt.

They parted and lay on their sides, still holding each other.

"Wow." She blinked at him, her lips parted, still glossy from his kiss.

"Yeah, wow." He smiled and traced her cheek. "We need to clean up."

"I know." She didn't move. "That was special. I liked it." She seemed shy now, adding yet another layer to the complex, beautiful, emotionally guarded woman.

He stared into her eyes, caught by the shadows the candlelight flickered over her face. "You know, I like you when you're mean."

She frowned. "I wasn't mean. Well, not today."

"But I especially like you like this. Soft, sexy. Naked," he added and earned a chuckle.

"Well, I love your kinky side. But this was great too." She stared at his mouth and leaned forward for a kiss. "I don't think we've done this before. Kissing like this."

"It's nice. Is it too vanilla for you?" he teased, but a part of him needed to know.

Shelby shook her head, and her hair trailed over her shoulder and over the slope of her breast, like a mink stole. "Not at all. I have to confess something."

"What?" he asked softly.

"Vanilla is my favorite flavor." She sighed. "I think I was born to be boring."

"Yeah, right. Honey, you are so damn sexy I about come in my pants whenever I'm near you. We've played doctor, house burglar, and you've seduced me in a red teddy you still need to wear for me again. You might like the flavor, but you're anything but ordinary."

She smiled at him. "So what does that make us?"

"Two sexed-up friends who like each other?" *Love each other?*

"Friends or fiends?"

"Oh, I like fiends better."

They laughed together and spent the next hour talking about anything and everything. The sex had become more. Shane just hoped Shelby could handle it, because he couldn't go back now. Not after he'd seen the warm, loving part of her.

Unfortunately, she left at midnight. And his bed had never felt lonelier.

He spent the next two days at work and did his best to pretend she didn't exist. They'd made plans to meet for breakfast Sunday morning. Just for food, not sex. They'd get to that Monday night.

Scheduling sex had been fun at first. Exciting trysts, an adventurous affair. But now it seemed a little tawdry considering he wanted Shelby to be a more permanent part of his life. It amazed him that after Lisa he could feel this way again, but there it was. He'd never been one to stick his head in the sand overlong, and his mourning for Lisa—or rather, the relationship he'd *thought* he'd had with Lisa—had ended.

Friday night rolled around, and he agreed to meet Mac at Botelli Mia's, a new steak and seafood restaurant in Queen Anne. Mac apparently knew the owner, because they were seated without a wait at a booth big enough to fit six comfortably.

"See, it pays to have friends in high places," Mac bragged as he looked at the line outside.

"Whatever." Shane indulged his friend's humor. Mac had been in a good mood all night. "You get laid or what?"

Mac's eyes widened. "Why do you say that?"

"You're smiling at me."

"Fuck you." Mac lowered his menu and narrowed his gaze. "Although, I should be asking you the same thing. You're different lately."

I'm in love.

The waiter arrived, and Shane ordered a beer. It seemed like a perfect night to drink his worries away. They made small talk until the waiter brought their drinks, then they ordered.

After the waiter left, Mac raised his glass. "To Shelby."

Shane paused with his glass in the air. "What?"

"You know, that chick you had a thing for?"

"Oh, her." Shane tapped Mac's glass. "To Shelby."

"May you finally find her and get some peace." Mac took a large swallow. "Come on, man. What's up? You're hot for this chick, then nothing? But you look content. More than you've been in a long time."

"So maybe I got lucky a few times."

"A few times?"

"Dude, lower your voice."

Mac leaned over the table. "What the hell, man? You never said anything."

"I'm past the age of kiss and tell, Mac."

"I don't need details, Mary. But a heads up would be nice. I've been trying to find a way to get you back with the Amazon, and here you're already plowing pleasureville."

Shane drank more. "You kill me with your language."

"Hey, I'm the product of a college degree." Mac was in fact a college graduate, but you'd never know it to talk to him. The guy acted like he'd been raised among wolves, or along the docks among sailors. God knew he swore like one. Typical Marine. "So no interest in Shelby anymore?"

"I didn't say that." *At all.* "But you know I'm not looking for anything permanent. Some sex did the trick though. I'm much more relaxed." Shane sighed happily. "I'll live to be ninety now, at least."

"Must have been some sex."

"You have *no* idea."

Mac teased him some more before he suddenly turned mute. He glanced over Shane's shoulder and swore. "Damn, that woman kills me."

Shane followed his glance and saw Maggie, Shelby's friend. The blonde wore tight jeans and a teal blue tank top that showed off toned shoulders and tanned arms. She was sexy, if a guy leaned toward soft blue eyes, a petite frame and nice breasts. But behind her came his idea of the ideal woman.

Shelby Vanzant. Her hair had been pulled back in a ponytail. Gold hoops hung from her earlobes, and her eyes sparkled like the topaz jewelry he'd bought his mother for Christmas last year. She wore jeans and a casual tee-shirt and managed to outshine every woman in the place.

Maggie spotted him and waved. She and Shelby joined them, Shelby looking as guarded as he suddenly felt.

"Hey Shane. Mac." She gave his friend a short nod.

"Maggie. Shelby." Mac's voice warmed.

Shane whipped back around. "You know Shelby?"

"You know Mac?" Shelby asked him, standing in front of their table with her friend.

"He's a friend of mine."

"His best friend," Mac added. To Shane he explained, "Shelby's been working on my knee. She's got great hands."

His suggestive leer didn't seem to sit well with Maggie. Or with Shane.

Maggie cut in, "There's a line outside. Could we join you two for dinner?"

Shane didn't think that was a good idea. They'd agreed to keep their relationship private. But after seeing the way Mac acted with her, he didn't mind if everyone knew about them. He would have said something then if he hadn't thought he might lose Shelby because of it. He didn't intend to do anything to screw up his chances with the woman if he could help it.

"Sure." Mac scooted toward the wall and Maggie sat next to him, leaving Shelby standing by herself.

With a helpless shrug, she joined Shane. When her leg touched his, the lower half of his body roared to life.

"You two been here before?" he asked, his concentration on Maggie, though he couldn't help noticing Mac's satisfied smile. The bastard was definitely up to something. Seeing Shelby without telling him? This unexpected invitation to a Friday night dinner that didn't include pizza?

"Nope. First time." Maggie blinked, all innocence.

Mac couldn't seem to take his gaze from her.

"You know Maggie works for Mac," Shelby added.

"Oh?" He turned to Mac. "Funny, you never mentioned you'd hired a new employee."

"Yeah? Well you haven't mentioned a few things to me either. Guess we'll call it even."

Hell. Mac had hired Shelby's best friend, and he was now one of her clients. Either his best friend had a thing for Shelby, or he was out to try to help Shane. Which meant there was a good chance the oaf might sabotage his relationship before it got off the ground. *Shit.*

"Oh no. I forgot to lock up at the gym." Maggie turned to Mac, her eyes wide. "I left all that expensive equipment out."

Shane had no clue what she was talking about, but Mac swore. "Come on." He prodded her out of the booth. "You two enjoy dinner, on me. Maggie and I have to fix a problem at the gym."

Maggie frowned at Shelby. "But she's my ride."

"I'll take you home. Shane, hitch a ride with Shelby. Later, guys."

Mac and Maggie left before Shane or Shelby could protest.

They sat next to each other for a moment before Shelby moved across the table. "Good. I can see you now."

"What the hell was that all about?"

She shook her head. "I have no idea, but Maggie dragged me here. I was planning on spending tonight curled up with a good book."

"A romance?"

She smiled. "What else?"

He knew what she liked to read, because they'd talked about her likes and dislikes. He remembered everything about her.

"Technically it's a romantic suspense. Romance with mystery." She tapped the table. "Like the mystery of our friends working on something we should probably know about. I had no idea Mac was your friend."

"Don't you remember me telling you about Jameson's Gym?"

She snapped. "That's where I heard that name. Maggie had me convinced she'd mentioned it." Shelby groaned. "They're onto us."

"They have to be," he agreed.

The waiter brought out their food. Well, his and Mac's.

"Oh, steak." Shelby winked at him. "My favorite."

"Dig in. Mac's paying." They both had a laugh and started eating.

"So what do we do about Mac and Maggie?" he asked. "He never told me your best friend was working for him. Or that he'd met you." And that last bit bothered him.

"Maggie dragged me to her aerobics class at his gym last Friday. She's really good, if you're into the step routine. I met Mac there. He's a funny guy. A little too pushy for my taste, but nice enough."

"Nice?" *Nice* was the kiss of death. He suddenly felt much better.

"Well, he's handsome too, if you're into brawny guys with too much muscle." She paused. "I mean that in the nicest way."

Another nice. His grin widened. "You know, you can order anything you want tonight. It's on Mac." He motioned to the waiter for another beer.

"He's a good friend of yours, isn't he?"

"Yep. Best buddy for years. We met in the Corps and reconnected out here. He's a hell of a guy. Rough on the outside, but a decent man. And he likes the ladies," he warned.

She raised a brow. "Jealous?"

"Of him or you?"

"Huh?"

"I don't want you to like him too much," he admitted. "But I don't care about his luck with women. Sexing it up with strangers isn't my thing." He winked at her. "I only like playing doctor with a sexy massage therapist I know." He loved her blush. "Shelby, do you want to come clean with the others?" And let everyone know she was his. Finally.

She toyed with her food. "I don't know. This thing between us is special. I guess I'm afraid they'll ruin it."

He'd wanted another answer, but he could respect her for the truth. "Your call. But how about another beer while we figure out how to handle our well-meaning but troublesome friends?" *Because I have a feeling it's going to be one of those nights.*

CHAPTER SIXTEEN

SHELBY DIDN'T WANT EVERYONE TO KNOW ABOUT THEM, because that would make her fantasy time with Shane all too real. She smiled and laughed, but inside she cringed. Maggie had been plotting, and Shelby hadn't seen it. Nor had she recognized Mac's pretense in coming in for massage work. Just like she hadn't seen Rick's perfidy until she'd caught him in the act. Would there be something about Shane as well? Something she'd learn too late to save her pitiful heart from breaking all over again?

And there was the truth—she'd fallen for Shane Collins. If she'd believed in love at first sight, which she didn't, she might have admitted her fascination with him when she'd called him Mr. Tall, Dark, and Rude.

"Shelby?"

"What?"

"Did you want dessert?" he asked, and she noticed the waiter hovering. "They have a terrific cheesecake."

"Sure." She softened even more toward him. The blasted man had remembered her favorite dessert. Everything about him added up to her dream man. When they talked, he listened. He'd been through his own relationship hell and had survived. He made love like he'd been built to please. He had a great job, family he loved, and friends she actually liked. His neatness nicely tailored her organized if slightly messy aesthetic. And they liked the same kinds of movies.

But he had yet to meet her mother and Ron.

"I hope dinner tonight wasn't too hard to bear." Shane must have noted her quiet. He looked way too serious for a guy who'd downed three beers.

"I'm fine." She forced a smile. "Honestly?"

"I always want you to be honest with me. Truth hurts, but it's better than a lie."

He had that right. "I'm worried about my mother."

"How's that?" He moved back when the waiter arrived to clear their plates. After the guy set down their dessert and coffee and left, Shelby explained.

"My mother is a whirlwind. She's loud, opinionated, and likes to think of herself as a hippie lost in the concept of free love. She married my dad, had me, and left him when he grew too boring for her, I guess. I haven't seen the man in twenty years."

"Sorry."

"Don't be. He faded away, but Ron took his place." She smiled. "He's the perfect fit for my mother. They design together, believe in the same weird stuff, and generally love me to death."

"So what's not to like?"

"They're overprotective. They check up on everything I do. And they are always involving themselves in my life. I love them. I do. But they're a lot to deal with." She swallowed audibly, taken by the compassion in his gaze.

"Afraid they won't like me?"

No, that they'll scare you away. "Not exactly."

"Shelby, we can keep our relationship, such as it is, to ourselves if that's what you want." He sounded so caring, she wanted to cry. God, if her mother ruined this thing she had going with Shane, she'd never forgive the woman.

"Could we?" Then what he'd said penetrated. "Wait, 'relationship, such as it is'?"

"Well, we have sex, and we've been on one—or if you count tonight—two dates. You said you only wanted something physical."

"So did you." Panic set in. What had she done wrong this time? He sounded as if he wanted to break it off with her. Was that why he was okay keeping everything a big secret?

"And maybe I changed my mind. I want the chance to be with you. Dating, Shelby." He cut a bite of cheesecake and lifted it for her to eat.

She blew out a breath she hadn't realized she'd been holding and took a bite, the flavor bursting on her tongue.

He watched her eat, looking satisfied.

"Boyfriend-girlfriend, hmm?" She took some dessert in her fork and lifted it to his lips.

He ate it, and the act became an intimacy tying them together. Giving and taking freely from each other.

"That's what I'd like, but I don't want to rush you."

She frowned. "You're being awfully gentle with me. Afraid I'll bolt?"

He chuckled. "We're being honest with each other, aren't we? Yeah, I'm afraid you'll leave. That I'm not what you signed on for. You wanted a no strings attached hook up, and like always, I fucked it up." He ran a hand through his hair. "I just… you make me happy."

"I do?"

"You really, really do. And I don't just mean in the bedroom. I want this to last for as long as it can, and I tend to go right for the things I want in life, a lot faster than most people are comfortable with. No, get that panicked look off your face. I'm not proposing." He grinned. "I'd like to go out with you in public. To call you my girlfriend. To hang around my family and hang around yours. That's a pretty big commitment right there."

"You got that right." *Especially because I'm falling in love with you. And it's not my mother I'm worried about screwing us up. It's me.*

"You need time. No problem. That's something I can give you. We stick to the plan for now."

"For now," she agreed and reached across the table for his hand. "I just…I need to think about this."

"Fine. But don't forget. Breakfast on Sunday at your house."

"And Monday night at your place. For the fun stuff."

He winked, and relieved she hadn't ruined anything by being honest, she polished off the cheesecake. Nice guy that he was, he let her.

When Shelby arrive with him at his house, she felt as though she'd come full circle. The sexual fling she'd intended had blossomed into a romance, and she planned to embrace it. She just needed to wrap her mind around it.

After he kissed her goodbye and went inside, she drove home, thinking hard. Would her mother approve of Shane? Hell yes. He had everything going for him, including a wonderful family. Shelby loved Lorraine and had liked what she'd seen during her brief meeting with Chad Collins. After overhearing him badger Shane about protection and spending time together, she knew she'd like him as much as she liked

Shane's mother.

George was terrific. And Shane… Scary as it was to feel, she loved him. It didn't make a lot of sense, and maybe she was blowing an intense crush into something more, but she respected him a lot more than she'd ever respected Rick. Shane didn't seem intimidated by her career or ability to think for herself. He liked being with her and didn't seem to expect her to change for him. And he listened to her, something Rick had pretended to do but never actually done.

Shane knew she liked cheesecake and romance books. He gave her the rough sex she craved. And he held her and kissed her like he cared, because he *did* care. He'd had her for sex from the beginning. There was no reason to pretend to like her to get into her pants, as he'd said. He genuinely liked her for herself, a novel idea.

She smiled as she pulled into her driveway. After letting herself into her house and locking up after herself, she fell asleep and dreamed about Shane.

Saturday passed too slowly, a mundane day spent doing chores she'd put off for too long. Then Sunday arrived, and with it came Shane, bright and *way* earlier than expected.

Never a morning person, she greeted him at the door wearing her robe and a scowl.

"Hey, sunshine." He held up a paper bag that smelled delicious. In his other hand, he held a holder carrying several cups of coffee.

"Now I know I love you," she murmured and took the coffee from his hands.

He held onto it, and she looked up at him.

He stared at her. "What did you say?"

"What?" She couldn't think past the need for coffee.

"Nothing." He kissed her on the cheek. "Nice hair."

"Screw you."

"Promises, promises."

She grunted at him and took her coffee to the counter, where she fixed it with cream and sugar. She inhaled it and felt almost human again. Until she realized Shane was seeing her in all her morning glory. If this didn't scare him away, nothing would.

"You're cute when you're half awake."

She frowned at him. "You said ten."

"It's ten fifteen." He chuckled when she whipped her gaze to the microwave clock. "Yeah. I can see I'm not the only one who's time-impaired. Just so you know, I'm always late."

"Oh. Well, as you can see, I'm not a morning person."

"Me either." He took a cup of coffee from the holder she hoarded by her side and drank it black. "But I cook."

"And clean." She made a face at him. "You're almost too neat to be a guy."

"Funny."

"That or you're secretly gay. Ron is so neat it makes my teeth ache."

"Now who's stereotyping?" He fished a pastry out of the bag and handed it to her.

She bit into it and groaned. "So good," she mumbled with her mouth full.

He shook his head. "That is the ugliest bathrobe I've ever seen. Neon green terrycloth? Didn't they stop making those in the eighties?"

"Hey!"

"Your hair is sticking up in the back. You have jelly on your lip, and you put way too much sugar in your coffee."

"Look, you idiot, I'll drink my coffee any way I—"

"So why do I have the urge to make love to you right

now? Right here?"

Her annoyance quickly faded. "Um, even with my morning breath?"

"So maybe we won't kiss."

She had to laugh. "Yeah, don't spoil the romance by cringing near my mouth."

"You know, there are other things you do very well with that mouth," he rasped. "I am *in love* with that tongue of yours."

She let him draw her close and ran a hand down his front to grip his erection.

He hissed and closed his eyes. "Yeah, like that. But I want your mouth over me. I want to watch you take me between your lips and see you suck me off."

"But we didn't schedule this. Isn't today a date day?"

"Fuck schedules." He unbuttoned his fly and unzipped his jeans. Then he lifted his cock out. He pulled on the collar of her robe, tugging her down. "Let me fuck that mouth."

She had no interest in her coffee or pastry anymore and set them down. She knelt before him, intrigued that she aroused him, even in her ratty bathrobe. Shane was a handsome, successful man. He could have had any woman he wanted for the asking. Yet he wanted *her*.

"Open your robe for me."

"I'm not wearing anything underneath," she warned.

"Let me see those tits."

She remembered that he'd said he wanted to fuck them and grew wet. She straightened and bent closer to his crotch. "Slide through me." She cupped her breasts and pushed them together, pleased when he moaned her name.

"Just a few times. I don't want to come on your tits. Not until tomorrow night," he said in a low voice. He thrust at an odd angle and positioned his cock between her breasts. He slid that thick, hot shaft between her mounds, his sac velvety smooth and taut when she felt him.

He swore and straightened. Then he grabbed himself with one hand and with the other palmed her head, pushing her back down. "Open up, baby. Blow me."

She knelt, quivering. The request was an order, because he knew how much she liked it when he was demanding. He pushed his cockhead between her lips, and she drew him in, licking with firm strokes of her tongue.

"Fuck, yes. That's good sweetheart. So sexy."

She could feel him staring at her as she took him deeper. Unlike the way she'd pleasured him before, this time he fucked her mouth. She opened wide and took what he gave her.

"Play with yourself," he said hoarsely and held her hair from her face so he could see himself fucking her. "I want you to get off while you I shoot down your throat."

She moaned and masturbated while taking as much of him as she could. Dirty, sweaty sex in the morning with the man of her dreams. Even when he came, filling her mouth and trickling down the back of her throat, she didn't mind, satisfied by his orgasm.

But he wouldn't let them be done. "Uh uh. You didn't come," he said, panting as he caught his breath. He withdrew from her lips and stood her up. Then he lifted her onto the kitchen counter and spread her thighs over the robe tucked beneath her. He latched onto her nipple with his mouth and fingered her pussy.

"God, Shane." She writhed under him, in lust and love and flying with feeling.

He added another finger while he toyed with her clit. And then he sucked her other nipple into a tight peak. She tightened around him without thought, clamping on those fingers that didn't fill her the way his cock did.

He released her breast to whispered into her ear, "Come, baby. All over me." Then he flicked his tongue into her sensitive canal.

She reached her pinnacle and drenched his fingers, her climax muddling her ability to think. He returned to sucking her nipple while she came down from such intense pleasure.

Slowly, he withdrew his fingers, a self-satisfied male watching his lover with possession, which she hadn't wanted. Or had she?

She was shaky and confused and in love. "I'll be back. I need a shower. Alone," she said before he could offer to join her.

He smirked and glanced at the pastries. "Don't blame me if there's nothing left when you're done."

She stuck her tongue out at him.

"Don't tease, baby."

With a laugh that ended in a groan, she left him in the kitchen. She returned twenty minutes later to find him snoozing on her couch. He'd left her coffee and several pastries. As she'd expected. The man didn't have it in him to be selfish.

Stupid thought. Of course he does. He's human. Her conscience demanded she not be blinded by lust and affection. No one was perfect, and there was no such person as her dream man.

Yeah, but Shane would never knowingly hurt me. I don't think. And that was the problem. She didn't know. But how could she? Only time would show her the real Shane Collins. And time was something he'd promised to give her. Why not take him up on his offer and see where this *relationship* took them? Because even she could see that there was more than outstanding sex between them.

She grabbed another cup of coffee, still warm in the container. As she fixed it and crossed to the couch, she watched Shane sleep. He seemed boyishly innocent in slumber, and she pushed a bit of hair from his eyes, taken with his handsome face.

"What am I going to do with you?"

Apparently, only time would tell.

She sipped her coffee and contemplated the future. Worst case, best case… Did she have the courage to try again? But wouldn't not trying make Rick the winner in the end? He'd been the one to spoil what could have been a deep and wonderful friendship between them. Why let him ruin her future with Shane?

The more she thought about it, the more she realized she didn't want to be the old cat lady at the end of the day, afraid to live her life and take a chance on love. She'd already been dumped once and lived through it. She could handle it again if push came to shove.

But as she stroked his hair, she knew Shane leaving would be different. It would hurt so much more, because she cared about him in a way she'd never been able to care for Rick.

What to do about her heart—that was the question. Because it already belonged to Shane.

CHAPTER SEVENTEEN

SHANE DIDN'T REGRET HIS TIME WITH SHELBY SUNDAY morning. Having unscripted sex had felt right. More like something a boyfriend—a lover—might do. He was sorry to have fallen asleep on her couch, though she didn't seem to mind. He'd woken up, his head in her lap, to see her watching an old movie. They'd spent half the day watching a Twilight Zone marathon on TV.

Monday evening had been like his other forays into the forbidden with Shelby. One smokin' hot sixty-nine that had him coming like a geyser between her soft lips. The woman had a way with her tongue that made him see stars with little effort. Now he had a hard time looking at her mouth without getting an erection.

But hell, there were worse ways to suffer.

The rest of the week dragged at work. Not being with Shelby was tough. He tried to keep his phone calls sparse because he didn't want to seem needy. He continued to question himself about her. Was he in love with her or responding so readily to a woman with whom he had chemistry? Sure he liked her. She was beautiful, driven, and successful. And she made love like a dream. But was his attachment just part of his pattern when it came to relationships?

He'd wanted to talk to Mac about it, but Mac didn't understand. Mr. Love 'em and Leave 'em didn't want connections. He wanted casual dates and one night stands. But that didn't work for Shane.

He thought about asking his mother or father for advice, but he didn't want to get their hopes up. If he wasn't careful, his mother would find a way to screen Shelby's medical transcripts looking for ways to improve fertility.

Shane wanted Shelby, sure, but a baby? The familiar panic he normally experienced when dealing with issues of marriage and all that followed didn't come. And he couldn't stop thinking about it, especially when he spent sexual and nonsexual time with Shelby.

They played miniature golf. He won. They bowled. She won and rubbed his nose in it, giving the word *competitive* new meaning. They liked Scrabble and Jeopardy, and he managed to drag her out for a few runs around Green Lake…after getting her to spend the night. A real treat considering she let him do whatever he wanted to her in the morning. He was no morning person, but God, the sex was incredible. But then, with her it always was, and he had to admit, the physical connection between them helped everything else fall into place.

They'd seen Maggie and Mac since their night at Botelli Mia's and played off their dinner. According to Shelby, Maggie said nothing more about her emergency at the gym, and Mac had been equally cagey about it. The liars. But Shane didn't mind their involvement, especially now that they seemed to be leaving well enough alone. He didn't trust it, but he decided not to question a good thing. And Shelby was a very good thing.

Staring at his office walls two weeks later on a Thursday morning, nonplused, he wondered when he'd first accepted the idea of Shelby in his life on a permanent basis. He wanted to spend time with her every day. Her staying the night was the highlight of his week, because it meant he got to cuddle with her after sex, something she'd been the one to suggest. But every time he came inside her, he wondered what it might be like to make new life. He didn't want kids with just anyone, but with Shelby.

He had a hard time remembering intimate details of his relationship with Lisa anymore, and Shelby openly joked about Rick, her ex, but no longer with the bitterness he'd once heard. He was glad the doctor had been a dickhead and that Lisa had cheated on him. He couldn't imagine a baby with a woman who thought compassion and loyalty were boring—vanilla.

But that left him with more questions about Shelby, because a baby sure as hell trumped her girlfriend status. To Shane, babies meant a wife, "I do," *forever.*

Their kids would be so pretty. Her looks and brains mixed with his? An ideal combination.

His computer chimed, taking his attention from Shelby. Hell, he'd be lucky if he didn't get fired with this attitude. He had work to do, deadlines to meet, and a hot brunette to convince to take a chance on him. No guesses as to which one had his priority lately.

"Excuse me, Shane? The Graces are here," the secretary said through the intercom. He groaned at the news and realigned his focus. Then he put on his game face, stood, and readied to meet the clients of his nightmares.

Mimi peered over the large, impressive desk of the

Harmon & Sons secretary while the poor woman scurried to find Thomas Harmon, Mimi's supposed reason for visiting. She and Ron had designed one of the corporate offices the company had built a few months ago. Today, she'd decided to stop by to check on the customer's satisfaction with their work. Such a small world to think her daughter's possible future and Mimi were connected. *Cosmic work, darling*, she thought with a smile.

"Do you see him yet?" Ron murmured as he thumbed through a copy of some architectural digest.

"Not yet."

A tall, handsome older man who looked like Thomas approached in his stead. He had crow's feet around his eyes, a sure sign of laughter and a fitting temperament for a man working around her daughter's possible future husband.

The secretary trailed after him, a pleasant mien over her previously harried expression.

"Hello." He held out a hand to Mimi, who took it and jangled as they shook—her bangles were a trademark she refused to leave at home. "I hear you're looking for my brother, Thomas. I'm Justin. The brains of the outfit." He had a nice firm handshake he didn't reserve just for men, she noted. She liked that.

"It's nice to meet you, Justin." She nodded.

"Hello there." Oh hell. Ron's *interested* voice. Though she couldn't blame him. She might set her sights on Justin when she'd finished interrogating Shane. Maybe for some added fun, she and Ron could fight over him.

"Hi. You must be Ron. Thomas told me all about you two." Justin took Ron's hand and grinned.

She'd just bet he did. Thomas recognized talent, thankfully, but he was a stick in the mud compared to this happy soul. Then she caught the look that passed between Justin and Ron and sighed. Another one bit the dust. It just proved to her, once again, that all the good ones were either unavailable or gay.

She cleared her throat, and they released each other's hands. As Mimi and Ron engaged Justin in conversation about their old client and sought information on new ones, she gave Ron a subtle nod.

Happy to take over with the gorgeous architect, Ron slapped him on the back. "Justin, I brought our portfolio with us. I was hoping to show Thomas our more recent work, since he'd mentioned you might have a few clients looking for designers of our caliber. Is there somewhere we could go where I could show you our stuff?"

Good God. She'd need to work with Ron on the word *subtlety*. The way he pushed past her to face Justin, batted his chocolate brown eyes, and used his deep bedroom voice was too personal too fast, even for Mimi. At least he dressed the part of a design professional. Skinny jeans that showed off his ass and a dark blue designer shirt with a while collar and cuffs added just the right contrast to his bronzed skin. It really was too bad Ron was gay. His looks complimented hers perfectly.

Justin blinked hard, looking like prey run to ground when Ron tapped his shoulder in a friendly gesture. "I-I, ah, sure. Come to my office."

"I'll be there in a minute," she added, irked that the pair seemed to have forgotten her. "I just need to use the ladies' room."

"It's down the hall," Justin said vaguely and walked away with Ron.

Men. She walked back down the hall, looking at the office nameplates, searching for Shane Collins. She'd met his mother already. Waiting on Maggie for information took too long. And while the girl pumped Shane's friend for information, she and Ron had scored with his mother. The father she still wasn't sure about, but Lorraine Collins had a take-charge attitude Mimi appreciated. Lorraine was blunt about wanting grandkids, which Mimi seconded. And when she'd learned who Mimi's daughter was, she'd been all over herself to welcome Ron and Mimi into her house.

It was with her blessing that Mimi had come down here to watch Shane in his "natural environment." Though Lorraine couldn't say enough about her son, she was obviously biased. But it helped Mimi to get a better picture of the man in whom her daughter had once expressed interest. And if she wasn't mistaken, her girl had done more than express interest with him.

Maggie was cute but not so bright, surprisingly. She was convinced Shelby was seeing someone. Of course she was. Shane Collins. Who else had her daughter run into who'd altered her aura so much? After he'd smacked into her at Green Lake, Shelby had been a fuzzy purple for days. And another reading after that odd lunch downtown a few weeks ago had turned up a picture of The Lovers in the cards.

Mimi nodded at a few men talking by an actual water cooler. How quaint. Then she turned the corner and spied a partially open door at the end of the hall, next to which a placard reading *Shane Collins* had been mounted. She quickly clamped down on her bangles, aiming for stealth, and stepped closer.

A husky feminine voice spilled out of the room. A look through the door showed Shane and the woman, and no one else. Mimi took the opportunity to eavesdrop.

"I'm glad you stopped by today, Gloria. I'm only sorry

Jonathan missed our meeting."

"But Shane, I wanted to see *you*."

The hussy. The woman sounded like she had asthma, breathing so hard.

Mimi peered through the crack, being careful not to get too close and give herself away. Uh oh. Gloria Grace was a knockout. Long black hair framed a delicate face, to which artfully applied makeup turned her features from pretty to dazzling. Her pouting lips looked cherry red, her blush was becoming, and her heavily lashed eyes were so blue they must have been contacts. Yet they captivated as well.

She looked to be about Shelby's age and had a terrific body that surgery or constant attention to exercise and diet kept in top shape. A repeat of Rick and his secretary came to mind, a terrible thing for Shelby to experience *again*. If it came to that, Mimi would skewer Collins herself.

Yet Shane didn't appear to be eager to step closer to the woman. If anything, he put his desk chair between them. It didn't prove much of an obstacle when she pushed it aside and backed him against the wall. Mimi approved of aggressive women. In this day and age, if you didn't go for it, it wouldn't come to you. Her mantra, and one she lived by. It would have been comical to watch this she-wolf corner Shane—a seemingly healthy, strong male in his prime—if he hadn't been the one Shelby wanted.

Shane braced his hands on Gloria's shoulders when she leaned in to kiss him. "Gloria, I'm sorry. I like your husband very much."

Good boy.

"I won't sleep with you, no matter how beautiful you are."

"Oh Shane. Johnny won't care."

"I will." He took a step away, his hands outstretched to

keep her back. "And besides, I'm seeing someone."

"Oh? Since when?" she asked, sounding annoyed.

He'd better be referring to Shelby.

"For about a month and a half now. She wouldn't like it knowing I threw my affections around."

"Affections?" Gloria snorted. "Honey, I just wanted some sex. If I want *affections*, I'll go to Johnny."

It sounded as if Shane had a conventional streak. Affections? Please. The younger generation was all about sex. Except for Shelby, and apparently Shane.

"Let's keep this between us, shall we?" Gloria fussed with her hair. "I must have misread your signals."

To Shane's credit, he didn't argue. "I apologize if I did or said anything to lead you on."

"Yes, well. We won't speak of this again. From now on, you can deal with Jonathan on your own."

"Whatever you want." Smart guy to put the power in her court, and from what she could see by Gloria's proud stance, the woman liked it as well.

"You're cute, Shane. And you're talented. I think if you keep at it, one day you'll have your own firm."

He smiled, and Mimi could see what her daughter saw in the man. A handsome straight-shooter with principles. A rarity in today's world.

Gloria turned and Mimi hurriedly backed away. She swore when her bracelets jangled and stopped, looking around her, pretending to be confused.

The door opened and Gloria walked out with a swagger that would set most men to staring. But not Shane. He smiled politely, told her goodbye, then turned to Mimi.

He just stared at her, his gaze lingering on her bracelets, her dress, and her face, then gave her a broad grin. "You're

Mimi Vanzant."

She inwardly groaned. If he told Shelby he'd met her at his office, there would be hell to pay. The girl never seemed to realize Mimi only wanted the best for her. Never to marry someone so unbearably wrong, like her father. He'd been dull, but Mimi had been in love. All his promises in the world hadn't changed the fact that the man couldn't give her the adventures he'd promised, nor had he the staying power she'd wanted to help raise her daughter. He'd crushed her girlish dreams of marriage and happily-ever-after in the same blow.

Mimi wanted true love for her girl, a love she still searched for daily. Had Shelby found it with this perceptive fellow?

"And you must be…" She squinted at the nameplate by his door and took her trendy reading glasses from her bag. After putting them on and making quite a show of it, she read his name. "Shane Collins."

He had the manners not to express his disbelief. Shelby would have been rolling her eyes. "Won't you come in?"

Shane invited her inside his office. She approved of the tasteful décor. Manly, professional, but not furnished with stock office equipment, which she detested. "Thank you. Actually, I was looking for the ladies' room, but my feet could use a rest."

"Sure thing."

He seated her across from his desk with a courtesy lost in most young men. "Can I get you something to drink?"

She considered Ron still busy with Justin and decided to give him time to connect with the fox who was anything but silver. Justin looked a little over fifty, maybe? A fitting age for Ron, as opposed to the young men he pretended to care about. Please. At their age, twenty-four was just too young.

She saw Shane waiting for her response and smiled. "An

espresso would be nice."

Shane buzzed through to the secretary for coffee and returned his attention to Mimi. "She has your face, you know." His gaze trailed to her bracelets and he smiled. "Not your eye for fashion, but it's nice to know what she'll look like in a few more years."

Oh, she liked this one. Mimi chuckled. "You're good."

"Not as good as you. Would you really have left me in here with Gloria if she'd attacked me like she planned?"

He had heard her. *Damn.* "I wanted to see what you were made of." No harm in being honest. "My girl deserves the best."

"Don't you think that's up to her to decide?" he asked softly.

"No."

He blinked. "No?"

"Look, Shane. I love my Shelby; I know her. She has stars in her eyes. She's a forever kind of woman who needs a white picket fence and babies to be happy." Might as well feel him out about all of it while she had him to herself. If he bolted after hearing the truth, he wasn't the man for Shelby after all. And it didn't matter that her daughter had only known him for a few weeks. Love was love. It didn't have time limits.

She read his stillness and looked beyond that. A part of her that Shelby had never believed in was attuned to energy, and though she couldn't read his aura the way Ron could, she felt a good vibe about the younger man. That and his eyes were a mossy green. She liked the color. It was vibrant, earthy, full of passion and life.

He and Shelby would give her beautiful grandchildren.

"I'm not sure about the picket fence," he said dryly.

"A euphemism. I'm not into fences either, unless you have

a dog. Have to contain the beasts."

"Ah, okay."

The secretary knocked and hustled in with Mimi's espresso. She left it in a hurry when Mimi waved and thanked her.

"She's skittish." Mimi took a sip. "But she makes a decent coffee."

Shane coughed but couldn't hide his smile from her. "Skittish? Laurie? I think she's just intimidated by all your color."

Mimi looked down at her fuchsia and orange print dress, that only a few women on this coast could have pulled off. It had more of an island zing, but she'd been in a tropical mood today. And it pulled the deeper red highlights from her hair.

"Well, the girl is beige bland. And she's pretty, which is sad. That color she's wearing does nothing for her." She sipped again. "So my daughter."

"Your daughter."

"And you?" Mimi pushed.

"Yep. And me." He leaned back in his chair and grinned at her. The smug look of a man in lust, and if she wasn't mistaken, in love. His energy seemed to flare when he mentioned Shelby, though she really needed Ron to be certain.

"Could you ring Justin's office and ask Ron to come in here?" she asked.

Shane chuckled as he punched a few numbers into the phone. "Justin? It's me." He paused. "Everything's good. Gloria's gone and we're still on track for the eighteenth. I told you so." He laughed. "Could you have Ron come down to my office? His partner in crime wants to see him." He laughed again and hung up. To Mimi he said, "He'll be right down."

She nodded. "You look good in a suit. Has Shelby seen

you wearing that?"

"Yeah. And jeans, and shorts. I like to run."

"So I hear."

"Oh? Shelby talks about me?" He perked up.

She felt bad about bursting his bubble. "Sorry, no. I heard about your run-in with Shelby at the park a few weeks ago."

"Maggie." He nodded.

"It's sad my own daughter won't share her life with me." She sniffed. "But at least I can see she's dating a wonderful man." She shot him a smile.

He chuckled. "You'd like my mother. She's a lot like you."

She knew that. Another reason Shane would make a fine addition to the family. The in-laws were more than tolerable. "If you break Shelby's heart, I'll string you up by your toes. I know people." Lorraine Collins was no one to screw with either.

"I think you'd be better off warning her not to break mine." His quiet words brought home how much they meant. "She's wonderful, and I'm not Rick."

She liked the fact he knew about the ex from hell.

"I'm loyal, honest, hardworking, and *not* a momma's boy," he warned. "I don't need anyone peering over my shoulder telling me how to behave with a girlfriend."

Mimi sagged a little. "Just girlfriend?" She'd been hoping for so much more.

His lips quirked. "Or fiancée or wife. However it happens, it'll be between me and Shelby. She loves you, but she's tired of you interfering." He leaned closer. "And you can tell my mother the same thing from me the next time you talk to her."

"How did you—Oh." She pursed her lips. "Smart boy, aren't you?"

"I try." He sat back, again looking satisfied. "For the

record, I do love your daughter. But she's not ready to hear it yet, and I'd appreciate it if you let us work it out."

"Oh sure. Right. Of course," she agreed, giddy to hear what she'd been praying for. She could almost see herself holding a grandchild with Shane's eyes and Shelby's smile. Mimi couldn't have said why, she just knew it was time to hold a baby again. And God knew it wasn't coming from her.

Ron appeared moments later with Justin behind him. "Mimi. There you are. We were getting worried."

"I just bet you were," she muttered and ignored the sparkle in his eyes. "I made a wrong turn and Shane was helping me adjust. The dear made sure I had coffee."

"Good man." Justin smiled.

There was an energy between Justin and Ron that told Mimi she'd be seeing more of him in the future. She could handle that, she supposed. Ron's romances never lasted long, and she liked Justin's positive attitude anyway.

She nodded toward Shane. Ron looked him over and shook his hand when Justin made introductions. She felt a decided shift of power, and then Ron took his hand away.

"Nice to meet you." Ron turned to her. "Mimi, we need to finish up with Justin. He has an appointment in half an hour."

She stood, clanging as the sweet chimes of brass, gold and silver bands collected at her wrists. "Wonderful. Thanks so much for your hospitality, Shane. I'm sure we'll meet again."

He escorted her to the door. In a low voice meant for her ears alone, he answered, "You can bet on it."

CHAPTER EIGHTEEN

GEO HAD JUST ABOUT HAD IT WITH HIS BROTHER. HE'D overheard his mother complaining to his father about Shane's lack of movement in Shelby's direction, which told him his mother knew more than she'd said about Shane liking Shelby. How she knew, he didn't question. His mother knew *everything*.

He was only glad she hadn't mentioned his sex life in any way after dumping a huge box of condoms on his bed the day he'd turned seventeen. Though she didn't condone his actions—and she'd told him just that in a loud, penetrating voice—she wasn't taking any chances.

Now that Gina was out of the picture and Amber in, he'd talked over the matter of his brother with her, and she'd come up with a brilliant idea. Mac had panned it and told him to butt out, that Mac had the situation under control…which was utter bullshit. From what Geo had seen, Mac wasn't paying attention to anything lately but that cute little blonde with the hot body, the new aerobics instructor at the gym. Geo understood the fascination, because yeah, he had a pulse, but that didn't help

Shane.

He had no intention of approaching his mother and asking for her advice. She'd tell him not to interfere, then make Shane's life a living hell. Hadn't she apologized to Gina on Geo's behalf? Seriously, the woman needed to back off a little.

His father told him to adjust and give in gracefully, that his mother was readying for an empty nest next summer and starting to hold too tight now to compensate. George felt for her, he did, but he was ready to fly the coop. Football, college, and college women consumed his thoughts. Gina had wanted to be exclusive after a few dates, and he didn't roll that way. Not like his brother, Mr. Steady Relationship Guy.

Boring, but hey, if it made Shane happy, he was okay with it. George loved his big brother. The guy supported him, covered for him, and had never treated him like a loser tag-along. They had fourteen years separating them, and George idolized Shane in so many ways.

So when Lisa had worked him over, he'd been angry, upset, and wanting badly to make it right. Shane had been listless for months. He'd finally started to come back to being fun to be around again. Happy even. But still alone and lonely, as Geo had heard Mac say. And then his brother had expressed interest in Shelby, a hot chick Geo liked. She'd never screw him over. She had a great heart, and she gave massages for a living. Talk about the perfect woman for Shane.

Knowing he could help his brother out gave him a renewed sense of purpose, and with Amber's wisdom in mind, he knocked on the window of Bodyworks that had a *Closed* sign by the door.

He'd purposely chosen this time after confirming with his source that Shelby would be finished and available to take another look at his knee. Denise succumbed to the Collins charm, like so many others. His superpowers might be subtle, but Geo used them to his advantage.

He grinned at the thought and knocked again.

Denise didn't answer the door, so obstacle number one wasn't a problem. Shelby finally answered. She opened the door a crack and scowled at him.

Obstacle number two.

"Okay, you little faker. What now?"

He put on a wounded look. "Shelby. I'm so sorry. I wanted to explain and apologize." He glanced down, the way he'd been practicing on Amber. "Could I come in?"

Shelby muttered under her breath about connivers and teenagers but stepped back to let him in anyway. "Touch nothing, Geo. I'm cleaning up."

The woman was always cleaning up. She'd make Shane the perfect girlfriend. Or wife.

Geo nodded to himself. Amber's idea would work, because something had to put a fire under these two. It had been two months since Shane had mentioned his attraction. But had he sought out Shelby? Had Shelby ever returned for pizza night or seen Shane socially? Hell no. Two duds at dating. He could tell without having to ask that Shelby wasn't seeing anyone. A guy knew these things.

"Well? I'm listening." She swept the main area, where a bunch of exercise balls and hand weights were stacked along supports on the wall.

"I'm sorry I lied about my knee, but I meant well."

She sighed. "I know you did, Geo."

"It's just, I think you and Shane would get along really well if you'd give him a chance."

"Geo—"

"There's someone else," he blurted. Amber had told him

that jealousy was a motivator. When she'd seen him dating Gina, it had driven her crazy. So it figured that Shelby, an independent, assertive woman, would possibly see Shane as unavailable and want him even more. He understood the psychology of it, because he always wanted what he couldn't have. He'd tried getting Shane and Shelby together once already and let nature take its course. But two slower people he'd never met. This had to spur her to action. He hoped.

"What?"

Her gaze sharpened. A good sign.

Geo tried his best to sound sincere. "Shane is really secretive about her and has been for weeks."

Shelby softened. "It's his life, Geo. You have to let him live it."

Not good, so he embellished, drawing inspiration from one of Mac's many women. "It's just… he met her at the gym. This ditzy redhead named Megan. She was all over him, and I think she wants to use him for his money. His last girlfriend, Lisa, dumped him almost a year ago and it hit him hard. He's a great guy, but I think this rebound chick is just using him."

She didn't blink. "Her name is Megan? You've actually met her?"

"A few times. One time he tried to pass it off, but I could tell what they'd been doing at his place. Her hair was mussed, and he looked like he'd been kissing her."

"At his place? His house?"

He nodded.

She frowned. "When was this?"

"A month ago? A few weeks at most," he said, getting into his story. "I've seen her at the house a few times when I popped over in the mornings to grab stuff I'd left at his place. She's not always there, but enough that I know something is going on, especially if Shane won't tell the family about it. I mean, he's his own guy, but we're a tight family. To not tell us about this new relationship proves there's something wrong with it."

He felt sure he'd gotten through to her, and then she went cold. "Thanks for the heads up, Geo. But if your brother found someone he likes, you need to accept it. Sometimes we get a taste of happiness, and you should let him enjoy it while he still can."

Okay, that sounded ominous. But then she was hustling him out the door, and somehow he found himself standing outside while she locked it and turned off the lights. He walked back to the car where Amber waited, looking so cute in her new Jeep. She had great parents, ones who rewarded their daughter for good grades.

He had a freakin' scholarship all but nailed, straight A's so far, and his dad's reward was to let Geo help him rebuild an old Mustang. Then maybe, if they got it to work, he could have it. Cool car, but jeez, was it worth the effort? Especially if Amber could take him where he wanted to go right now?

"Well? How did it go?"

He frowned. "I don't know. She got all weird at the end. Maybe she's not as into my brother as I'd hoped she'd be."

Amber shook her head. "I've seen him. Your brother is smokin'. If she doesn't want him, that's her loss."

"I guess." Geo sighed. "I hope I'm not as pathetic when I hit my thirties. I won't have a little brother to help me out."

"Yeah. But hey, at least there's no one stealing your clothes all the time." She pouted.

Amber's younger sister wanted to be Amber. He thought it was funny. She thought it was annoying.

"Come on. I'll treat you to a latte downtown. I think

there's an open mike night at Tova's."

She smiled. "You're on."

♥

Shelby saw red. It didn't seem possible that she could have been so wrong about a man a second time, but it made sense. Why Shane didn't pressure her to tell everyone they were dating, when he'd admitted he wanted them to be boyfriend/girlfriend close. Why he never insisted she spend the night, but acceded if she wanted to. How someone so perfect, so handsome and successful, might want her.

Because he didn't. He wanted sex and cuddling from her while he had better sex on the side. Just like Rick. Smart guy that he was, Shane took to heart all her complaints about Rick and acted the complete opposite. Supportive, fun loving, confident without being arrogant.

Tears filled her eyes, and she tried to make some sense of this. Why would Shane need to hide another woman? She'd been giving him plenty of sex. But then, she'd given Rick plenty too and he'd sought his secretary.

She'd expected Shane to be committed solely to her while they played around, so he would have to lie to keep her. Oh God. They hadn't been using protection. What if he'd been with another woman who had something, and he'd given it to her?

She felt sick.

Then her Mimi-tendencies toward the dramatic subsided and she calmed. What proof did she have that George had been telling the truth? It totally went against everything she knew about Shane to think he'd cheated, especially after being cheated on by Lisa. Everyone she'd talked to about Shane had let slip he'd had a hard time with her. But maybe he was playing the field too? She'd wanted to, but then she'd met Shane and was happy to be with him and only him. But weren't men more fickle in general?

And what if George had lied and none of this was true? That would be a happy answer to her present dilemma. But *why* would he lie? George didn't know they were dating. If he had, he never would have mentioned another woman. Would he? But if he truly wanted her to go out with his brother, why mention a sexpot sleeping over?

She thought she recognized the name and description, though, and that made it hard to refute George's story as anything but truth. A bimbo of a redhead named Megan frequented Jameson's Gym, where Shane worked out. She knew because Maggie had complained about the exercise groupie a time or two, not liking how the woman latched onto *anything with muscles and a penis*—Maggie's words, apparently now true.

Shelby let herself cry. She'd earned it after putting aside her mistrust and opening herself to Shane. She'd believed him when he said he cared, when he said he wanted them to be closer. Hell, she'd thought he'd said he loved her a time or two, then decided it must have been a heat of the moment thing during sex. And really, they'd only been together a few months. That was much too soon to feel this overwhelming sadness for a relationship fizzling before it could really get started.

Yet her brain and heart had a disconnect, because Shelby had actually believed he might be The One, with a capital *O*. This time, no one had interfered in her love life, and once again she'd fucked it all up. Had she not been good enough in bed, after all? Was Rick right about her? One relationship down the drain could be attributed to Rick's issues, but twice now?

Seemed like maybe she wasn't as good in bed as she thought.

Then her spine snapped straight and she remembered what it meant to be her own person. The groveling and whining were all well and good for a pity party, but damn it, Shane had promised that if he was with her, he wouldn't be with anyone else.

She deserved an explanation. And unlike the way she'd ended things with Rick, walking away with her tail between her legs, hurt and betrayed, this time she'd go out in a blaze of anger and scorn. Fuck Shane Collins for turning out to be so much less than she'd hoped.

After wiping her eyes dry, she grabbed a hold of her fury and her keys and drove over to his house. They had a date scheduled for this evening. One he'd probably end early so he could make time with the redheaded slut.

She fed her rage with images of them sleeping together as she parked in front of his house and raced up the steps to his front porch. She knocked hard on the door, surprised to see Mac there.

"Where's Shane?"

"Upstairs getting ready for a…date." His eyes widened. "You? Really? Son of a bitch." But his smile didn't fully form as he looked into her face. "Hey. You okay?"

She brushed past him and stormed up the stairs. She heard the shower running but didn't care. She slammed into Shane's bedroom and moved quickly through to the bathroom, where steam fogged the shower.

"Mac?" Shane called out, his sexy voice making her heart ache even worse.

"No, me." She ripped the shower curtain back, and he swore. "Expecting someone else? Megan maybe?"

He didn't look guilty or shocked or scared. Just surprised.

"What are you talking about? Shit, is it seven already? I thought I had more time to get ready for you. I was going to kick Mac out before you got here, I swear."

"I want an explanation." Her heart beat so loudly she couldn't hear much else.

He turned off the shower and grabbed a towel, which he wrapped around himself. It bothered the hell out of her that she noticed how terrific he looked naked, with water dripping down his impressive six-pack. "Okay, Shelby. Try again. What are you talking about, and why do you seem so upset?"

She couldn't cry. She was too knotted up to shed another tear. "I know about Megan."

He frowned. "Megan? The only Megan I know is Mac's old girlfriend from the gym."

"Ha! You admit it."

"Admit what?" He looked concerned. "What's up, baby?"

"I know about you and her. How you've been seeing another woman while you were supposed to be faithful to me." The tears started again. *Damn it.* "After all that talk about Lisa and how she fucked you over. And Rick did the same thing to me. How could you?"

She wanted to hear him say it. To listen to the truth and watch him with a straight face admit his lying, cheating ways. God, she wanted this hurt to turn to anger.

"Are you drunk?" He stepped out of the shower, and she hit him. Hard in the stomach.

He grunted but didn't double over, as she'd hoped. So much for brutality making her feel better. Instead she felt worse.

"You're losing it. I have no idea what this mess with Megan is about, but if she did anything to hurt you, I'll—"

"George told me," she shouted, finally stopping him.

"What?"

"Your little brother swung by my work this evening and told me all about Megan and your sex on the side. I can't believe you'd do that to me, but I shouldn't be surprised," she said bitterly. "You're all alike. Using women for sex, even when you don't have to."

"Shut up for a minute," he cut in, his voice low and filled with an anger she'd never before. Sure they'd argued from time to time, but he'd never been really mad at her. "I don't know what fucked up story my brother is spouting, but I have been into you one hundred percent from day one. I don't cheat. I don't need to," he said, his arrogance pissing her off all over again.

She wanted to belt him in that sexy mouth, and her overwhelming temper scared her. "I'm leaving." She hurried out of there before she did something she'd regret and fell to his level. If she hadn't known it before, this pain clearly told her she'd loved the asshole. *With her whole heart.* Rick's defection had hurt, but she'd known she'd carry on. Shane… She just didn't know.

She skirted Mac and left in a rush. With nowhere else to go, she hurried home, not wanting to talk to anyone right now. Later she'd call Maggie, and maybe her mother. But right now, she needed a good cry, solitude, and a pint of coffee ice cream.

Mac still couldn't believe his best friend had been tapping such a fine piece of ass—attached to a fine woman—and he hadn't known. No wonder Shane hadn't been chafing to find Shelby. He'd been doing her for a while, apparently. That lucky SOB.

Loud voices from upstairs told him something was wrong. If Shelby's drawn face hadn't clued him in, her shouts would have. And then to hear his calm buddy shouting back? The argument didn't last long, though, because Shelby raced out of the house with tears in her eyes. That bothered him. A lot. He liked Shelby. She'd done a hell of a job on his knee, which was doing better than it had been in months, and from what he'd seen of her, she was perfect for Shane.

His buddy came storming down the stairs dripping wet and hugging a towel to his waist. He seemed leaner than the last time Mac had seen him, but then Shane was a nut about running. Too bad he wasn't fast enough to catch Shelby before she raced away, squealing tires down the road.

"What the hell, man?" Mac stared in fascination, not sure what he was looking at. Shane looked pissed, sad, and frustrated all at once. Definitely woman problems, but Shelby didn't seem like the type to play games. And Mac knew Shane wasn't that kind of guy. So what—

"I'm going to *kill* my brother!" Shane slammed the door shut. "Go find him, or your interfering ass is next!"

CHAPTER NINETEEN

WHILE SHELBY RAN AWAY, SHANE HURRIEDLY DRIED OFF, dressed and shot out of his house on a mission to fix things. He gathered he'd supposedly cheated on Shelby with Megan, and that she'd gotten that insane idea from George. What he didn't know was why his little brother would strive to fuck up his life, and more importantly, how Shelby could think Shane capable of cheating on her.

He *loved* the woman. Had all but said out it loud, and a few times he'd slipped during sex and yelled it while he came. He would never imagine she'd cheat on him, but then, he loved her. After dealing with Lisa, he knew the difference between quality and flash. Shelby had heart. He knew she'd been faithful. She was too honest and responsive to him. She shared herself more and more, and he'd started to believe she might love him back.

And now this.

He pulled up to her front door, saw her car in the drive, and parked behind it. Then he walked around the house to the backdoor, grabbed the key from the hideaway she'd shown him, and let himself inside.

He heard angsty music playing and saw a pint of ice cream with a spoon sticking out of it on the kitchen counter. Then he saw her exit the bathroom. Her eyes were red and puffy and she was blowing her nose. A dozen or more crumpled tissues littered the floor by the couch.

"Get out," she growled, apparently still seething through her tears.

"I can't believe you would think I could do that to you," he said quietly, feeling the hurt she must have been feeling. "I understand why you would, since my brother loves me and is a pretty decent kid. But we both know he's told a few lies to get what he wants."

She opened her mouth—to argue, no doubt—then snapped it closed. "So you're saying he made it all up? There's no Megan, no gym, no affair?"

"No. Megan's real. She's a groupie at the gym, and my brother had a thing for her big time until Maggie started working there. Now he's into blondes. I'm surprised he didn't use her instead of Megan as my supposed lover." He wanted to hug Shelby and offer comfort. And he wanted to spank her for believing such terrible things about him. "What the hell did my brother say to convince you I was cheating with Megan, of all people?"

Her eyes filled again. "It's just… He said he wanted us to be together. That you were making a mistake with some gold digging witch," she added nastily. "And that I should make a move to save you from yourself. Not those exact words, but that was the intent."

"And after fucking my brains out every time we make love, you thought I'd go to another woman?" His voice rose. "For what?"

"How the hell should I know?" she cried. "Rick did it. Why wouldn't you?"

He figured as much. "Damn it, Shelby. I'm not Rick! I thought we'd been honest with each other. Lisa ripped my heart out when she cheated on me, and I never loved her as much as I do you."

Her eyes widened. "What?"

"I love you, but God knows you don't deserve it." He fed the anger building inside *him*. "Do you have any idea how hard it's been for me to trust *you*? Lisa lived with me. I saw her every fucking day, and she had an affair under my nose. But you and I don't see each other as much, and it's all I can do to convince you to spend a rare night at my place. You don't want to tell anyone about us, and I'm trying to give you the space you asked for, but it's fucking hard. Then you have the nerve to accuse *me* of cheating?" He paced around her dining room. "When would I have the time? When I'm not with you, I'm working out or doing one of three projects I've been assigned at work."

"I don't know." She sounded miserable.

Good.

"I trusted you before I ever saw your physical results. I trust that you're on birth control, though I've never seen it. I trust that you'll eventually tell me how you really feel about me, because I thought the way you responded in bed meant something." And how wrong he'd been.

"Shane. I'm sorry, but George—"

"Is my brother. Yeah, I know. I also know if Maggie or Mac told me you'd been cheating, the first thing I'd do would be to hear your side of the story before accusing you of anything. And maybe I'm an asshole for believing in someone after being screwed over like I was, but I love you. You trust the people you love." He let out a disgusted breath. "Obviously I'm the only one feeling that way." He turned around and headed back out the door.

"Shane, wait."

"Now I need time to cool off. I'll talk to you later. Maybe. Fuck if I know." He slammed out of the house, having said his piece. But he didn't feel any better for it. Instead, he felt worse.

♥

A week had passed, and Shane refused to talk to her. George had made an apology. Apparently the actor had thought he was doing Shane a favor. In what world that stupid story was a favor, Shelby had no idea. But he looked despondent about the whole thing, so she forgave him. It went without saying he broke up with Amber over the incident.

Her mother had been amazingly quiet about everything. She didn't comment or criticize when the ugly mess poured out of Shelby one night at dinner. And Ron had been silent as well. For the pair of them to not offer advice was like entering her own little alternate universe, and their attempt at kindness made her cry more.

Maggie, bless her, commiserated. Of course Shelby should have been hurt. Sure she'd believed Shane's own flesh and blood. Why wouldn't she? And Maggie wasn't talking to Mac, though she continued to work for him. Mac had stupidly taken Shane's side in this, and Maggie, loyal friend that she was, took Shelby's.

Shelby didn't tell anyone, but she'd left a message for Shane to call her yesterday. He hadn't responded yet.

Another week went by without contact. She missed him. *So much.*

No more wisecracks about her being a book nerd. No more arguments over what to watch. Now she had her choice of Lifetime movies but continued to linger over the stupid car channel, wondering if he was watching it. And she missed the intimacies they shared. He'd never made her feel ashamed for wanting exciting sex. For all that he loathed the word *vanilla*, their slow lovemaking, missionary style, often made her feel like a part of him. Like a real girlfriend and lover, half of a whole.

It all wouldn't have been so bad if she wasn't aware she'd hurt him with her doubts. After all he'd been through, then she'd added to it, knowing what a bitch Lisa had been. She wanted to apologize again and make things right, but she also understood he needed to be alone. If only she'd trusted him more.

No. If only she'd trusted herself.

Days went by, until she realized it had been almost three weeks and no word from Shane. Her mother and Ron remained mute about the subject. Maggie wouldn't speak his name, and George no longer visited her at work. Mac continued to come in for his weekly appointments, but he wisely refrained from mentioning Shane. Once he'd remarked that Shane looked like shit, and she'd let it stand, glad that he wasn't living it up without her.

Thursday—exactly three weeks after their huge blow up—arrived. The man was sulking. There was no other explanation for it since he hadn't called, texted or left her a message stating they were broken up, finished, kaput.

Shelby had run the gamut from sadness to frustration to anger and back to grief. But three weeks? Enough was enough. It was one thing to be mad at her, but to withdraw completely from her life? So she'd made a mistake. She was human, and she was bound to screw up royally again. If he *really* loved her, as he'd claimed, he'd give her the chance to explain. That had been the point behind his upset, that she hadn't trusted him. Well, now he was doing the same thing to her, not trusting her to come to her senses.

She'd realized what she'd done to him, and she felt worse than awful.

She didn't leave another message on his home or cell phone. As soon as she finished work tonight, she planned to take control of the situation, because Shelby was a doer, and sitting around waiting for Shane to make a move was driving her insane.

Denise had the day off and Ann finished her exercise ball class at noon. For three more hours Shelby saw clients, then started to clean up. Before she could turn the sign over to *Closed*, the front door opened. Great. Another customer. She sighed and turned with her broom. And froze.

Shane stood there in a suit, his tie loose around his neck, holding his suit jacket over his shoulder. He looked haggard… and so good to her she wanted to gobble him up. Instead she remained in place and waited for him to say something.

He locked the door behind him and turned the sign to *Closed*. Then he walked past her, checked on the other rooms, and locked the back door. He didn't speak, but entered her massage room, where she'd just finished changing the sheets. She had the bathroom to clean and laundry to do. But she couldn't stop herself from following him around.

Inside her room, he hung up his jacket, removed his tie, and rolled up his sleeves. Then he turned to her.

"You look terrible."

She scowled. "Yeah, back at ya, hot stuff."

He didn't grin, but she the twitch at his lips set her at ease. "I'm here for my appointment."

"Funny, I don't remember booking it."

"Denise booked it for me. *She* likes me."

Her temper got the better of her. "I like you, you jackass. I've been trying to talk to you for days but you—What the hell are you doing?"

He slathered her massage butter over his hands. "Strip and get on the table."

She blinked in confusion. "What?"

"You heard me. I booked an hour and a half of your time."

"For a massage."

"I didn't specify who was giving it. You look like crap. You've lost weight, and you're too tense. Get naked and hop up here."

So much for some make-up sex to relieve at least one ache.

He waited for her, one brow raised. So sexy and domineering. And like that, she missed him all over again. Blinking away the tears, she grumbled but dropped her broom, her clothes, and her pride, and moved belly-down onto the table.

He put warm hands over her shoulders and rubbed, and she sighed through the opening of the pillow.

"Okay. I'm ready to hear you now," came his deep voice from far away.

"Now?"

"I'm here, aren't I?" His hands moved to her neck, and she hysterically wondered if he meant to choke the answers out of her. But he only rubbed the tension from her aching body. She'd tried to work her way past the pain of his leaving when he wouldn't talk to her. She'd earned more money, but she'd also worked herself to the bone.

Weariness pulled at her.

"I missed you, Shelby," he said softly.

"Oh hell." She blinked hard and kept her eyes shut, hoping and praying she'd remain tear-free through her explanation. "I was falling in love with you, and it scared me, okay? So when George told me you were seeing someone else, it was easier to believe that and cut you loose than try to reason crap out."

His hands tightened over her arms then released, stimulating blood flow.

She sighed. "You're pretty good at this."

"Keep going."

She groaned. She'd had weeks to think about what she'd done and why. "Isn't it enough I'm sorry for not trusting you?"

"No. I want to understand."

How could she fault him for that? "When Rick dumped me, I was floored. I really did love him. At least, I loved who I wanted him to be. He was funny and successful and handsome, and people liked him. But he wasn't that nice to me. I didn't notice it at first. But then I was too fat, too skinny, my makeup wasn't right. I laughed too loud, was too aggressive. All of it delivered with a smile or a joke. I was tired of changing to please him."

"He was a dick," Shane growled and ran his hands down her back.

"I see that now. He lusted after Maggie and hated my mom and Ron. But I thought he'd grow to tolerate them for me. Instead I found him with a prettier, shorter, skinnier blonde sucking him off."

"Had to make you mad."

"I was humiliated. All the things he said about me not being good enough came back, and I ended us without a whimper. I just walked away. I had nothing at his place and he had nothing at mine. After a year of dating, I just walked away."

She remained silent for a moment, still stunned at that fact. "And then I was hurt. A lot. I hated men, I admit. But I started getting mad."

"Good. He was a horse's ass."

She warmed at his support but needed to explain. "No, I was mad at me for putting up with his shit for so long. I hate to say this, because I sound like I need therapy, but I think it has to do with my dad leaving when I was a kid."

His hands changed direction on her back, moving back up in butterfly strokes. "Relax, Shelby. Just breathe." He continued to work on her upper back and arms. "The thing about your dad… Once I calmed down, I thought a lot about why you went off on me. And after I talked to your mom about—"

"What?" She started to rise from the table, wanting to see him, but he shoved her back down.

"Just lay there, would you?"

She didn't want to upset him and have him leave again, so she stayed flat.

"Anyway, your mother helped me understand a lot. But I wanted you to realize it too."

"Oh, so you being a martyr and staying away from me, after accusing me of not trusting you, that was for my own good?"

"And mine."

She didn't get that.

He went to work on her feet, and she moaned at the heavenly touch.

He chuckled. "I've missed that moan."

"Not as much as I've missed you."

He stopped for a moment.

"What? You wanted honestly, you got it."

He rubbed again and spoke. "I like domesticity. When Lisa

and I were a couple, it felt like home. No bars or wild orgies, no hanging from the chandelier. I guess I was too comfortable, in love with love more than I was in love with Lisa. And I was cheated on and nearly swindled by the woman. It made me question my judgment and shook my confidence."

"I never would have guessed. You seem self-assured to me."

"About my career or my ability to run a mile, yeah. But I move too fast in relationships. I realized that. I can't just fuck and be done with it. I get attached."

"That means you're not a horn dog like most of the men I know. Nothing wrong with that."

"But because of that, I moved too fast with you. I should have stuck around and heard you out. It hurt when you believed what George, that idiot, said about me. And he's really, really sorry, by the way."

"I know. He told me."

"Good." His tone was grim, but his hands were gentle as he ran them over her feet to her calves. "I'm sorry I took so long to hear you out, and that I wasn't more understanding about what you heard. Hell, I went through Lisa's infidelity. I should have been right there with you, understanding your concern. Instead I felt under attack. Honey, I'm the last guy to cheat on you. I might argue or leave your ass, but no way would I destroy your trust like that. I can't stand it, and I won't tolerate it."

"Neither will I."

"Yeah, I get that."

So where did that leave them?

"Anyway, I got over my anger in a few days. But I needed to make sure I was doing the right thing with you. Loving you after a few months, that's crazy, right?"

"Yeah."

"But it's real." He sounded surprised. "I can't eat, I can't sleep. Work is killing me because I'm making so many mistakes it's taking me forever to get it right before I turn my shit in. Even Gloria Grace is pitying me."

She chuckled, and it felt good to laugh. "Is that so?"

"I wanted to come back to you whole and for the right reasons. I had to make sure I wasn't just with you because that's my M.O. with women. Have sex, date, move in together. But I don't want anyone else. Just you."

"Well, I wasn't out screwing half the town while you were gone either."

"No kidding. Not with that bad energy, as your mother calls it."

She groaned.

"Don't worry. I like her and Ron, and they know where I stand."

"Where's that?"

"With you, baby. I'm here, aren't I?"

"So you forgive me, even though you admit I had a right to believe what George told me?"

Shane snorted. "Isn't that kind of an *I told you so* mixed in with a questioning apology?"

"What?"

"Never mind. Yes, I forgive you. Yes, in your shoes, I might have believed you'd fooled around if your own brother said so."

"Thank you." Finally. Vindication and forgiveness. It was like Christmas come early.

"But Shelby, I've been miserable without you." He leaned closer and kissed the back of her neck. "I still love you."

She squirmed under him, her body reawakening to his

touch. Though the massage had been relaxing, he'd also stirred her up just by being near. And those hands on her body... Their chemistry had yet to fade. If anything, distance made him more potent.

"I love you too. You're hearing me through this stupid pillow, right?"

"Oh yeah." He paused for a few moments. She heard the rustle of clothing and prayed that meant what she thought it did. "This is going to be tricky, but I have confidence in you."

He massaged her buttocks. The deep rub was magical, and she moaned in pleasure and arousal as his thumbs pressed closer to her inner thighs, grazing her wet cleft.

"You smell good," he murmured and leaned down to kiss her neck again. Then he moved away. "Lift your head up."

She did and started to ask why when he suddenly grabbed her ankles. He tugged, pulling her back so that her pelvis rested against the end of the table. She felt off balanced and clutched at the sheets under her.

"What are you doing?"

"You in just a second." He spread her legs and gripped her hips, pulling her back and slightly up, so that her pussy aligned with his cockhead. And then he thrust inside her.

He drove so deep and hard, he shocked her into an immediate orgasm. As she keened and clamped down tight around him, he fucked her faster and shuddered.

"Oh yeah. Coming hard, baby." He jerked and continued to thrust, spilling into her with muttered words of love and distress that he'd come too soon.

He remained locked inside her and leaned over her back. Planting small kisses along her spine, he had yet to grow slack inside her.

"God, I missed you. So much. And not just your tight

pussy."

"Or your thick cock."

His breath came faster. "Or your slick mouth. I haven't come in anything but my hand once, and that was two days ago because I was so pent up with anger and frustration I couldn't wait any longer. Damn it. I missed you."

He'd said that. But she liked him repeating it.

"So what now?"

"Now you know I love you, and I know you love me." He sounded smug, but she'd grant he had a right to be, especially after giving her that rush. She felt so boneless she could barely breathe. "I'm probably moving too fast again, but I'll trust you to slow me down."

"You're good so far," she said sleepily.

"Great. Then I'll tell you we're dating. Committing only to each other. Boyfriend/girlfriend all the way, and I'm telling everyone I know."

"Okay."

"And if you don't freak out on me in another month or two, we're making it official."

Shane pulled out, flipped her onto her back, and entered her once more, watching her as he moved. "Yeah, I'm gonna put a collar on you and keep you."

"Collar?" She groaned and reveled in his lips around her nipple. She loved him watching her, because it added a hint of naughty to their loving. "Shane…"

He bit her, hard enough to jolt a dart of need in her core. "Not a literal collar. I want everyone to know you're mine. And that I'm yours." He began making love to her, slowly, and each inch of him was a precious part she wanted to hold onto. Connected physically and now emotionally. *Finally*.

"I don't know. I was thinking a collar might be fun. Not

vanilla." She bit her lip when he turned to her other breast and sucked her nipple with rough pulls. He pillowed his head between her mounds and nuzzled, inhaling her scent. Then he returned to her breasts and made love to them. To her, while he moved in and out of her with a slowness that drove her insane.

Shane leaned up and watched her while he took forever to thrust back inside her. "I love your tits. Your body. Hell, I love you, Ms. Vanilla."

"Soon to be Mrs. Vanilla, hmm?" She put her arms around his neck and hung on while he increased his pace.

"Damn right." He snapped his hips, and he brushed something tingly inside her. "You have to say yes."

"Yes, yes."

His laughter faded into a groan when she squeezed him inside her.

She gripped his neck and threaded her fingers through his soft hair. "God, I'm coming again."

"Good, because I can't stop. Touch yourself, baby. Come with me."

She moved a hand between them and rubbed herself, and in seconds, they both crested another wave of pleasure. Together.

CHAPTER TWENTY

A MONTH LATER, NOVEMBER HAD TURNED THE SKIES gray and the weather *colder than a witch's tit.* George used the phrase around his family whenever he could, making sure to include Shelby in his antics.

She rolled her eyes at him and met Shane's pained expression, aware they looked goofy. They'd dressed as matching ice cream cones at Vanzant Interior's quarterly gala. Since Shelby had been depressed over Shane during Halloween—her favorite holiday—Ron had suggested they make their party a costume bash, and not a week from Thanksgiving. But Shelby didn't mind.

Her Halloween had been spent lamenting the loss of a wonderful man. So tonight she planned to make up for her lost celebration. It was a perfect night for them to give each other treats. Chocolate syrup they could lick off each other, and maybe some hot wax for fun. She'd never been so happy, and everyone she knew commented on it.

She had a feeling Shane was gearing up to ask her something special. Not an engagement, but they'd been talking a lot about moving in together. In her mind, a true step toward commitment. She still had instances of panic, waiting for the other shoe to drop on her relationship, but Shane talked her down off the ledge. And on those occasions when he started talking babies and 401Ks for their grandkids, she reined him in without breaking a sweat.

Shelby had no doubt Shane was *it* for her. They promised to keep each other honest, and to never lose that spark that had brought them together in the first place. Lots of bodywork in and out of the massage clinic, and plenty of non-vanilla dates.

"I can't believe you came as ice cream cones. That is so revoltingly couple-like." Maggie sneered at her costume.

"Please. I'm cute. You're… What are you, exactly?"

Maggie opened her large beige overcoat. Instead of a sexy teddy or vampy vixen costume, Maggie wore a flowered frock that looked like something her Aunt May might have worn, loose knee-highs pooling around her ankles, and Mary Janes. She also had stuffed animals strapped to her arms and legs. "I'm now officially the cat lady."

Shelby burst out laughing, and Shane ambled closer to her, Mac hard on his heels. Wherever Maggie went, Mac seemed to be near. Shelby had a feeling her friend was due to get run over by big bad Mac Jameson. And that pleased her, because she happened to like him. A gruff, teddy bear of a guy who looked like he ate small children for breakfast, Mac might be exactly what Maggie needed, someone who wouldn't cater to her every whim. And he wasn't a loser. From what Shane had said, his friend wasn't even playing around with random women anymore.

Shane attributed the loss of Mac's harem to "one smart-mouthed blonde who looks like God's personal hooker in pink aerobic tights." That Mac. He really had a way with compliments. He'd come as a biker, and he wore his jeans and leather vest very well. Shelby had noticed Maggie keeping a wary eye on him throughout the night.

Interesting things were heating up in Seattle, that was for sure.

"What the hell is strapped to your thigh?" Mac asked Maggie, his eyes the size of quarters.

"One of my many cats. I'm the neighborhood cat lady."

"You are not." Shelby sighed. Maggie and her dire predictions about being an old maid.

Mac choked on laughter and whispered something to Shane, who broke down in tears.

"What's so funny?" Shelby had to know.

Maggie planted her hands on her hips, clearly annoyed. "Yeah. What are you idiots laughing at?" Shelby liked that her best friend and boyfriend got along so well. Maggie treated him like her brother, and he teased her the way he did George.

Mac wiped his eyes and had a hard time explaining through more laughter. "You have a *pussy* right near your, um, your, ah…"

"For God's sake." Maggie yanked free the velcroed cat nestled almost between her thighs and threw it at Mac's head. Then she stalked off to join Shelby's mother, Ron, and Ron's new boyfriend—Justin Harmon. Shane's boss.

"You have to admit that's funny as hell." Shane chuckled and watched Mac trying to placate the temperamental blonde by giving her back the stuffed cat.

Shelby bit back a grin, but Shane saw it. "Okay, it's funny. You know what's also funny?"

"What?" He pulled her as close as their puffy cone costumes would allow.

"You realize Mac now has his hand on Maggie's pussy."

Shane died laughing again, and Shelby joined him. They

had so much fun together, and their humor meshed. Hell, everything about them meshed. She spent so much time at his place and he at hers that they were all but living together. She tolerated his neat tendencies, and he allowed her to stack piles of crap everywhere, so long as it remained organized.

As Shelby glanced around at her friends and family, she couldn't wait for the holidays. This year was special. She longed to share festivities with Shane, to see what he thought of the Christmas present she'd already bought for them.

Matching wedding bands and a save-the-date invitation for August 2nd, the anniversary of the day Shane had run into her and turned her world, and her coffee, upside-down.

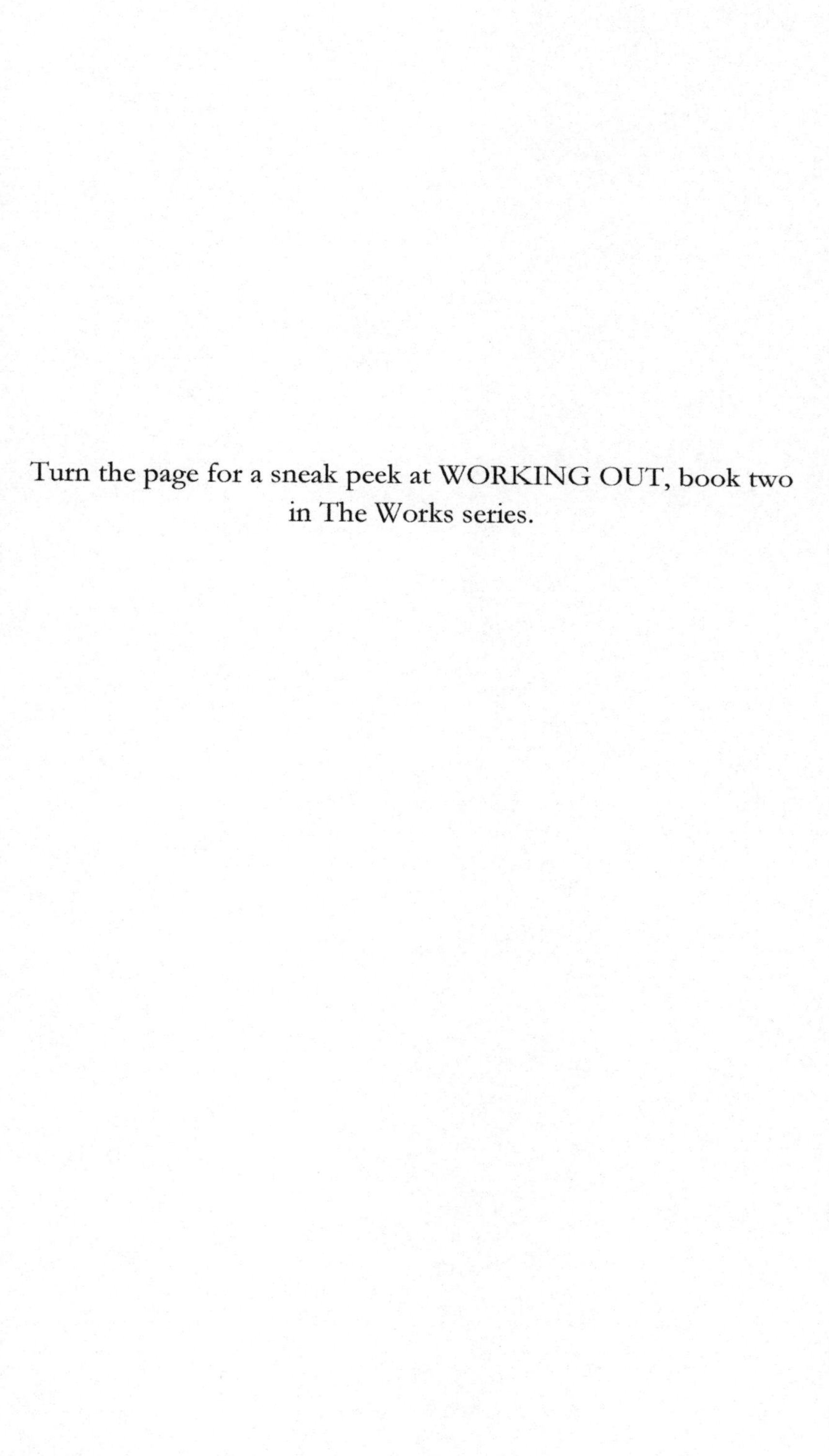

Turn the page for a sneak peek at WORKING OUT, book two in The Works series.

WORKING OUT

December in Seattle

He'd known it was coming to this. For four long-ass months, he'd been doing his best to handle the situation, and for four months he'd been fooling himself.

Mac Jameson gripped the neck of his beer bottle and glared across the bar at the bane of his existence. He could no longer ignore those big blue eyes, that killer rack, or the platinum blond hair that framed a face that haunted his dreams. She worked for him, but it didn't stop her from sniping, scowling, or blatantly ignoring him when she didn't like what he had to say. A smarter man would have taken her signals as uninterested and run the other way.

But not Mac. He thrived on challenge, and Maggie Doran had *dare* written all over her. Aside from her smart mouth and incredible looks, she had a work ethic he truly respected. To make matters worse, she was far from perfect, which he would have found boring. No woman could look like she did without carrying some massive baggage.

He hadn't yet figured out how to unload her issues long enough to sleep with her and put himself out of his misery.

A solid clap to his back reminded himself he wasn't

drinking alone.

"So what's your excuse this time?" his best friend asked as he joined Mac at the bar. "The redhead not hot enough? The brunette who wanted your number too clingy?"

Mac refused to pay attention to the end of the bar where two sexy women continued to glance at him in between high-pitched laughter and cocktails. "I don't date women who giggle. Christ, I'm thirty-six, too old for games."

"Since when?" Shane, as usual, ignored the scowl Mac shot him and continued to talk. "The Mac I know has no problem serial dating. What was it you said to me not so long ago? To indulge in the holy trinity and forget my problems? Tits, ass and an orgasm. There you go, buddy. You have two more-than-willing candidates still making eyes at you." Shane discreetly nodded toward Mac's new groupies.

"No fault with the trinity. You have me there." Mac had to smile. His grin faded when he noticed his recent obsession now sandwiched between two guys pointing fingers at one another.

Shane followed Mac's attention and sighed. "Figures. That woman is trouble." And Shane would know. Now dating Shelby, Maggie's best friend, Shane spent more time with Maggie than Mac did—a fact that annoyed the crap out of him, not that he'd ever admit it out loud.

"Don't get me wrong, I like her a lot," Shane continued, "but that stupid vow of celibacy is like a neon sign on her forehead. It's like Maggie's secretly calling out to anyone with a dick to help end her plight."

Mac blinked. "What did you say?"

"Oh, sorry. *Plight* means problem. As in, she has something troubling her."

"Dickhead. No, what you said about her vow of celibacy."

"Oh that. Maggie is off men, or so Shelby told me. I'm

sworn to secrecy, so don't say anything." Shane shrugged and drank his beer. "Oh hell. Looks like I'm going to have to help her out. Those guys don't look like they're playing."

Mac wanted to get back to Maggie's issue about not having sex, but Shane was right. "You stay here in case I need someone to bail me out of jail. I'll handle those guys."

Shane stared at him a moment, then nodded. "Yeah. Just flex a few times and they'll scatter like mice."

Mac shot him a not-so-nice grin.

"And do that. The smile that's more a grimace. Great intimidation factor, there."

In a mood to crack some skulls together, Mac muscled through the crowding bar and reached Maggie in time to hear her telling both guys off.

"… if you'd even bothered to ask, you'd know I never drink tequila. And I don't like grabby men. Period."

When Maggie grew angry, her voice turned huskier, sexier. It put Mac in mind of satin sheets and naked limbs entangled with his. Unfortunately, her voice seemed to have the same effect on the morons fighting over her. Morons that looked somehow familiar.

The redhead poked the dark-haired guy in the belly. Both appeared of equal weight and height, yet neither had the same mass as Mac. Of the two, the dark-haired man looked meaner, so Mac kept an eye on him.

Maggie turned to the redhead. "Brent, it's okay—"

Brent cut her off. "She's with me, Wilson."

"Yeah, right." Wilson made a face. "Why would she want you when she could have me? I can buy and sell you twice over, and you…what? You own a nice little home in Green Lake and bench press twenty more pounds in the gym? Please."

Brent had patience, because he took a deep breath and let

it out without slugging the guy. "Wilson, don't be such a dick. Maggie and I were talking before you interrupted."

"Talking? Brent, she was backing away and trying to be polite about it." Wilson huffed. "Poor thing just doesn't know how to reject you without hurting your feelings."

Mac suddenly realized where he'd seen the men before. They were members of Jameson's Gym—his uncle's pride and joy, and his current employer. It should have made him reconsider his need to pound both of them into tomorrow. Brent had been a member for a few months and wasn't a bad guy, but Wilson was new. He also appeared to be a conceited jerk.

Maggie opened her mouth, no doubt to say something snarky. She might be little, but she didn't tolerate fools well at all. Then she spotted Mac and snapped her mouth closed. The fire in her blue eyes went straight to his gut. Damn, she was pretty, especially when riled.

"Maggie." He smiled through his teeth.

"Oh hell." She groaned.

ABOUT THE AUTHOR

Caffeine addict, boy referee, and romance aficionado, *New York Times* and *USA Today* bestselling author Marie Harte has over 100 books published with more constantly on the way. She's a confessed bibliophile and devotee of action movies. Whether hiking in Central Oregon, biking around town, or hanging at the local tea shop, she's constantly plotting to give everyone a happily ever after. Visit **http://marieharte.com** and fall in love.

Made in the USA
Las Vegas, NV
17 April 2025